EVERLAND

BOOK 1

WENDY SPINALE

SCHOLASTIC PRESS
NEW YORK

Library of Congress Control Number: 2015027027

ISBN 978-0-545-83694-4

10 9 8 7 6 5 4 3 2 1   16 17 18 19 20

Printed in the U.S.A.   23
First edition, May 2016

Book design by Christopher Stengel

To all the Lost Girls whose
adventures ended way too soon and
cheer for me from beyond the stars—
Harriet, Shirley, and Andreae

· GWEN ·

Outside my window, plumes of gray smoke and steam rise from the decimated city into the polluted midnight sky. There they linger like ghosts of those who once walked the streets of London before the arrival of the Marauders. I briefly wonder what life was like before the German monarch's reign began and the world was without steam power.

In the distance, the faint glow of kerosene lanterns illuminates the remains of the city I once called home, daring me to venture beyond the safety of our dusty hideout above an old furniture warehouse. My heart aches to return to the house in which all of my childhood memories were made, but there is nothing left of it. Taking in a breath, I swing my legs through the broken window and onto the rusty fire escape, answering the city's quiet call.

"Where do you think you're going?" Her accusing whisper startles me.

Looking over my shoulder, I find my twelve-year-old sister, Joanna. She stares at me with reproachful eyes, her arms folded across her chest. Her small face scowls, reminding me of the look my mother used to give me after I had been caught doing something wrong. Now all that remains of my mother is my sister's uncanny resemblance to her: corkscrew curls, a turned-up nose, and high cheekbones.

"We're almost out of rice and are down to a few liters of water," I say, adjusting the leather straps on my rucksack. "I'm heading out to scavenge. I won't be gone long."

"Gwen, the Marauders are patrolling closer," she says, pointing out the window. A zeppelin flies low, skirting the rooftops of the mangled buildings in the distance. The city's lamplight casts a golden glow on its wooden hull. Even from here I can hear the whir of its engines and propellers. "It's too dangerous."

"I know," I say with a sigh. "It's time to move again. We should probably head north toward Cambridge. There is not much left this far outside of the city anyway. We'll pack up and leave in the morning, but I have to find something for us to eat."

Joanna reaches toward a shelf. She grabs an aluminum pot, turns it over, and places it on her head. Under the window's ledge, she pulls out her chest armor, made of two cookie sheets held together with copper wire. My sister slips the armor over her head. "I'm coming with you."

"Not this time, Joanna." I place her makeshift helmet back on the shelf. Tilting her chin, our eyes meet. "You need to look after Mikey. He's been having night terrors again."

Joanna squints. "You know Mum and Dad wouldn't approve of this."

This again? I've lost count how many times Joanna has used our parents to try to stop me from venturing out alone. "We're not going to discuss this."

"You know I'm right," she says with defiance.

Impatience wells up inside me and my words spill out harsher than I intend. "Mum and Dad are gone. I'm the oldest. I'm in charge now. We've been through this a hundred times."

Joanna jerks her chin from my grip. "You don't know that for sure. They could still be out there waiting for us," she says, waving a hand toward the window.

"It's been a year since the invasion. If they were alive, they would have come for us. They are not waiting, nor are they coming back," I say, trying to keep my voice calm but not succeeding. "Our parents are dead."

Joanna is quiet, the sting of my words evident as her bottom lip quivers. She stares at her small bare feet and twirls the copper-button bracelet on her wrist. The military insignia on each button is worn. They once lined the lapel of one of our father's uniforms. It is the only token my sister has left of him. Instinctively, I reach for my father's military tags around my neck, comforted by the keepsake he left me.

"I'm sorry. I didn't mean . . . ," I say, silently berating myself. After a year of caring for my siblings, my temper has become increasingly short. It seems to take so little to set me off lately. I try to pull her into a hug, but she recoils, unwilling to meet my gaze.

"You've changed," Joanna says, her words hot and bitter. "You're not the same. You promised, Gwen. What happened to our Sister Pact?"

Visions of our early childhood wash over me like an unexpected storm on a clear day. Dozens of stinging raindrops, each carrying a memory, invade my thoughts. Nights of sneaking from my bed and into hers to tell her stories of fairies, pirates, and mermaids. Pinkie-sworn promises to never grow up. Promises I couldn't keep.

"That was then, this is now." My voice is too loud, I warn myself, but I cannot contain the frustration bubbling inside me like an unattended pot of water over an open fire. "Do you think I like this any better than you do? Do you think I enjoy being the responsible one taking care of you and Mikey? I would give anything, anything at all, to have my life back, to have just one more day being a child and not your guardian. Look!" I point toward the city's blackened remains, a boneyard landscape of fragmented buildings. "London is gone! And by the fact that no one has come to England's aid, I think it's safe to assume the aftermath of the invasion has extended beyond the country's borders. It's time to face reality: There are no more private schools or fancy parties." My words spill too quick and harsh from my lips, but I can't stop them. "No more ballet or equestrian lessons. Our parents are gone. We are trying to survive, and this is not a childhood game or make-believe. This is real life. It's time to grow up."

An injured expression replaces the scowl on Joanna's face. My stomach groans with hunger, but the ache is nothing compared with the immediate pang of guilt that fills me. I wish I could take back what I said. "Look," I whisper. "Joanna, I . . ."

"You were a much better sister than you are a mother," she says softly, tracing pictures in the layer of dust on the floor with her big toe.

A stab of pain pierces my heart like the tip of a sharpened sword. A mother? I had never intended to be her mother, but the stern tone in my voice echoes like a parent chiding her children. I am about to correct her, to convince her I am still her sister, only a child like her, when Mikey, our six-year-old brother, appears, rubbing his eyes. Dirt dusts his blond hair, making it look brown. I can't remember the last time I bathed him. In fact, I can't remember the last time I bathed myself.

"What's going on? Why are you guys fighting?" he asks through a yawn.

"Never mind, go back to bed," I say too sharply.

"I can't sleep. Bad dreams." He takes Joanna's bandaged hand. She winces but doesn't complain. The blisters on her fingers have worsened over the weeks and seem excruciatingly painful. Bloody and infected, the sores haven't responded to any treatment: warm baths, tubes of salve, bandages, or an expired bottle of antibiotics I scavenged. I've tried to convince myself that it's nothing to worry about. That her wounds will heal with time. Refusing to believe that she has contracted what has ravaged the adult population and left many of the children untouched. But even through the denial, the truth still haunts me with every corpse I stumble upon.

"Come on, I'll lie down with you. Have I told you the stories about the mermaids in the city?" Joanna says, leading Mikey by the hand.

"Are they real mermaids?" Mikey asks with curious, wide eyes.

"Joanna," I say, gently touching her shoulder. I want to apologize, to convince her that I am just looking out for her well-being, but the words stick in my throat, filtered by uncertainty. Instead I hear myself saying, "Don't keep him up too late with those silly fairy tales. And no pirate stories, he'll be awake all night. It's late. Blow that candle out. We're leaving when I return."

She looks away. "I wish you'd never grown up," she mumbles. I shudder, her words twisting a sharp blade in my chest. Joanna leads Mikey to our filthy mattresses and tattered blankets. They settle into the lumpy beds, whispering under the dancing flicker of dim candlelight. Mikey giggles as Joanna waves her hands around as if she were in an imaginary sword fight.

Shaking my head, I turn back to the open window and take one final glance at England's structural ruins. A gray haze hovers over the city like a cloak of death and disease. The blackened remains of the once-bustling town of London provide mute evidence of the carnage and destruction caused by the Marauders, the pirate soldiers sent by Queen Katherina of Germany.

Years ago, Queen Katherina ascended the German throne after the unexpected death of her husband. But it soon became clear that ruling just one country would not be enough for her. England tried to stop her, working to have the International Peace Accords signed by the world's nations. It was meant to unify and create a utopic society for all time. It was a hollow gesture at best. Queen Katherina quickly defied the treaty, leaving the countries surrounding her kingdom in a bloodbath, earning her the nickname the Bloodred Queen.

So we are not her first invasion and certainly not her last.

I descend the fire escape to the rain-soaked streets below. Leaving my sister and brother to their fairy tales, I travel east on foot for an hour outside of our hideout before reaching a dilapidated suburban community.

A full moon casts its eerie glow through a break in the gloomy clouds, chasing away dark shadows in the alleys. The stench of death and rotting corpses still lingers in the muggy air, evidence of diseased bodies discarded into the sewage system by survivors and soldiers alike. Rumors of crocodiles let loose within the sewers to devour the dead circulated among the survivors in the days following the bombs. Even after all this time, the smell makes me want to retch. Crouching behind the rubble of bomb-shelled buildings, I watch for movement. Other than scavenging rodents, the night is silent. Most of the houses lie in ruins, casualties of the war. Those buildings still standing loom with windowless gapes and graffiti-painted walls, an indication that they have already been looted. Weeds grow tall in the front lawns and through the thick cracks of the buckling streets as nature reclaims what once was hers.

My hopes rise as I stumble upon a single-story house that appears untouched. Other than a pile of bricks and mortar from what was a chimney, the structure seems undamaged. Thankfully, the windows remain intact, a sure sign that no one has scavenged the place. Still, I know I must be cautious. Assumptions will get me killed.

I step out of the shadows and into the milky moonlight. Glass crushes beneath my black leather boots. I cringe, cursing my careless mistake. The stillness of the night air remains unbroken, at least this time. I make my way to the side of the house, slipping through a broken board in the backyard fence.

With the palm of my hand, I wipe dirt from a dingy window on the garage door. It's too dark inside to see anything. Placing my rucksack on the ground, I pull out a small kerosene lantern and a book of matches. The cover flips open, revealing a single match.

Afraid of accidentally blowing it out, I hold my breath, run the match along the strike strip, and light the lamp. It sparks and the warmth chases away the chill from my fingers.

Once more, I survey my surroundings to be sure no one is watching, even though I know I'd hear the hiss of the military's steam tanks from a mile away. Searching the ground, I select a loose brick from the crumbled chimney and hurl it at the window. The glass shatters, breaking into a thousand tiny shards, littering the stone walkway in a puddle of fragmented tears and leaving jagged teeth in the frame. I reach inside to unlock the door, careful not to cut myself. As I let myself into the garage, rusty hinges wail in protest.

Like most of the homes I have searched, empty boxes and plastic containers lay strewn about the dusty floor, evidence of a family fleeing for their lives from the bombs, the deadly virus, and the Marauders. More than likely, there will be nothing left to salvage, but I rummage through the shelves and drawers anyway. Other than a rusted torque ratchet and spool of copper wire, everything else is useless. I slip the treasures into my pack before trying the door into the house. Fortunately, it gives way with little resistance, allowing me to enter the living room.

Photos of a family hang on a pale yellow wall above a sofa. Naïve smiles greet me from the frames: a man with a square chin; a doe-eyed woman; and two kids, a boy and a girl. I trace my finger over the faces. Where are they now? Did they make it? Did they get out of the city in time? Questions I often ask about my own parents, but like the silent, ghostly images staring at me through these family photos, I'm left with more uncertainties than answers.

Stepping away from the pictures, I catch a glimpse of my own reflection in the glass. Blue eyes stare back at me, hollow and distant with dark circles beneath them. Loose tendrils of light brown, curly hair, having fallen out of my plait, frame my dirt-streaked cheeks. I pull out the hair ribbon and rake my fingers through my kinky waves, but it doesn't help. Rubbing my fingertips over the smudges on my face, I notice the dirt under my fingernails. My breath catches as I remember that only a year ago I obsessed about perfect manicures. Now those worries seem frivolous as I inspect my calloused, filthy palms covered in cuts and scars. Another glance at my reflection and I notice that although I am just shy of my sixteenth birthday, I look as if I am twice my age.

A noise to my right startles me. Two yellow eyes peer at me before disappearing beneath a broken china hutch: a rat. *Figures,* I think. Along with cockroaches and children, rodents are among the last survivors of the war.

As expected, most of the food is gone or eaten by the rats. I'm lucky enough to find a tin of tuna packaged in spring water and a half-full canister of pasta in an upper cupboard. I add them to my pack. Placing a canteen beneath the sink faucet, I try to turn the water on. Pipes rumble for a moment, then go quiet. A few drops of muddy brown water drip from the dusty silver mouth, but hardly enough for a sip. I slam the handle.

I continue to search the house for other items to add to my stash: a kitchen knife, a colander, and an umbrella, a necessity for England regardless of the time of year. The master bedroom is empty aside from a metal bed frame and a broken kerosene lantern. A black frock with decorative silver knob buttons on the lapel hangs in the back of the closet. It's big, but it will suffice. I slip my arms through the sleeves and sling my pack over my shoulders.

Lying in the center of a bedroom painted flamingo pink is a tattered brown bear peering at me with a single black button eye. I pick it up and hold it to my chest, remembering my own room filled with too many stuffed animals. My nose tingles with the faint smell of chocolate, and I recall the strawberry-scented bunny that sat at the head of my bed. I add the bear to my stash. If nothing else, it will be good kindling for a fire.

A shrill scream shatters the silence. I extinguish my lantern and race back to the sitting room. Leaning up against a wall, I hide from the window's view. The lantern rattles in my trembling grip. I sneak a glance through the single-pane glass. Footsteps hammer on the wet cobblestone street, soaked from the late evening's shower. A dozen Marauders in dark military attire halt in front of the sitting room window. Bronze chest and shoulder plates cover their uniforms. Full leather and metal helmets complete with night-vision goggles and gas masks obscure their faces. They scan the street, their geared and cogged metal rifles reflecting the full moon. My heart races at the terrifying sight of them as sweat prickles at my neck. One soldier gives an order, his voice almost mechanical through his helmet. The group splits into teams, smashing down the doors of the adjacent homes. I duck below the windowsill but keep my attention fixed on the soldiers storming through the houses.

Something shifts across the street, catching my attention. A girl with long blond hair peeks from a shrub. She looks to be about Joanna's age, just a child really. The girl scans her surroundings before dashing down the street. I bolt upright, watching her stop several houses down and jump onto a rubbish bin. On her back is a leather and metal rocket pack. She pulls a lever and a large brass cog, not unlike those found inside a clock, spins on the outside of the pack. Two delicate copper wings spring open. Steam spills from the bottom of the rockets and her feet leave the ground. Her petite frame flies over a wooden fence.

Something in me wants to follow her, a longing for human connection other than my own family. But I remind myself that Joanna and Mikey are waiting for me at home. They are my responsibility. Still, I haven't seen anyone else in months. Like me, they must hide in the shadows if they haven't already succumbed to the virus or been caught by the Marauders. I stare into the dark alley that the girl disappeared into, when suddenly two green eyes lined with black powder peer at me, separated from me only by glass. Alarmed, I fall back, catching myself with my hands. A teenage boy gazes through the window, unblinking. His wide eyes look me up and down, as if he is as shocked to see me as I am him. He looks back at his pursuers, then at me.

"Let me in," he pleads, the glass muffling his words as he pounds on the windowpane with his fists.

Immobilized by fear, I shake my head as my pulse quickens. My quaking hand reaches for my dagger. I unsheathe the blade and point it at him. He slaps both of his palms on the window, making the glass vibrate. Startled, I inch back farther from the window. He stares with such intensity my breath catches. The gruff voices in the street grow louder, drawing his attention. His clenched, stubbled jaw twitches and he turns his jade gaze back to me one last time. His face expresses something akin to frustration or disappointment—which, I am not sure. It ignites the sickening feeling of guilt I've become so accustomed to. He is not the first I have turned away, sacrificed for the good of my own family. Nor will he be the last, of this I am sure.

The boy pushes off the glass and darts across the residential street. Effortlessly, he leaps over the wooden fence, lands on the top of a rubbish bin, springs onto a second-story balcony, and with the expertise of a gymnast, pulls himself onto the rooftop. Standing on the peak of the two-story Victorian home, he looks back at me with a curious expression. Other than his forest-green coat, its tails fluttering in the wind, he is dressed entirely in black.

The glow of the moon shines on his handsome face. Fixing his gaze on me, he bows and slips a pair of goggles dangling from his neck over his eyes. He holds his cupped hands to his mouth. With the call of a rooster, he cries into the broken clouds and star-embezzled night sky before vanishing over the roof peaks of this suburb. Puzzled, I sit back on my heels and stare at the spot where he stood, half expecting him to reappear. The angry shouts grow louder and another group of military men passes the house. I duck below the sill, risking another glance out the window.

Two soldiers, only a few years older than me, stop just outside of the house.

"Which way did they go?" one of the Marauders asks, peering through the window.

I press my body and face to the dusty carpet. Fear chokes me as I listen to the other soldier respond.

"The girl took off up the street and the boy went over the roof," the other soldier growls menacingly with a thick, deep German accent behind his helmet.

"Check the backyards for Immunes," the first soldier says.

"Yes, sir."

The two Marauders race across the street and climb the fence, disappearing behind the house. I sigh, letting go of the breath I did not know I was holding.

Immunes: the vile name they've given to children who have not died of the Horologia virus. We are the survivors of the outbreak and valued for our antibodies. The Marauders are our abductors.

Ten restless minutes slip by before I make my way to the alley behind the house. Sprinting, I keep to the rubbish-littered backstreets, haunted by ethereal shadows cast by jagged rooftops. With the Marauders out patrolling, I backtrack through unfamiliar passageways and find alternative routes. For the last few months, they have hunted for survivors, children orphaned and left on their own in the streets. However, I have never seen soldiers search the suburbs this far outside the borders of what once was London proper. Not London anymore, I remind myself; they call it Everland now.

After an hour, I hide behind a row of hedges and watch for movement along the dark street. I have the uneasy feeling that I am being watched, but see no one. Sprinting to the fire-escape ladder, I scramble as fast as I can, the cold metal leaving its bitter bite on my fingers. When I reach the landing of the fifth floor, I climb through the window frame and throw myself to the concrete floor. I sink my teeth down on my lip, trying to quiet my rapid breathing as I listen for anyone following behind. The night echoes my silence.

I let out a breath, relieved to be greeted with the quiet of our refuge, our sanctuary . . . for now, at least. Standing, I brush off the dust from my coat. A candle sputters on the far side of the room next to three empty mattresses. The sweet smell of rum stings my nose, and I know instantly something is wrong.

Joanna and Mikey are nowhere to be found.

My gaze darts throughout the room, searching for my brother and sister. I tiptoe across the floor, being as silent as possible. Something large rustles near the shelves to my right. An icy chill races up my spine. My fingers graze the copper hilts of the daggers sheathed on my hips. A whimper emanates from inside the metal rubbish bin. With caution, I lift the lid.

Two watery brown eyes glisten at me, the moonlight reflecting in their frightened gleam.

"Mikey!" I reach for him, pulling him from the bin. A colander covers his head like a helmet and he wears makeshift armor over his tattered pajamas. He looks like he's ready for war.

"They came, the pirates!" he says, sniffling.

"Not the Marauders," I beg, my voice weak.

"Joanna said they were pirates. She told me to hide. I did just what she said. I hid in the bin and was as quiet as a dormouse. Even quieter."

My pulse races and my cheeks flush with panic as I settle Mikey to the floor and dart across the room, searching other hiding spots for my sister.

"Where's Joanna?" I ask frantically, lifting one of the mattresses.

"They took her," Mikey says in a fresh burst of tears. "They took her away."

I run to the window, but the streets are quiet and there is no sign of the Marauders. Mikey rushes me, jumping back in my arms and burying his face in my neck. I look out into the distance and a deep ache festers in the pit of my stomach as a new realization settles over me.

To get my sister back, I will have to return to Everland.

· HOOK ·

The eight-legged Steam Crawler roars as it maneuvers around the rubble of what was formerly the Victoria Memorial. Its steel and chrome gears shriek to a stop in front of Buckingham Palace, one of the few buildings untouched by the bombs and currently my central command station. While it is nothing like Lohr Castle, the only home I've ever known, the palace has served me well for nearly a year.

Sliding the passenger door up, I step from the vehicle and am engulfed in a haze of warm steam bursting from the vehicle's boiler. The brisk wind of a looming storm whips through my hair, obscuring the vision in my only functioning eye.

Threatening clouds blanket the darkened, early morning sky. Although the gloom has left the spirits of my men restless, I feel charged with anticipation, knowing our days left in Everland are numbered. There is very little reason left to stay. Everland is nothing but rubble.

In the distance, my zeppelin, the *Jolly Roger*, is being loaded with supplies by dozens of Marauders. The wicked grin of the skull carved into the stern of the ship calls to me, beckoning me to take her away from this ruined city. Metallic gears serving as eyes glitter, reflecting the torches lit within the royal gardens. Propellers spin, and the whir of the zeppelin's engines serenades the desolate remains of London. Its hum is a symphony to my ears, a tune that vibrates throughout my soul, renewing my resolve.

I am grateful to be granted not only the finest of Queen Katherina's fleet, but given her personal ship as well. It was a token of her appreciation for my service, she told me. A "gift." It is the only offering my mother has ever given to me, mute evidence that she wasn't as evil as I had believed when she took my eye. Perhaps her gift is a gesture of her remorse, but a confession would never cross her lips.

My second-in-command, Bartholomew Smeeth, stumbles behind me droning on and on about something insignificant and extraordinarily annoying. I despise it when he mumbles. He is only a temporary pawn in the grand design. For now, I tolerate him, pretending that I was the fortunate one to have found him trembling in his ridiculous Royal Guard costume beneath the ornate dining room table in Buckingham Palace, sparing his life as he pledged his allegiance to me. A man swayed so easily is a liability. His time as a Marauder will soon be coming to an end.

As we climb the steps to the palace, one of the soldiers coughs within his helmet. I stop and stare, but he's unwilling to meet my gaze. Like all the Marauders, he, too, will eventually succumb to the Horologia virus, his fingers and lungs ravaged by the disease. A virus that took on a life of its own the day the first bombs dropped, destroying Europe's largest biological weapons lab. The beginning of the countdown to the end. Within a month, two-thirds of my soldiers were dead. Only the youngest survived, leaving the inexperienced to finish this war. Although no one is older than eighteen, they fight on with fierce determination until it is their turn to meet their maker, a fate none of us will escape.

Unless I have something to say about it.

We pass the masked soldiers guarding the entrance and stop at the gilded front doors of Buckingham Palace.

"The ship's almost full, Captain. She should be ready to travel soon. The sooner we get out of Everland, the better," Smeeth says.

"Agreed. Prepare them for departure," I say, storming through the entrance, leaving Smeeth in my wake. The lock gives an audible snap, sealing the palace doors behind me. I push the glass door of the inner chamber and step into the main room.

Gazing out the window, I watch the boilers hiss and columns of mist rise above the army of Steam Crawlers and zeppelins as they prepare for our departure. I reach for my copper-adorned eye patch, the socket as empty as my heart became the day I lost it. My fingers skim the three scars, scratching an itch that never seems to be satisfied. The ridges spark the childhood memory of my mother peering into her mirror, her once-unblemished and smooth skin mocking her as new lines of aging marked the corners of her eyes. Even as the years continued, I thought she was more beautiful with every one that passed.

The reflection next to hers was that of a young boy. It was my thirteenth birthday. After celebrating with the help, my instructors and only friends, I had brought her a gift since she was unable to join the festivities. Cupped in my small hands, I offered her a shiny green apple from the Forbidden Garden. Unbeknownst to me, a lethal substance lay within its peel. It was the last time I recognized the boy who reflected back at me. It was the last time my right eye ever saw her gold, bladelike fingernails that I once admired as they glittered in the sunlight. I never stepped foot into the orchard again.

Happy birthday to me.

I continue farther into the palace, until I reach a steel door. The tumblers click as I turn the key in the lock. When I enter the lab, a fine mist bathes me, washing away any outside contamination. The white walls, floor tiles, and countertops appear orange under the lantern light in the sterile room. Cabinets line the walls, their glass doors revealing bottles of medicine and other medical supplies. A single hospital bed sits against the wall. The stainless steel sink reflects the twinkle of lamp fire.

The Professor doesn't flinch as I step inside the room. She doesn't startle like she did during the early days of her imprisonment. Instead, she simply refuses to acknowledge my presence and studies her notes in a spiral binder, her auburn hair pulled back from her face. I often wonder if she's become comfortable with my company, or if she's so engrossed in her studies that she doesn't hear me enter. Either way, I can't help but find myself staring at her, infuriated by her lack of interest in my presence.

She is the same age as my mother, but other than that the Professor is nothing like her. As dark as my mother's hair, eyes, and heart are, the Professor is equally the opposite. She possesses wild hair, bright eyes, and a nurturing demeanor with the kids my men bring to her. Her kindness to the children both maddens and intrigues me.

"Pack the lab up. We're leaving Everland for good," I say.

The Professor's gaze flicks toward me and she does a double take, suddenly noticing me. Her eyes become wide and glassy.

"Leaving?" she asks.

"I've done what I came here to do. We will return to the Bloodred Queen tonight!"

She shakes her head and presses her lips together. "I am not going anywhere with you."

"Trust me, I'd leave you here in a heartbeat. You've accomplished nothing close to finding a cure. Consider it an act of mercy that I don't abandon you in Everland," I say, tamping down a burst of fury. I head to the door, afraid to turn back. Afraid she'll call my bluff. Even after all her failures, she's still the best chance at finding a cure.

She follows behind, grips my arm, and spins me toward her. "We can't leave yet. Your soldiers are dying, along with the remaining children of Everland. This virus is bound to kill all of us unless I find a cure. I have to stay!"

Her defiance stirs a burning ember within me, threatening to erupt into an infernal rage. No one challenges me and lives to tell about it. I slam my hand onto the counter. She takes several steps back.

"You've had months to figure it out. The best you've come up with is a means to treat the symptoms. All this time you've searched for immunity in the kids and you've come up with nothing! I'm tired of this forsaken city. We go home now!"

She glances down at her scarred and scabbed hands, evidence of her own infection, which she's managed to keep at bay. For how much longer, I am not sure. I start again for the door.

"Wait!" she says, her voice hitching. "If we leave today, there will be no hope for any of us, not without a cure. I know how to develop it, but what I need is here . . . in Everland."

"Why?" I ask, meeting her gaze. "What's here that you so desperately need?"

The Professor bites her bottom lip.

Fury explodes within me and before I know it, I have stormed toward the Professor, peering down at her. My hands grip her shoulders and she whimpers. "Tell me!"

She hesitates. I dig my fingers into her flesh. "Now!" I shout.

"If we leave, we will all die. But there is one person, one child, who can save us all."

Rage due to her months of lying boils over, and I shout, "Who? Who is it?"

Her eyes search mine and reluctance gives way. "Immunity lies in a single girl, the only one who was vaccinated for the virus."

"A girl? And you can't create a cure without her?" I ask, releasing the Professor.

She straightens her lab coat. Her eyes meet mine and the fear is gone. She takes a breath before she speaks.

"I've tried. Without her, we're all as good as dead."

· GWEN ·

I gently set Mikey down and slip my rucksack off my shoulders. Despite the chill of the early morning air, beads of sweat trickle down my face. I wipe them away with the back of my hand, trying to hide the mounting alarm racing through me.

"What are we going to do?" Mikey says. He rubs his nose on the sleeve of his threadbare blue pajamas.

"Don't worry. We're going to go find her," I say, hearing the apprehension in my voice.

"How?" Mikey asks. "There must be a bazillion pirates out there."

"I don't know. We'll figure it out," I say, attempting to reassure him. Frantically, I untie the top of my rucksack and empty its contents onto the floor to make room for only the essential supplies. Mikey pushes the umbrella aside and picks up the dusty old teddy bear, snuggling it to his chest.

"Can I keep it?" he asks, his eyes still red and swollen.

I consider telling him to leave it behind, that we can only afford to carry necessary supplies. But looking into his tear-streaked face and the single button eye on the bear, I don't have the heart to deny him this simple luxury. I nod and continue to fill my rucksack with the supplies from the shelf. As I lift a small sack of rice, a family of cockroaches scurries for cover. I brush away one that clings to the bag. In spite of the bugs, my mouth waters over our meager amount of food, but I push away my overwhelming desire to eat. This food is for Joanna and Mikey. I can live on less, have lived on less.

As if on cue, my stomach gives an audible growl while I'm putting a tin of tuna into my bag, reminding me that it's been days since my last meal. There is no time to worry about the small discomfort of hunger, though. The Marauders could be back at any time and the coal-black night is beginning to fade as the first hint of dawn paints the horizon. Giant clouds in the distance warn of an impending storm.

Mikey tugs my sleeve with a trembling hand. "Gwen, I don't want to go out there. What if they catch us? They'll feed us to the crocodiles!"

I pull him into my arms and hug him tight. "They won't get us, I promise. I'll keep you safe. And there are no crocodiles running around Everland. That is just a silly tale."

Something stirs to my left, sending a renewed dose of hot adrenaline coursing through my veins.

"Hide," I whisper to Mikey, shoving him aside. He runs and fades into the dark shadows on the other side of the room. Snatching my dagger, I whirl toward the noise. In the window, a person sits with his back against the metal frame. The small amount of moonlight still left in the early morning lights up his silhouette, casting his long shadow on the concrete floor. It stretches toward me and falls on my leather boots. I aim my blade at him.

"Who are you?" I demand.

The boy, not much older than me, seventeen at the most, steps close enough that I can make out his sharp facial features. His lips turn up in a cocky grin, and I immediately recognize him.

"It's you," I say with surprise. "You're the boy the Marauders were chasing."

He gives a dramatic bow. "In the flesh."

Noticing that I have let my blade drop, I point it back at him.

"Well, that's no way to treat a guest in your home," the boy says, lifting his aviator goggles from his face and perching them atop his head. He surveys our cramped home, wrinkling his nose in disapproval. "If that's what you call this landfill. Not much of a house at all, is it? And it stinks."

"What do you want? Supplies? Food? We have barely enough for ourselves. You might as well leave or . . ." My threat sounds unconvincing even to me. Biting the inside of my cheek, I remind myself that I must protect Mikey. "I'll kill you!"

He folds his arms, his face still shadowed in the dark room. "Kill me? I hardly think anyone could leave a scratch on me, much less a girl like you."

"You underestimate me," I say, jabbing my dagger toward him. He doesn't flinch.

"Do I?" he asks, pacing in front of the window. "First, you leave me at the mercy of Captain Hook's dirty dogs. Now you have a blade on me. A dull one, from what I can see. Is that how you normally thank someone who's saved your hide?"

"Saved my hide? You did nothing of the sort. What do you want?"

He doesn't have time to answer before footfalls clatter on the fire escape outside the window. I pull a second dagger from the sheath on my hip, aiming it at the window.

"Did you find anything, Pete?" asks a high-pitched voice from the gap in the wall. I glance around the boy's frame and see a young blond girl hop through the opening. It's the girl from the alley. Now that she's in front of me, I notice her mirrored goggles perched on top of her head, her dirty white tunic, dusty trousers, and heavy leather boots. The outline of her mechanical wings peeks above her tiny shoulders, their metallic sheen glittering in the moonlight.

When she sees me, the girl sprints forward, positioning herself between me and the boy. She pulls a slingshot from her belt. Her brows furrow and bright blue eyes narrow as she studies me.

"You'd better not touch him or else you're going to have to deal with me," she says, pulling the elastic back on her slingshot. A steel ball sits in the pocket, aimed at my head. "I assure you, I'm the best shot in all of Everland. Perhaps all of England."

The boy laughs, placing a hand on her shoulder. "It's all right, Bella. She isn't going to hurt us." She doesn't drop her aim. He steps around the little girl and holds his hand out, unfazed by my knives. "I'm Pete. This is Bella."

I take another step back, nearly tripping over the umbrella lying on the floor. Steadying myself, I kick the umbrella and the rest of my scavenged supplies out of my way. "How did you find me?"

Pete drops his hand and frowns. "I followed you, of course." He strides to the shelves and rifles through our supplies. "You really ought to cover your tracks better," he says, picking up a tin of corn. He shakes the container next to his ear, grimaces, sets it back on the shelf, and starts to grab another.

I step in front of him, gripping my daggers tightly. "I'd advise you to step away from our supplies, boy," I say through gritted teeth.

He brushes my weapons away with a swipe of his hand and reaches over my shoulder for another tin. Again he listens to the contents rattle inside. "My name is Pete, not 'boy,' and didn't we already go over that part? You're planning to slice and dice me with those butter knives of yours, yada yada."

He's called my bluff. I've done a number of things in order to survive, but I've never hurt anyone. I had hoped I'd never have to. Unable to bring myself to stab him, I kick him in the shin with the toe of my boot instead.

"Ow!" he yelps, dropping the tin and clutching his leg. "What was that for?"

Bella raises her slingshot again. "You really are asking for trouble, Immune."

I stand a little straighter and ignore Bella's threat. "What did you mean when you said I ought to cover my tracks? I've managed to outwit the Marauders for the past year," I say, sheathing one of my daggers but keeping the other pointed at him, just in case.

"Is that so? It's a bloody miracle you've lasted at all. Explain those to me," he says, pointing at the concrete floor. Shoe prints dance across the cement in a clumsy display. Now my own muddy boot prints overlap them. Something sour blooms in my stomach as I silently berate myself. I practically led the Marauders to our hideout. It's my fault Joanna is gone. How could I have been so careless?

"You left a trail of them behind you, and no offense, but if you don't want to be found, you might consider showering the next time the rain comes in. I could smell you from three blocks away. When was the last time you washed your . . ." He takes my hand in his and shock spreads across his face as he examines my fingers. I jerk back and push him away.

Bella drops her aim and smirks at me. "True story," she says with a wrinkle of her freckled nose.

My cheeks flame as I remember my reflection in the mirror earlier, and I hug myself, hoping to hide the scent I must have become so familiar with that I hardly smell it anymore.

Pete stares at my hands folded into my arms. When his gaze doesn't shift, I hide my hands behind my back. His eyes flick to mine before he turns his attention back to our meager supplies and steps around me.

"Another thing: It's polite to say thank you when someone saves your life," he says, tossing a tin to Bella. She begins to place it in a pouch attached to her hip.

"Hey! That belongs to me!" I seize the tin from her and put it in my own bag. She squints in anger. I ignore her and turn my dagger to Pete. "And what do you mean you saved my life?"

Pete sifts through the contents on the shelves. "First off, quit pointing that thing at me," he says, sounding more amused than annoyed. "Second, we aren't here to hurt you. Third, do you really think I would be crowing on a rooftop in an attempt to draw the Marauders' attention away from you if I wasn't trying to help you? If I had slunk away unseen, Hook's Marauders would have found you in a heartbeat. You'd be in Everland strapped to a cot with tubes snaking out of you. Unless you aspire to become a human pincushion, you should be thanking us, Immune."

He picks up the half-full canister of pasta and tosses it to Bella. I catch it in midair, stashing it in my rucksack.

"Don't call me that!" I say, pushing Pete aside. "Get out of my way." I grab a small first aid kit, a tin of beans, and what's left of the rice, shoving them in my bag.

"Call you what?" Pete gives me a mocking grin that screams to be slapped, but I refrain.

"Do. Not. Call. Me. Immune." I enunciate each word with a jab of my finger into his chest.

Bella cocks her head to one side. "That is what you are, isn't it? That's what Hook would call you," she says, grabbing the rice from my bag and stuffing it into hers.

"And who is Hook anyway?" I continue, clutching my rucksack to my chest.

Bella puts her hands on her hips and stares at me incredulously. "Who's Hook? For an Immune, you sure don't know much, do you?"

I stare at her, speechless.

Bella gives an exaggerated sigh. "The leader of the Marauders. Hanz Otto Oswald Kretschmer. H-O-O-K," she says, spelling out each letter. "Get it now? HOOK. Or at least that's what we call him."

"Kretschmer? You've nicknamed Captain Kretschmer? Is she serious?" I ask.

Pete laughs. "Entirely, and I wouldn't question Bella if I were you, Immune. You don't want to be on her bad side. She might be small for a twelve-year-old, but she's a fighter."

"I told you to stop calling me that."

"I don't know what else to call you," Pete says, draping an arm over Bella's shoulder. "Here Bella and I have been polite, introduced ourselves, saved you, and you still haven't told us your name." He clicks his tongue. "What poor manners you have. Didn't your mother teach you anything? Where are your folks, anyway? Did they run like the others?" He grabs a book of matches from the shelf and hands it to Bella.

My face grows warm with anger. I clutch my father's military tags, feeling the bite of the chain in the palm of my hand. The metal brings forth my last memory of my father. Just before the first bombs dropped over London, he kissed my forehead, slipped his military tags around my neck, and told me he must protect the Queen of England. Pride glistened in his eyes as the front door shut, leaving me behind to care for my siblings. Promises of returning never fulfilled.

I swallow my rage. "Dead," I say under my breath to keep Mikey from hearing, not wanting to dash his hopes of their survival. For now at least. The truth is much too painful.

Bella and Pete exchange an odd glance and stare back at me.

I sigh and go back to packing my bag. "Aren't all the adults dead? Parents, soldiers . . . even Her Majesty hasn't been seen or heard from since the war started."

Pete and Bella remain quiet, as if waiting for me to continue.

"Dad was a staff sergeant in Her Majesty's Armed Forces. Mum was a doctor, a researcher of some sort. Neither came home the day the war started. End of story. What concern is it of yours, anyway?"

Pete swallows and dips his chin to his chest, seeming to contemplate what to say next. "I'm sorry for your loss," he says in almost a whisper. It is the first time his voice is devoid of sarcasm, which takes me by surprise. He grips Bella by the hand and she gazes up at him with affection. "Mine are gone, too. Have been for several years now. And Bella here, I found her hiding in a hollowed-out tree trunk a few days after the bombs fell. Her parents didn't make it either."

The hurt on his face reflects the same deep ache I feel: a dark, vacant chasm my parents once filled. Bella kicks at a clump of mud on the floor and doesn't look up. I think of the numerous nights my brother cried in his sleep, calling out for our parents and being comforted by both Joanna and me. I can't imagine what Bella, just a child herself, must have felt hiding all alone with no one to reassure her everything would be all right. She would've been eleven. Not nearly old enough to care for herself alone.

"I'm sorry for your loss, too," I say softly. Another uncomfortable silence hangs in the air. Finally, I notice the book of matches in Bella's hand and snatch it from her. "But that doesn't mean you can take our supplies."

"Gwen?" Mikey whispers from around the corner of the shelves.

"I told you to hide," I hiss. An injured expression crosses his face, and he shrinks back into the darkened corner, hiding behind the dirty teddy bear. I immediately regret snapping at him. When did I become so quick to hostility?

"Gwen?" Pete asks, looking at me quizzically. "That's not much better than Immune, if you ask me."

Glaring at him, I grab another item from the shelf, a photograph of my family. "How did you two survive, anyway? Most of the children have been abducted or fled with their families. I haven't seen anyone in months," I say.

Pete peers over my shoulder at the picture without answering.

"Hmm, you have a sister, too? She's cute for a Little. Is she hiding in here also?" Pete asks, stealing the photo from my hand. "Come out, come out, wherever you are, Little."

Searching the bottom shelf, Bella groans and tosses a thimble, which she seems to deem useless. She stashes a sewing kit into her satchel.

"A Little?" I ask, reaching for the photograph. Pete holds it out of my reach, inspecting it carefully.

"That's what Pete calls all the kids who aren't teenagers," Bella says, peering over his shoulder. "Kids like me. At least until next year."

"So where is she?" Pete asks, his brows raised.

"She's not here," I say, snatching the photo from Pete's hand. I glide my finger over the familiar face in the picture. Joanna's curly hair hangs haphazardly in her face. She smiles brightly as she leans her head on our Newfoundland puppy, Nanny, another casualty of the war. A lump grows in my throat and tears spring to my eyes. I shove the photo into my pack and swallow back the pain. There's no time for tears.

"Not that it's any of your business, but Joanna's been taken." I brush Pete aside, sheathe my dagger, fling my rucksack over my shoulders, and take Mikey by the hand. "Now if you'll excuse us, we need to find our sister."

I swing a leg over the window ledge, but a hand jerks me back, sending me crashing to the floor. When I look up, Pete has my bag in his hand. He kneels, his eyes drilling into me.

"You're coming with us," he says matter-of-factly.

"What?" I stare at him, stunned. Anxiety prickles my skin like a swarm of fire ants, and my fingers graze my daggers.

His face draws close to mine. "You don't plan to march into the city and rescue your sister with a couple of dull daggers, do you?"

"I'll find another weapon on the way." I grab for my pack, but he brushes my hand aside.

"Do you really believe you and your kid brother can get her back all by yourself? It's only a matter of time before you're caught, too." Pete hands me my bag. "Most survivors have learned the two rules to staying alive. Number one: Don't leave behind a footprint. Bella and I stick to the rooftops. Others, those that are skilled with weapons and can run fast . . ."

"And have stomachs of steel," Bella interjects, wrinkling her nose.

"Those Scavengers utilize the sewage systems," Pete finishes.

"There are other people?" Mikey asks, tugging on Pete's coattail.

"Of course there are others," Bella says with exasperation in her voice. "Lots of them. All kids, obviously. You don't think the four of us are the only ones left in England, do you?"

"Where are the other kids?" Mikey asks, his expression wild with curiosity.

Pete beckons us to the window. Mikey follows and, with reluctance, I join them. In the distance, the crumbled buildings of Everland rise toward the sky like steel, concrete, and brick tombstones. The navy-blue hues of night have faded into lavender as the sun on the horizon chases away what is left of the evening stars. Only two twinkling points remain. Pete points to the west.

"Second to the right," he says. "Just below it."

"You're telling me there are children hiding in Everland?" I ask in disbelief. "Why would they remain in the city? That's the first place the Marauders would search. The children are practically right under Kretschmer's nose."

"Not Kretschmer. Hook," Bella corrects.

Pete rubs his stubbled chin. "Quite literally under his nose, in fact. They're not *in* Everland, they're *beneath* it."

Staring out into the distance, I try to imagine orphaned children living underneath the decimated city. "How is that remotely possible?"

Bella shrugs and says, "We live in the Underground and within the Lost City."

"The Underground? As in the railway? I thought the tunnels were destroyed during the war," I say.

"That's only partially true," Pete says, sitting on the frame, his legs dangling outside the window. "Many were destroyed, but some of the tunnels survived the bombing. A few of the secret bunkers are still intact, too."

He leans forward, his eyes gleaming. "The bunkers and tunnels are much more than concrete holes in the earth now. We have a team of Tinkers, engineers who have built an entire city beneath Everland. A city in which a hundred kids thrive. Clean water, food, shelter." He glances down at Mikey. "Safety."

When he looks back at me, his gaze locks with mine. "You are going to be our guests."

"Guests?" Mikey asks, excitement brightening his expression.

Pete smiles, the first rays of morning lighting the left side of his face in a golden radiance. "We're taking you to the Lost City." He stands in the window frame and extends his hand out to me.

Bella, blowing a puff of air, ruffles the fringe hanging in her face. "We? More like *you*. I didn't invite them," she says, climbing into the window frame.

"The Lost City?" I ask in wonder. The thought of a city run by children seems unimaginable, like a fairy tale.

"It's where all of the orphans go," Pete says. "It's where Bella and I call home. The Lost City is all that's left for us, or at least what the Marauders haven't claimed as their own. Luckily, they have no idea that it exists. It's a place for the survivors of the war and the Horologia virus, the children who have no parents. They can, they *will*, help get your sister back."

Doubtful, I eye him warily. "You're kidding. How can a bunch of children help get Joanna back?"

He beams. "I guess you're just going to have to trust me."

"Trust *you*? You must be mad. How do I know you're being truthful about the Lost City? For all I know this is a trick and you're aligned with the Marauders. You could take us straight to Hook. And even if you're not one of those horrid pirates, two less people in the city to fight over supplies would only benefit you, isn't that right?" I say, brushing Mikey behind me.

Pete crosses his arms. "If I were in with Hook or wanted less competition, I would've made sure Hook's men found you in that abandoned home, and Mikey would be fending for himself."

Mikey peeks around me, frowns, and grips my hand tighter.

Bella sighs. "While I would like to see you left behind, I don't want to wait around here any longer." She reaches into her leather satchel and holds out a clenched fist. Her tiny gloved fingers open slowly. Gold powder shimmers in morning rays of sunlight like fairy dust. Speechless, I look at Bella and back at Pete.

"It looks like gold," Mikey says, running a finger through the sparkling powder. "Did you find a pirate's treasure chest?"

"Sort of. You've heard of the Bank of England, right?" Bella asks.

Mikey nods.

"Well, this is only a bit of the thousands of gold bars beneath the building. Cogs says the gold is too soft to make anything practical. He ground the gold bars into powder for me so when I scavenge, I dust the path ahead of me to decide how far I have to jump. All I need is a bit of moon or lamplight to reflect off it." Bella pulls the lever on the straps of the rocket pack and her wings eject, sputtering to life. From far away, I didn't realize how truly remarkable they were, but up close I'm awestruck by their beauty. Her wings are made of copper piping intricately designed with sweeping loops, brightly polished cogs, and a stunning mechanical clock. A thin film covers the mechanisms in each wing, and as the early morning light hits it, the coating shimmers in a show of bright colors.

"Who's Cogs?" Mikey asks.

"He's a Tinker, a boffin of sorts. Our chief engineer, to be exact," Pete says. "Cogs is a smart chap who fiddled in robotics and electronics before the war. He's in charge of operations in the Lost City."

Shouts erupt in the distance. The familiar squeal of gears grinding against one another from the Marauder's Steam Crawlers echoes through the labyrinth of buildings. Pete stands taller in the window, searching the streets. His forehead wrinkles. "It's time to go," he says, adjusting the straps of his pack over his shoulders.

"I don't know," I reply, hesitant as I turn toward Mikey. He stares at me with an anxious expression and pulls his teddy into his chest, fiddling with the single button eye. "How can I trust you?" I ask Pete.

"What more is left here for you but faith?" Pete says, extending a hand to me from the open window. The sunlight halos him an amber glow.

"And a little bit of pixie dust," Bella adds, pouring the rest of the gold into my hand.

The shouts from the street grow louder. I swallow the lump of fear in my throat, torn between taking my brother and running for safety on our own or joining Pete and Bella. Mikey tugs at my hand and waves a finger at me, gesturing for me to come closer. I bend toward him.

"Can't we go with them, Gwen?" he whispers. "They have all of our food anyway."

He has a point. If I reject their offer, they'll leave with our supplies and we will have nothing but what is in my pack. If we go with them and the Lost City is real, Mikey will have a safe place to stay while I rescue our sister.

I turn back to Pete and Bella, who both stand in the window, silhouetted in the sun's early glow. Bella's glittering wings flutter. "Pete, they're getting close!"

"So, are you coming?" Pete says, leaning toward me.

I peek through the window. Shadows creep between the warehouses. The metal clang of military vehicles crawling along the broken streets echoes through the maze of buildings. Steam rises between the buildings and the vehicles let out an ominous hiss.

Bella's eyes flash with worry. "Pete? We have to go!" she urges, waving my brother toward the window. I lift Mikey, and Bella helps him through the opening. As I reach for Pete's outstretched hand, I hesitate.

"Wait. What was the second rule to surviving?" I ask.

Pete smiles, his perfect white teeth flashing with confidence. He places his goggles back over his brilliant green eyes, and I see my worried reflection stare back at me in the lenses. He pulls me into the window frame with both hands, drawing me close enough that I can feel his breath against my cheeks.

"Rule number two: I am always right."

· H O O K ·

Smeeth's breath crackles in a wet wheeze as he struggles to keep up. As if the fires, ash, and dust in Everland weren't bad enough, the cigars he insists on inhaling have only made his asthma worse. But I say nothing. Maybe he'll kill himself before I have to do the dirty deed myself.

"But, Captain, you were scheduled to return to the Bloodred Queen six months ago with a progress report. Why are we still chasing orphans? We've gained nothing from them."

"Those orphans, or rather one orphan in particular, are vital to my plan," I say, marching through the ornate palace hallway to the front entrance, stopping at a window.

Smeeth wrings his hands. "They were never part of the objective. Your mother will have all of our heads if we don't return to Lohr Castle soon."

Outside, the shadowed rubble renews my resolve. There is only one thing left to do in Everland before we leave. Just one.

"Mother will have my head anyway, along with my lungs, liver, and anything else she desires. We were supposed to claim England as ours, to establish our own governorship over the country. What good is our report now? We have single-handedly destroyed the heart of England and in turn released a deadly virus. If we leave now, what news do we have to bring her? That we took over London, renamed it Everland, and that the city is only a fraction of the metropolis it once was? She already knows what I've done. If the report from Germany is true, if the Bloodred Queen has contracted the virus, too, then this disease has spread well beyond England's borders. Not only that, but I've failed her . . . twice."

My fingers bite into the windowsill, the pain calming the humiliation brewing within me. "I have to find the cure. I will not return to Lohr Castle without it."

"You've done what the Bloodred Queen has asked," Smeeth says. "You've conquered England. Let us give her the report she's asked for and leave with the money, travel the world away from this dump. Queen Katherina can deal with coming back and cleaning up the mess herself."

"It won't be enough," I say.

"What do you mean it won't be enough? England is defeated and two billion as payment is hardly something to scoff at."

Spinning, I lunge toward Smeeth, towering over him until I am close enough that I can smell the wretched stink from his last cigar. "And what if the rest of the world looks like this? Aside from the single report on the Queen's condition, no one outside of England has made contact since the attack. Not even by telegraph or carrier pigeon. England's allies would never let this go unpunished unless . . . unless the virus spread. That's the only reasonable explanation for the silence from them, from the world, really. We know that the Horologia virus has drifted beyond England's borders, but how far?"

"I don't know, Captain," Smeeth says, taking a few steps back. "But I still think you ought to take the money and run."

I reach inside the pocket of my black leather military coat. I pull out a fiver along with a book of matches, then set the bill on fire. It bursts into a vibrant flame and then extinguishes, leaving a dusting of ashes on the floor. "If the virus has spread and left the world's leading countries immobilized, this note is nothing more than a measly piece of paper. What is the money worth now? Nothing!"

"Then we'll ask for payment in precious metals and gems," Smeeth says.

As I gaze at what remains of the once-magnificent palace, my eyes fall upon the torn tapestries hanging from the faded walls, remnants from the day when I claimed it as my headquarters. "No, we are on the brink of having something worth more than rocks and crystals. Something the world leaders will sacrifice anything for to save the citizens they have left. A service—a gift, really— that even my mother can't provide her people. A prize that will award me the respect I'm long overdue."

"What's that?" Smeeth says, furrowing his brow.

"The cure."

I spin on my heels and head toward the palace doors. "Sound the signal. I want those Crawlers and zeppelins ready to go in five."

"Yes, Captain." Smeeth salutes and hurries from the palace.

Within minutes the alarm's shrill cry breaks the silence of the misty early morning. Armed men scatter like ants retreating from a stomped-on anthill. They form perfect lines, each a mirror image of the other. Their only form of identification is their names clumsily scratched into the metal of their full helmets. Fools. They think etching their name on their helmet so no other soldier accidentally wears it will keep them from contracting the virus. They'll all be as good as dead if I don't succeed.

Dozens of Steam Crawlers fill the palace courtyard, an army of spiderlike machines. Brigades of masked soldiers file in formation as they flank the armored vehicles. I stand at the entrance of Buckingham Palace. Towering over the army of men, I scan the mass, my heart beating wildly beneath my coat. The sight of the soldiers, their dark uniforms adorned with bits of metal that reflect an orange glow from the dawn sunlight, stirs a flicker within me, like a candle chasing away the darkness of despair.

"Marauders, this is our time, the moment we have waited for. We came to London to seize it, to establish Everland for the Bloodred Queen. And today is a new step toward real power, absolute supremacy. Our treasure is not gold, but the crowns from each of the world's leaders."

My voice is swept away by the soldiers' cheer. Their shouts feed the flame in my gut, fueling my confidence. I clutch an empty glass vial and hold it high for the soldiers to see.

"This is all we need. The blood of the Immune will send the strongest leaders of the world to their knees, even the Bloodred Queen herself. The Immune lies here within Everland. Find the girls. Find them all! Find the female whose veins pulse with the antidote to the Horologia virus."

Again the Marauders roar with solidarity, their deep voices almost mechanical beneath their helmets. Gunshots ring through the chilly morning air.

"Find Pete! He knows where they're hiding. Search every street, building, rubbish bin, crack, hole, crevice, rooftop, and basement. She's out there. Bring me the cure!"

The army thunders in approval. With clenched fists pumping, they burst into chants. "Hook! Hook! Hook!"

I ball my fists, cringing at the nickname they have given me. "It's Captain Kretschmer," I mutter through gritted teeth.

"I'd go with it, Captain," Smeeth says. "It has a nice ring to it. Don't you think?"

My eyes skim the Marauders, taking in the rows of men cheering for me. For me! Not my mother, the Queen of Germany. They're not shouting out the surname that I was unfortunate to have been born with. No. Not Captain Kretschmer.

Hook!

Tucking the vial into the pocket of my coat, I feel the tug of a smile pull at my lips. "Perhaps you're right, Smeeth. It's a new beginning, not just for me, but for all of us." I spin the gold ring adorned with the seal of the Bloodred Queen on my finger. "A new era."

Slipping the ring from my finger, I hold it for the soldiers to see. "Long live the Bloodred Queen!" I shout. I toss the ring into the air, and with my pistol, I shoot the band of gold. It fragments into two pieces before clinking on the brick ground. The last link of choking resentment slips from the heavy chain wrapped tightly around my neck.

The soldiers chant my name, feeding the embers of determination deep inside of me. I reach inside my pocket, pull out another ring, and slip it on my gloved finger. With a balled fist, I hold it up for my army to see. The gold skull and crossbones shimmer in the sunlight.

"We will rule the world!" I shout.

The Marauders roar as they climb into their vehicles. I rush down the steps and slide into my Steam Crawler. With a hiss of the boiler, the military vehicle rumbles to life. The tank howls as its mechanical legs creep forward into the broken city.

· GWEN ·

Having ventured out only at night in the last year, my eyes sting in the daylight. Mikey fares better as he peeks through the holes of a colander neatly tied to his head with twine. An old, rusty pot lid serves as a chest plate. Bronze cogs, bolts, and wheels attach kettle lids to his makeshift shoulder pads and spin as he swings his arms. His brown teddy bear peers out of the top of the small rucksack on his back. Seeing his petite frame in the crude armor reminds me of the hours Joanna spent constructing it. I miss her terribly and wish I could take back all the things I said the last time I was with her.

Mikey struggles to keep up, and finally stumbles, his worn shoes tripping on the buckled concrete street.

"Mikey!" I sprint to him and kneel. Blood seeps through a scrape on his knee, staining his tattered pajamas. "Are you okay?"

"It hurts and I'm tired," he says, sniffling back tears.

We've been traveling toward the city for an hour. I'm worn out from walking, crawling under fences, and hiding under what is left of expressway overpasses. Mikey must be exhausted.

Bella pulls the teddy bear from Mikey's rucksack, kneels by my brother, and hands the stuffed animal to him. "Here, this will help you feel better," she says. Mikey takes the ragged toy with some reluctance, worry creasing his forehead. He snuggles the bear to his chest, and I notice the corners of Bella's lips turn up in a slight smile. In that moment, her fierceness disappears, and I see a trace of the girl she must have been before the war changed us all. I can't help but smile at her attempt to comfort him in spite of her pride.

When she catches me staring at her, she grimaces and stands. "You really ought to be more careful. It's no wonder you fell with all that shuffling you've been doing," she says, flipping the lever on her rocket pack. The contraption gives a loud hiss as steam rises from the pack. Her wings deploy with an audible click. They glitter brightly beneath the faintest ray of sunlight peeking through broken storm clouds. Bella's feet lift from the ground and she floats to Pete's side.

"Can't we rest awhile?" I ask, wrapping an arm around my brother.

Pete stops, shakes his head, and walks toward us. "If we rest, we die. You just don't get it, do you, Immune?" he says. His tone is sharp and jarring, sending a fresh wave of anxiety through me. My cheeks grow warm. When I say nothing, Pete walks away with Bella flying just above his right shoulder.

"Why do you keep calling me that?" I ask, gathering myself as I help Mikey to his feet. We sprint to catch up with Pete and Bella.

"Keep calling you what?" he replies, obviously toying with me.

"Immune. Aren't you and Bella Immunes, too?"

Bella wrinkles her nose, as if the suggestion has left a bitter taste in her mouth. "No way. We're Lost Kids."

"Lost whats?" Mikey asks, letting go of my hand and staggering alongside Pete.

Pete whirls around. "A Lost Kid. A member of the Lost City. Can we move on now?"

"But you're still an Immune, aren't you? What, precisely, is the difference?" I ask.

"The difference is precisely this: Lost Kids never get caught," Pete says, standing a little taller. He spins, walking backward, and points a finger at me. "Immunes, on the other hand, eventually end up as one of Hook's lab rats." Pete turns and continues marching up the street. "Without Bella and me, you'd be in Hook's lab as we speak."

I roll my eyes. "This is ridiculous," I mutter.

"I don't want to get caught," Mikey says, scurrying in front of Pete. "I want to be a Lost Kid like you and Bella."

Pete stops and crouches. "Well, there you go," he says, giving Mikey a gentle tap on the nose. "You're well on your way to being a Lost Boy. Stick with me, kid, and you will be a Lost Boy in no time. In fact . . ." Pete unsheathes his dagger and taps each of Mikey's shoulders with the flat surface of the blade. "I dub you, Mikey, Lost Boy in training." He turns the knife and offers the ornate hilt to my little brother.

Mikey's mouth gapes as he reaches for the chrome dagger. I snatch it from his hand and give it back to Pete. Mikey scowls, but it quickly fades. He throws his bear into the air, catches it, and dances around in circles. "I'm going to be a Lost Boy!" he sings.

Bella blows a breath through puffed cheeks and flicks the lever on her rocket pack. Her wings flutter slower and she glides to the ground. "Did you have to go and make him a trainee?"

"You are completely mad." I throw my rucksack over my shoulder and stomp off, irritated with his nonsensical talk.

"Hey, wait," Pete says. He runs next to me.

I trudge forward, unwilling to stop. "What? Now that you've knighted my brother, are you going to tell me you can fly, too?" I gesture to Bella, who folds her arms and narrows her eyes.

He drapes an arm over my shoulders. "Maybe I can."

I shrug off his arm and march away from him.

"Oh, and one more thing," he says.

Whirling around, I stare at the boy. "What now?" I ask, annoyed.

"You," he says, stepping closer to me and poking a finger into my shoulder, "are still an Immune."

Before I can retort, deep, metallic voices resound from the buildings nearby. Pete shoves me behind a smelly shrub, and Bella and Mikey race after us. I glance around the edge of the bush, careful not to touch the leaves. A group of Marauders hurries up the street. They shout orders through their gas masks, their words indecipherable from this far away. My stomach rolls as I watch one soldier drag a dead body from a building by a laced boot. Empathy settles over me as the soldiers joke about her pink knickers peeking out from her ripped skirt. I am glad she is no longer alive to face the embarrassment of their crude comments.

The soldier lifts a manhole cover, and she is rolled into the sewer by the heel of his boot.

"Lunchtime," the soldier shouts into the hole.

I swallow back the urge to vomit. My throat is dry and my hands tremble. I have no idea what the soldier meant, but I'm terrified to entertain the thought. I pull Mikey close. "What are we going to do?"

"We need to split up," Pete says, peeking through the bush. "Bella, take Mikey. Meet us at Beckton Station."

Bella nods, pulls her slingshot from her belt, and grips Mikey's hand. He doesn't resist, but his bottom lip quivers.

I brush Mikey behind me. "No! I'm not leaving him."

"We are going to distract those soldiers. Mikey is too little to outrun them," Pete explains with quick, quiet words. "You and I have the best chance of evading them, and Bella knows every hiding spot from here to the first tunnel entrance. It's our best option."

"I want to come with you," Mikey whines into the fur of his bear.

Placing a finger against his pink lips, I shush him. The twigs of the bush scratch my cheek as I peer through the maze of branches. Hook's men search the empty, run-down buildings with their weapons drawn, sunlight reflecting in the metal gleam of their guns. One soldier breaks a window with the butt of his gun and kicks at the remaining shards, sending glass tinkling onto the concrete. He raises the weapon, looking through the brass scope mounted on top before stepping through the gaping hole.

"It's either now or never. If we don't go, we'll all be caught," Pete says, flicking his gaze at me and back at the soldiers.

The soldiers are two buildings away and approaching quickly. "Mikey, you stay with Bella. Don't leave her side for even a minute," I insist. I take a deep breath, trying to loosen the growing tightness in my chest. "Do whatever she tells you to. No arguing."

Mikey frowns and tears pool in his eyes. "But, Gwen, I'm scared. Let me come with you." I'm tempted to change my mind when Pete stoops in front of Mikey.

"I need you to look after her," he says, tilting his head toward Bella. "She needs a brave soldier, a Lost Boy, to protect her. I know you can do it. Can I count on you?"

His kindness surprises me, and I feel the ire brewing in me shift.

"I don't need looking after," Bella argues. Her voice teeters on revealing our hiding spot.

Pete takes her petite hand into his. "We all could use an extra pair of eyes watching our backs. Where would I be without you? How many times have you gotten me out of a jam? Once? Twice?"

"More like a thousand," she mutters. Bella kicks at a pile of stones from the crumbled structure behind us and curses under her breath. "Okay, fine. I am a damsel in distress and need your help. Without you, I'm bound to become Hook's next victim, and I'll never ever get away," she says in a quiet singsong tone, waving a gloved hand in the air. "So, what'll it be? You with me or not?" She playfully punches Mikey's shoulder.

Mikey tilts his head and looks at me, seeking my approval. Even though I know he's frightened, he rolls his shoulders back and stands up a little straighter. There's a change in his expression, and suddenly he's not a little boy but something stronger, braver.

I nod my consent, even though my stomach aches at the thought of leaving him behind.

Squeezing his bear to his chest with one arm, Mikey pulls the umbrella from the pack on his back with his other hand. He holds it in front of him as if it were a sword. "I will guard her with my life," he says, his small voice unwavering.

I wrap my arms around him, hugging him tight as the nagging feeling that this might be the last time I will ever see him whispers in my head. "Mum and Dad would be so proud of you," I say quietly. "If they could only see how grown up . . ." My words catch in my throat. I swallow them back. He's too little to be a grown-up. I am supposed to be the brave one. Mikey's sad face reflects the ache within me. Dropping my arms, I step back to take one last look at him, but I don't get the opportunity.

"We need to go now!" Pete says, shoving me out of the bushes. I stumble from our hiding place before regaining my balance. The sting of sheer terror adds to the dull pang of hunger. A half-dozen soldiers stare at us through their goggled helmets, a few of them stopping midstride, as if unsure what to do next.

I step back, panic imploring me to run. "What have you done? They've spotted us!"

"That's the whole point." Pete crosses his arms and gives a bellowing laugh that echoes through the narrow street. "It's about time you yobs arrived. What took you so long? Hide-and-seek gets awfully boring waiting for you to show up." Pete taps the leather cuff watch on his wrist, his fingernail audibly clicking against the intricate gears. "Tick tick."

The soldiers lift their weapons, their chrome barrels taking aim at us. I struggle to catch a breath as two other soldiers emerge from the crowd: a tall, muscular boy a bit older than me and a short, maskless boy. Both have bronze-and-chrome Gatling guns wrapping around a single arm. While the shorter one is dressed in a similar dark and metallic uniform as the other Marauders, the other wears a long, leather military coat adorned with brass buckles and buttons. Although the soldiers' armor is intimidating, the sight of the leather-clad boy makes the hair on the back of my neck stand up. I know immediately who he is.

Up until today he has been the faceless boogeyman from my nightmares, a distorted illusion formed by rumors on the streets the days after the bombs fell. Seeing him up close for the first time, he is more terrifying than I imagined. I can make out every detail, including his tan skin, square jaw, and black hair. Three long scars rake across the right side of his face, disappearing beneath an eye patch. Despite his ominous demeanor, it is his dark, single eye that frightens me most.

I have no doubt that the boy who stands before me is the leader of the Marauders. Hook. My heart sinks and my limbs feel heavy, unable to move. The Marauder's good eye grows wide before he bursts into a fit of laughter. The shorter soldier steps next to him.

"Blimey, it's him, Captain!" the soldier says. His English dialect betrays him. He is one of our own. My stomach lurches at his treachery. "It's Pete!"

"Indeed, it is, Mr. Smeeth, and a girl," the Captain says in a mocking tone, his dark eye narrowing on me.

"A girl?" Pete says, staring at me with a quizzical expression. "Who? Her? Or are you referring to that pathetic sidekick of yours?"

Smeeth lunges toward us but is stopped by Hook's outstretched arm. The Captain rubs his chin. "You keep foul company for a girl." He tilts his face toward the sky, as if sniffing the air. "I thought I smelled chicken."

The other soldiers snicker in unison. A few howl a rooster call, mockingly.

Pete cackles, unintimidated by the Marauders. "Let me introduce you to Captain Hook himself and his little trollop. Nice to run into you again, Bartholomew."

I try to distance myself from the soldiers, walking backward slowly, but Pete grips my elbow tightly. A tremble rips through my body as terror floods my veins. I had hoped I'd never have to meet the Captain beyond my nightmares.

Smeeth flinches. "That would be Mr. Smeeth to you," he says, lifting his arm and aiming the menacing Gatling gun at us.

"Aww, I thought we were over the formalities and on a first-name basis," Pete mocks.

I bite my lip, tasting the coppery hint of blood, and realize I'm being pathetic. If I'm going to be Hook's next abduction, I'll at least go out fighting. I grip my knives and steel myself.

"Capturing you has become much easier than I had anticipated. We'll be back to the palace by high tea," Smeeth says.

"Let's not make this difficult. Why don't you and your little girlfriend just come with us," Hook says, taking a careful step toward us and holding up his gloved hands.

Pete elbows me in the ribs. "Girlfriend? Did you hear that? I had no idea you had feelings for me, although it is hardly surprising. I *am* irresistible."

My cheeks flush, the heat spreading to my ears and neck. I blink at him, incredulous and unsure what to say. I've never been anyone's girlfriend.

"What do you say?" Pete continues. "Hide-and-seek was not much fun. We're much too good at hiding. Are you up for a game of follow-the-leader? Although I ought to warn you, Captain Hook and Bartholomew are lousy leaders, and I would avoid standing downwind from them. They smell like codfish."

I shake my head more in disbelief than as an actual response.

"Yeah, me neither." He shrugs, leans near me, and holds a hand up to his mouth. "They don't play fair anyway," he says in an exaggerated whisper.

Before I have a chance to respond, Pete snatches something

from inside his coat and launches it toward the soldiers. A tin can bounces several times before stopping in front of Hook and exploding into a red, smoky haze. Pete clutches my hand and we are running. My feet trip as I attempt to keep up with him. Adrenaline pulses through me like fuel, pumping blood to my wobbly legs. I glance back at the bewildered soldiers as the buildings blur past.

"Get her!" Hook screams, covering his good eye from the smoke.

A hurricane of sounds bombards me: military boots running, shouting voices muffled by masks, and the panting of my own breath as we sprint around a corner.

"What are you doing?" I ask, my hand gripped so tight in his that my fingers tingle.

"Saving your hide, again," he says through quick breaths. "The first time was free. This one will cost you. I'm sure you'll think of some way to thank me later. Back massage, foot rub, I might even let you kiss me."

I ignore his insinuation and pick up my pace as boots pound the street behind us. "They'll shoot us, won't they?" I ask, expecting hot pain to flood through my body at any moment.

"No, they won't hurt us. They need us in decent health. We're no good to them bleeding and at death's door."

Bullets ricochet off the brick storefront next to us, sending up plumes of dust and rocks. I duck and shield my face as pebbles pelt me. Pete pulls me around the corner of the building as the sound of shots follows our path.

"I thought you said they wouldn't shoot at us," I yell over the cacophony of gunfire.

A brick wall blocks our way. Pete scrambles up it effortlessly. "I've been known to be wrong before," Pete grunts as he pulls himself to the top and reaches his hand down to help me up.

"But what about rule number two?" I say, swinging my legs over the top of the wall.

"It appears with you here, rule number two is null and void," he says. He leaps down and helps me from the wall. "Enough with the talking and more with the running. That canister of ground chili peppers will stall them, but not for long," he says, dragging me onto an abandoned street. Rats scatter past puddles left over from last night's rain. The stench of death and rot rises from the manholes in the humid summer heat. Our boots tread over unidentifiable rubbish, splashing pungent brown liquid onto my trouser legs.

We zigzag through the alleyways as the Marauders pursue us. Finally, Pete pulls me onto a narrow side street between two rundown brick structures. He grunts as he lifts a manhole cover from the street.

"Quick, climb in," he says.

I hesitate, covering my mouth and nose as a vile smell wafts from the opening.

"Now!" Pete growls, giving me a hard shove.

As the soldiers draw near, I sit on the edge of the manhole and drop into the sewage system, my boots kicking up a splash of murky water. I lean against the wall, panting. Pete climbs down the ladder, replaces the cover, and joins me, peering through the holes in the cover. Footsteps stop just above. I slump against the brick wall. A foul odor prickles the inside of my nose. My stomach gurgles in protest and my eyes sting. I blink back burning tears.

Something sticky and squishy seeps between my fingers. With the sleeve of my coat, I wipe away tears and blink down at the object. A guttural scream erupts from me, but Pete clamps his hand over my mouth. His fingers press so tightly into my flesh, the bones in my cheeks ache. I recoil from the decomposing skeleton and into Pete. Looking away, I bury my face into his chest. His arms squeeze me tight.

"Shh!" Pete warns in a hushed voice. "You're going to get us caught!"

Nodding, I shift my gaze back to the body. Empty eye sockets stare lifelessly up as beetles writhe on the remaining bits of flesh. The buzz of flies rings in my ears. Blood stains the almond-colored dress, the lace of the woman's corset having frayed. Two skeletal legs stick out from beneath her voluminous skirts. I turn my gaze away and wipe my hand on the brick wall, resisting the urge to gag. The stench is overwhelming.

Something crashes just above our hiding spot. Hook growls. "How does that boy keep getting away?" There is another bang.

"Captain, orders?" a soldier says.

"Search the buildings. Don't forget to check closets, basements, crawl spaces, anywhere a couple of street rats would hide. Find that girl!" Hook declares.

"Yes, sir!" The soldier orders the men in various directions.

Hook roars and I flinch, but Pete rubs my shoulder, his arms still wrapped around me.

"Pete, I know you can hear me." The Captain pauses, as if waiting for a response. "Pete! All I want is the girl."

Pete gives me a puzzled look. "He wants just you?"

"Why not you, too?" I ask.

Pete quickly drops his gaze from mine, shrugs, and holds a finger to his lips, reminding me to keep quiet. He's hiding something.

"Bring her to me, or so help me, when you are found, I will personally strap you to the cold steel table. I'll enjoy watching every agonizing moment as you writhe in pain, the tubes and needles sucking every ounce of life from your pathetic body. You will curse the day you ever crossed my path."

"That bloke has some serious anger issues," Pete whispers in my ear. His face is close to mine. His breath tickles my neck and is warm against my skin. It smells peculiar, like bubble gum. My cheeks grow hot.

"Do you hear me?" Hook screams.

Other than the scurrying of a few rodents in the tunnel, everything remains quiet. The sound of boots walking above us makes the tension in my body grow. My eyes and jaw clench shut as if I could disappear. The footsteps stop at the manhole cover. Pete quietly leaps up and tugs me to a shadowed corner as Hook peers through the holes. Another familiar and menacing voice draws his attention away.

"Captain, my men are in pursuit of a couple of children," Smeeth says. "We may have them cornered in an alley a few blocks from here. A boy and that pixie-lookin' girl we always see with Pete."

Mikey! My heart stops and I try to bolt, but Pete pulls me back. I struggle against his hold as he clasps a hand over my mouth. With bulging eyes, he shakes his head. "Shh! Stay quiet!"

"It's Bella," Hook says, his words clipped. "Do what you have to do to get the girl, even if it means incapacitating the boy. Just don't kill her."

"We'll do what we can, Captain," Smeeth says. "That girl's half bird with those wings of hers. She's struggling to hold on to the boy."

"Who's the other kid?" Hook says.

"I don't know," Smeeth says. "Boy's maybe six, seven at the most. It doesn't look like Bella is going to be able to carry him much longer, and he is having a hard time keeping up on his own."

My body tenses and I jerk, trying to escape from Pete's grasp again. I hear Hook respond, but his words are lost as I thrash violently against Pete's hold. Seething, I elbow the Lost Boy in the ribs. He grunts, his arms release me, and I dart from his grasp. Doubled over and wincing, he manages to hold a finger to his lips, reminding me to be silent.

"When the men capture them, do whatever you want with the boy. But take Bella straight to the Professor's lab for testing," Hook says, his voice fading as he walks away.

"I'm going to kill them," I declare. Enraged, I grab my dagger as I start up the ladder.

Pete jumps to his feet and wraps his arms around my waist, restraining me as I step onto the first rung. "Seriously, you need to control your slice 'em, dice 'em attitude when someone pisses you off." I pull from his grip, but he snatches my wrist, forcing me to drop my knife. It lands in the disgusting water with a plunk.

"Let me go. I'm going to cut them into teeny-tiny bits and feed them to the rats," I growl.

"I know, I know, rat food. I get it, but we need to get to the Lost City. We can't take them on by ourselves. We'll need help. Besides, Bella would never let them near Mikey," Pete grunts against my flailing arms.

"They will regret it if they lay one single finger on my brother."
Bella's small face comes to my mind as I imagine her struggling to
hold my brother up, her wings straining against the extra load.
"On either of those kids," I say through gritted teeth.

Pete sighs, spins me around, and holds me at arm's length.
"Enough! No need to get your knickers in a twist. Listen, Immune,
I'd really like to help you, but you need to get one thing straight. I
know their weaknesses better than you do. How are you going to
take on an army of Marauders with a pocketknife?"

I shove him hard, sending him stumbling backward, nearly
falling into the nasty sewer water. "You're the one who got us into
this mess. I knew I shouldn't have trusted you. If I had stuck with
my gut, if I had gone after Joanna myself, Mikey wouldn't be running in the streets unprotected and alone. I'm done following you."
I fish my knife out of the water, sheathe it, and start toward the
ladder again, determined to get my siblings back myself.

Pete chases after me. "Unprotected and alone? Have you met
Bella?" He grabs my arm, whirling me to face him. "She's the best
bet he's got right now. Besides, you were on the brink of starvation.
Your stomach hasn't stopped growling since we left your hideout,
which tells me you weren't eating much. And my guess is that you
weren't eating your share just so you could keep those kids alive.
Do you really believe you can take Hook and the soldiers on your
own, especially with a Little in tow? You're mad if you do."

I raise a hand to slap him. He grabs my wrist before my palm
makes contact. Pulling from his grip, I glare at him, wanting to
blow him out like the flame of a candle. Wishing he'd just disappear. "I don't see how this situation has gotten any better since

you've come along. In fact, it's gotten much worse. At least if I had gone alone, if it was just Mikey and me, we would still be together. Now both of my siblings are out there, no thanks to you."

"Joanna wasn't my fault, was it?" he yells back. "And as far as Mikey is concerned, you're lucky he isn't in Hook's lab as we speak. It was you who led the Marauders to your hideout, not me!"

I purse my lips, biting back the barrage of expletives running through my head.

Pete rubs his forehead wearily. "Look, Bella would rather die than let anything happen to Mikey. She is a little rough around the edges, but she's smart. If they outrun the Marauders, they'll be at our meeting point. As for Joanna, we'll get her back. I intend to help, but you have to do what I say, when I say to do it," he says. "No questions asked."

"And why would I do that?" I cross my arms in front of me indignantly. "Listening to you has caused me nothing but grief."

"Frankly, I'm fed up with your princess attitude. Maybe I ought to let you go on your way. I'm certainly not benefiting at all from this," Pete barks.

His words sting, but I press my lips together, unwilling to let him see the hurt boiling within me. "The feeling is mutual," I mutter as I climb the ladder.

"Wait!" Pete says, grabbing my ankle.

Clutching my knife, I jump down, grip his shirt collar, and throw him against the brick wall. I hold the tip of my dagger to his neck. "Don't. You. Touch. Me!"

"Whoa! Hold on!" Pete says, holding up his hands, his eyes wide with actual fright. "The truth is . . . the truth is I need you."

Surprised, I loosen my grasp on his shirt. "What? Why?"

He hesitates. His reluctance to share his thoughts stirs a sick feeling within me. I grip his shirt again, shaking him. "Talk!" I shout, gritting my teeth.

He grimaces and lets out a breath. "You see, there aren't really Immunes, or at least not any I have found until I came across you."

"What do you mean by 'aren't really Immunes'? That's what you've been calling me this whole time," I accuse.

"It's complicated, but what you need to know is this: Not all children are resistant to the Horologia virus. Especially not girls, it seems," Pete explains. Running a hand through his hair, he paces, stops, and steps toward me. "Look, I won't lie to you. The few girls we have found, they don't last long. In fact, they rarely last a month. When we find them, they are already showing symptoms and . . ."

My hammering heart skips a beat. "And then what?" I demand.

Pete stares at me, his gaze intense. "They die."

Time stands still and my vision blurs. I back up, placing my hand on the hilt of my second dagger. "So if girls aren't immune, what use am I to you?"

Pete looks away. "Because . . . Bella is dying."

His words strike me like a stray bullet piercing my heart. I meet his glassy gaze. He swallows. The muscles in his face grow taut. He's not lying.

"What do you mean? She looks perfectly healthy," I say.

"Bella is alive only because of Doc." He winces and shakes his head, as if saying those words is painful. "The virus is like some bizarre, cancerous, flesh-eating disease. Her fingers and toes are black, blistered, and the flesh is peeling away. The only reason she appears well is because her gloves and stockings are lined with medication to dull the pain. Doc also came up with some sort of a booster shot from the antibodies of us Lost Boys, but it only slows the progress; it doesn't cure it." Pete pulls up the sleeve of his jacket. A macramé of dark tattoos gives his skin the illusion of machine parts. The intricate details permanently etched in ink are stunning. I reach for his arm, hoping to get a better look, but something catches my eye and my breath hitches. A colorful display of blue, purple, and yellow bruises in varying stages of healing tint the inked gears, springs, and other mechanical gadgets. Before I have a chance to really inspect the tattoos and injuries, Pete pulls his sleeve back down and continues, "But you . . . you show no signs of infection. You may really be immune, and if you are . . . well, maybe . . . just maybe . . ."

A thousand thoughts flood my mind, but only one renders me speechless. I can't utter the words that are about to make me crumble like the rubble along the street.

Pete lets out an audible breath. "I believe you are an Immune, a *real* Immune. That's why Hook wants you, I'm certain of it. You're the only girl I've seen who actually seems unaffected by the virus. How you lived out there without showing symptoms is a miracle. Judging by the fact you have a sister who has also survived, there has to be something about you two. Something genetic, I suppose. Maybe the cure lies in you and your sister."

Unable to catch my breath, I rest my hand on my chest, lean against the ladder, and will myself to inhale slow and steady breaths. "Joanna's not immune." My words barely tumble out as a whisper.

Pete places a firm hand on my shoulder. "What?"

I meet his gaze, his green eyes searching mine with confusion. "She's not immune," I say, shaking my head, accepting the truth I've known all along but have denied until now. "Joanna has sores on her hands. They've only recently appeared, maybe a few weeks or so ago. I didn't know what they were. I was trying to treat it with antibiotics, but the blisters weren't responding to treatment."

Panic glasses over Pete's eyes. "Even more reason to get her back soon. The sooner the better. She needs to see Doc."

"Who is this Doc person?" I ask, sheathing my dagger.

"He's our physician, a prodigy of sorts," he says with a wave of his hand. "We have to get to the Lost City as soon as possible. We're going to need help getting Joanna out of the palace. Let's find Bella and Mikey. If they dodged Hook's men, they'll be at the eastern tunnel entrance just outside of Everland's border. It isn't too much farther." Pete starts to climb the ladder when something large splashes into the murky sewer water just up the tunnel in the inky darkness.

"We'd better hurry. There are things more sinister down here than those twits," Pete says, nodding toward the manhole above. He scrambles up the ladder and pushes the cover off, climbing back through the hole. A second loud splash sends chills up my spine. I climb the ladder and Pete reaches a hand out to me. I grip it, a lifeline keeping me from shattering into a million little shards.

· G W E N ·

Rain stings my cheeks as a fresh storm erupts from the dreary sky. My hair clings to my skin, obscuring my vision, and hangs limply on my soaked clothes. The scents of the wet asphalt and damp vegetation mingle in the air. We trudge through an overgrown meadow, which appears to have once been a park. Twisted and rusty monkey bars of a playground structure rise from the tall grass, providing cover when the Marauders' zeppelins buzz overhead, patrolling the outskirts of Everland.

I am thankful for the bit of warmth the scavenged coat provides. Wishing I had Mikey's umbrella, I blink away the rain from my vision. Pete appears unfazed by the weather, although it is hard to tell with his goggles concealing his eyes.

While the heavy shower is loud enough to drown out any noise, we travel without speaking. In the distance, a thick, smoky haze hangs heavy over the city, mingling with dark, stormy clouds.

"Why were you so far from the Lost City?" I ask as we trudge through the mud, breaking the lengthy silence. "It seems like it'd be easier to pillage close to Everland."

"There's nothing useful left inside the city limits. What supplies haven't already been scavenged, Hook's men have taken for themselves. Other than what the Marauders have confiscated, there's nothing left."

"How do you and the other Lost Kids survive? There can't be nearly enough food in your rucksack to supply an entire city of kids."

"Nonperishables and supplies come from the scavenges," Pete says. "Scavengers are teamed in pairs and given designated neighborhoods to scour. That's why we were so far from Everland."

"But there's hardly anything left in the outskirts," I say. "I could barely support myself and my sister and brother, much less hundreds of other children."

"We also live off of whatever is easily accessible: underground mushrooms, stray animals, rats, insects," Pete says, snatching a grasshopper from the tall grass. He pops the bug into his mouth. It crunches like the sound of potato crisps, sending a shiver through my body.

"You don't at least cook them?" I ask as he picks up another. My stomach rolls when he bites it in two.

"And there's also the underground garden that Spade, our horticulturist, and the Harvesters tend to," Pete says, ignoring my question.

"Underground garden? How is that possible?"

"Cogs and his team of Tinkers tapped into the Thames and created the hydropowered something-or-other with a monstrous steam turbine. I don't understand all the fancy science behind it, but it fuels the ecolanterns used to simulate sunlight, irrigates the crops, and funnels into the water-purifying system. It's quite a sophisticated design for a chap who's only sixteen."

"A sixteen-year-old engineer? A teenage doctor? Did the war and virus spare only the geniuses?" I ask.

"Well, you know what they say: Only the strong and the paranoid survive." Pete eyes me, a peculiar expression crossing his face. "Which makes me wonder, how have you lasted so long?"

"I'm strong and certainly not paranoid," I reply with defiance.

Pete's brows raise, as if I've spoken nonsense. "We also rely on the fish in the Thames when we can manage to find them. The riverbanks are heavily guarded, though. Most days we can't fish without risk of being caught, but you are right, it is getting harder to find provisions."

"What will you do when the supplies run out?" I ask. "The provisions from the scavenges, I mean. Surely a garden isn't enough to sustain you all."

Pete grimaces and shakes his head but doesn't answer. Instead, he trudges on.

We travel for a little while longer, quietly sneaking by a group of soldiers on patrol and ducking past parked Steam Crawlers. The overgrown shrubs and tall grass shield us from their view. We stop only once: to eat fresh berries we find growing on a small bush. The bright tartness bursts on my tongue, and my stomach rumbles for more even after we've devoured them all. Eventually, we reach the end of the railway, its tracks buckled and rusty. Broken beams and shattered glass from what appears to have been a station platform litter the ground. A search zeppelin flies overhead; its boilers hiss and propellers whir, rustling the weeds that have taken over the abandoned lots. We wait for it to pass. I hold my breath, afraid the simple act of breathing might bring an army of Marauders. As the zeppelin's engine fades, I let out a sigh.

"We're here," Pete whispers. Cautiously, he steps out from our hiding place.

Alarmed, I grab his arm, tugging him back into the brush. "What are you doing?"

"Just watch," he whispers, stepping into the open. Pete makes his way to the train tracks. His rooster call shatters the early afternoon silence. I shrink down into the prickly brush, expecting dozens of Marauders to descend upon us.

"It's about time you guys got here." Her voice chastises us from somewhere high in a grove of tall oaks. She floats down from a tree like a butterfly as her wings flutter, steam from her rocket pack haloing her. When her boots touch the ground, she pulls a lever on the straps over her shoulders and the wings close with a snap. "I was beginning to wonder if the Immune was holding you back. I'm surprised she wasn't caught."

Despite my relief at seeing Bella, I still scowl. She smirks, obviously glad her jab at me has hit its mark.

"Where's Mikey?" I ask, ineffectively trying to cover the worry in my voice.

Bella sighs. "Stupid Bartholomew Smeeth found us. He really needs to find a new hobby. Why can't that bloke just leave me alone? Creepy guy needs some therapy or something. Who chases little kids? That's the kind of person my parents warned me about in primary school."

"Bella, where's Mikey?" Pete asks, sternly.

Bella ruffles her fringe with an exaggerated breath. "Don't get your britches in a bunch. He's fine. He's right there." She points to an overgrown field of tall grass dotted with white, yellow, and purple wild pansies.

"Can I come out now?" Mikey's small voice says through the thicket of grass. "It's itchy and there's something with a long tail in here with me. I hope it isn't a crocodile."

I move toward the voice and brush aside the foliage. "Mikey?"

"Right here!" he says.

It takes a moment before I see his brown eyes staring at me. Mud, grass, and flowers cake his entire body. Had he not blinked, I would never have seen him.

"Mikey, what happened to you?" I ask, stifling a laugh. I help him from the dense brush and attempt to wipe dirt and blades of grass from his face, but my efforts are in vain.

"It was Bella's idea. I couldn't climb way up in the tree and didn't have wings like her, so she camouflaged me. Did I fool you?" Bright white teeth grin at me, contrasting with his fragrant, earthy disguise.

"Yes, you did," I say, chuckling. "But now you desperately could use a bath."

Mikey scratches his head. "Aw, but I took a bath last week. Or was it two weeks ago?"

Again, the guilt of not being more diligent about his hygiene—or mine, in fact—rakes over my conscience.

"Good job looking after him, Bella," Pete says, opening his arms. She leaps to him and wraps her tiny arms around his waist. He kisses her on the top of the head. "I knew he'd be in good hands."

I'm surprised to see the softer side of them when they usually exude such ferocity. Their affection for each other is a bittersweet reminder of Joanna, her stubbornness, bravery, and warmth. When Pete notices me staring, he pulls away and straightens his coat, as if brushing away that single moment of vulnerability.

Mikey frowns and balls his fists. "Hey, what about me?"

Pete's face brightens, appearing grateful to turn the attention away from his affection for Bella. "You? Well, you are the real hero. You protected her just like you said you would. I owe you my gratitude for that." Pete gives a deep bow. "Well done, Lost Boy."

My brother grins wide, cracking the mud packed on his chubby face into a dozen fissures.

"What happened to you guys?" I ask, plucking a white pansy from his dirty blond hair.

"Turns out stupid old Smeeth was waiting behind the corner of a house when you ran. When he saw us slip from the bushes, he chased us down. Fortunately, the fool could stand to lose some weight and apparently has a wheezing problem. You should have heard him. I wonder if he was a pug in another lifetime."

"Very funny," Pete says, patting Bella on the shoulder.

The screech of metal breaks the moment of calm. Pete stiffens and places a hand on Bella's and Mikey's backs, urging them forward. "Come on. We need to get out of the open."

We run along remnants of track with Pete leading the way. Finally, we reach numerous boulders that block the entrance to the Underground. Pete slips his hand inside a large shrub. I can barely make out a copper switch beyond the brambles. As he flicks the lever, a rumble emanates from the pile of boulders. The stones shudder and move toward us. It is then I realize the boulders are only an illusion, camouflaging a steel door. A gap large enough for a person to step through opens.

"Everyone inside!" Pete hisses, his eyes darting behind us.

Hearing voices behind me, I turn my head. Farther up the track, there is movement in the tall brush. The warmth of panic blankets me as I push Mikey and Bella through the gap. I follow behind, taking in the large gears and chains above my head that appear to control the mechanized door. Pete follows behind, turning a rusty wheel attached to the chains along the wall. The steel door closes and Pete flips another lever. The machine clanks loudly and three sliding locks snap into place.

Inside, the air is stale and musty, humid against my skin. I can hardly see anything. The sounds of small, scampering feet surround me, but the echo within the narrow cavern makes it difficult to tell if the feet belong to one or multiple rodents.

"Are you sure about this?" I ask, turning back to Pete, unable to see him in the darkness. "You have been in here before, haven't you?"

"Oh brother," Bella says. I can almost hear her rolling her eyes. "Please tell me you're not afraid of the dark."

"No, I'm not afraid of the dark," I say, annoyed by the insinuation.

"Knock it off, Bella," Pete scolds. He strikes a match along the rocks. In the dim light, he reaches for a lantern on a ledge chipped into the wall. Pete lights the lamp, casting the tunnel in a golden radiance. "I don't think they saw us."

"Of course they didn't," Bella says. "Come on, kid. Let me show you around." She reaches inside her satchel and pulls out a handful of gold dust, handing it to my brother. "Here. Leave a trail for your sister so she doesn't get lost. She doesn't seem too bright," Bella whispers within earshot of me. She pulls Mikey by the hand and together they skip ahead, uninhibited by the inky blackness as Mikey scatters a trail of gold in front of him.

I take in the tunnels around me. Unlit lanterns hang from the ceiling from tarnished pipes that fizzle, steam escaping from the joints.

"Don't worry." Pete takes my hand and guides me along the descending tracks, leading with a lantern tightly gripped in his hand. The light casts eerie shadows on the broken walls. Bugs scurry ahead of the lamp, a few crunching beneath my feet like the sound of broken glass. Eventually, we catch up with Mikey and Bella, who are chattering endlessly about the boys of the Lost City.

"I can't wait to not be a Little anymore," she says, skipping pebbles along the tracks. "The Biggers get privileges the Littles don't get."

"Like what?" Mikey asks.

"Dessert, a whole minute longer in the shower, and Pete lets the Biggers stay up an hour after the Littles go to bed for an evening nightcap," Bella says.

"Dessert! I want to be a Bigger," Mikey replies in wonder. I can't blame him. It's been so long since we've had anything sweet, even a single bite of dessert would be heavenly.

As we continue descending, hand-drawn caricatures adorn the cracked concrete surfaces, reminding me of hieroglyphics. Stick figures with dark masks and military gear crowd together as smaller characters throw stones at them.

"What is this?" I ask, running my hand along the drawings.

Pete stops suddenly. "Shh," he says, holding a hand up.

I listen but hear nothing. A bullet rockets from the pitch-black tunnel in front of us, ricochets off the wall to our right, and barely misses Bella as she hops out of the way. A small rock whizzes past my head and I duck.

"Hey!" Bella shouts. "Watch where you're aiming those things!"

"Who's there?" a boy's deep voice says from the darkness. "Identify yourselves!"

"Whoa! Who gave you clearance to guard this tunnel?" Pete hollers. "Bobbies are to guard the northern and western tunnels. The eastern and southern tunnels are for the Scavengers only!"

"Pete!" someone says, enthusiasm lacing the tone of his small voice. "It's Pete!"

"Pete's back!" yells another young boy's voice farther down the tunnel.

Murmurings erupt from the passageway as lights rip through the darkness. I shield my face, wincing against the blinding light. A redheaded boy no older than Bella approaches Pete. His freckled face crinkles with uncertainty.

"Hey, Pete," he says. "Sorry 'bout that. I didn't know it was you."

Pete slaps the boy on the back. "No problem, kid. But we gotta work on your aim. You're lucky we weren't the Marauders."

"We're lucky he has bad aim," Bella retorts.

Another boy, a teenager with dark eyes, hair, and skin emerges from the shadows wearing a brown jacket adorned with brass buttons. His brow creases in a scowl and he slips his revolver into the holster on his hip. He inhales the butt of a hand-rolled cigarette, tosses it to the ground, and puts the embers out with the toe of his boot. He tilts his head, blowing the smoke toward the ceiling of the cavern.

"Scout, who gave you permission to patrol these tunnels? You could've killed someone," Pete says.

"We received orders to guard all of the tunnels. Marauders have been spotted near every entrance. They're on the move. I've never seen anything like it before," he says.

"Who gave the order?" Pete asks sternly.

Scout rolls his eyes and snorts. "Who do you think?"

Pete balls both fists and places them on his hips, dropping his chin to his chest and shaking his head. "Jack."

"Sorry, Pete," Scout says. "You know how he gets when you're out scavenging. You might be the leader, but when you aren't around he makes sure we all know who's in charge."

"Leader?" I say, staring at Bella.

"Yep, Pete's the leader of the Lost Kids," she says matter-of-factly. "Jack's been vying for the spot since he arrived. If you ask me, Pete should've kicked his bum out to Everland a long time ago." She scrambles onto a boulder, giving her a bird's-eye view.

Pete straightens, adjusting his green coat, and spins. "Lost Boys, gather around. We have guests!"

Four more pairs of eyes emerge from the shadows, belonging to boys anywhere from ten to sixteen. Mikey hides behind me as I back up against the rock Bella has climbed.

"It's a girl!" one boy says in disbelief, seeming to have just noticed me.

"Of course it's a girl, knucklehead," Bella says from her perch. "It's not like you haven't seen one before."

"Where'd you find her?" Scout asks, stepping closer to me and reaching for a loose curl.

I brush his hands away. "What's he talking about?"

"I told you, we don't get girls here much. You're the first girl other than Bella that we've seen in months," Pete says, leaning against the wall with his arms folded.

Surrounded by hushed chatter, I pick Mikey up to keep him from being squished by the crowd. "But they've had Bella. What's so interesting about me?"

"Oh, Bella's just our sister, she doesn't count," one of the younger boys says, tying off the opening to his rock pouch.

A light-eyed boy peers up at me. "You're much too big to be a sister."

"Oh boy," Bella says, slapping her forehead with a hand. She leaps off the boulder, landing in front of me. "I haven't seen this much drama since Girl Guides. She's just a dumb girl. Can we move on?" She marches over to Pete and takes his hand. "Let's go, Pete."

Pete pulls his hand from Bella's and steps toward me. "Go on ahead, Bella. Take Mikey and the boys with you. We'll be along soon. Scout, make sure Mikey gets settled in."

Bella's cheeks flush and she balls up her fists. Whirling, she stomps off.

"Sure thing, Pete!" Scout puts a hand on Mikey's shoulder. "Follow me, kid. You're going to like the Lost City. It beats topside hands down."

Mikey peers up at me. I glance at Pete.

"It's okay. You're safe with Scout," Pete says, ruffling Mikey's hair.

When Mikey looks back at me, I nod. I put him down and he follows the chattering Lost Boys, who trail behind Scout. Mikey takes one last look at me before disappearing behind a corner.

I am alone in the tunnel with Pete. My stomach flutters as he places a lamp on the ground and leans against the rock next to me.

"Sorry about Bella," Pete says. "She's been rather attached to me since I first found her. I think she might fancy me." His cheeks grow pink as he shoves his hands into his pockets. "I probably should have warned you that you'd be sort of a celebrity."

"I'm not a celebrity," I say. "I'm just like the rest of you."

"But you're not like the rest of us," Pete says, turning to face me, his shoulder leaning against the rock. "This whole time these boys, especially the Littles, have only had the influence of one another. In some ways they are all brothers. In other ways we're a tribe. The stronger, faster, and bigger determine the pecking order. There is no semblance of the old life they once knew, of having the strong father figure *and* the nurturing mother figure. You're the closest thing to a mother any of these kids has seen in a year."

My cheeks flush and a sense of déjà vu comes over me as I recall my conversation with Joanna before she was taken. *You were a much better sister than you are a mother.*

"But I'm not a mother of any sort."

"For months I have been surrounded by orphaned boys, children who have no family to go home to. No fathers, no mothers, and other than Bella, not even sisters." Pete runs a hand through his messy hair and drops his gaze to the ground. "Becoming an orphan changes a person, especially the way these kids have become parentless. They're not typical kids. Something was stolen from them when they watched their parents die, like a piece of what makes them children perished with their folks. Survival becomes instinct and they lose what makes them, I don't know"—he pauses—"kids. The Biggers and I do our best to provide the Littles with some likeness of family, but it just isn't the same. With you here, maybe, just maybe, they can have some of that back. Joanna and Mikey have you. These kids have no one."

A pang of sympathy grips me as I contemplate his words. I never considered how fortunate my siblings and I were; not only were we spared witnessing our parents' final breaths, but we've had each other. "I'm just their sister, and not a very good one at that," I say, reflecting on my last conversation with Joanna. "I'm practically a child myself."

"You are their family, and whether you accept it or not, you are the closest thing they've got to family," he says.

The weight of his words hangs in the air, and I struggle to find a response.

Pete rubs the back of his neck. "Look, there's something else I need to tell you and you're not going to like it."

"I don't know," I say, my voice a little snarkier than I intend. "None of today has been much fun. I highly doubt any news you have could make it worse."

Pete scratches his stubbled chin and studies me. "I'm not sure how to put this delicately, so I'll just come out with it." He takes in a big breath and blows it out. "Our dwindling supplies and the Marauders are the least of my worries."

"What do you mean?" I ask, bewildered.

"If Bella and your sister die . . . if you are truly what Hook believes you are, the only Immune girl, you are the only chance for survival that humankind has. Your gender is endangered, and if Bella and Joanna die, you *will* be the last woman, the last chance for our species' survival."

My stomach twists in a million knots. The ache of hunger is replaced with sickening revulsion as the implication sinks in. I place my hand on the wall to steady myself. "You don't know that. We have no idea if the virus made it beyond England."

"All communication has been lost. England is silent. It has been a year. Don't you think our allies would've come by now? No one would let England fall like this without retaliation, without sending support. And yet we've seen no sea ships, no zeppelins. The steam railways were significantly damaged, but you'd think the rest of the United Kingdom would find a way to connect with England. The only reasonable answer is that the virus has not just killed England, but possibly everyone beyond her borders. The entire world, for all we know."

I swallow the lump in my throat. That can't be possible.

"We have to find a cure and get Joanna back immediately," I say, my words spilling out quickly. "We need to find out how far this virus has spread."

"One thing at a time," Pete says, rubbing my shoulder. "The good news is that Hook will give her the best treatment to ensure she survives. However, I'm sure she's in a high-security facility where she will very likely stay for the rest of her life, until she's old enough to . . ."

I cover his mouth with my hand. "No! Don't say it!" I cannot bear to hear him finish the sentence. She may only be twelve, but if what he says is true, by the time she is able to conceive children of her own, of course they would use her to save humanity. I choke back the growing nausea and wipe an angry tear from my cheek.

Pete sighs. "I wish I had better news. I promise you this: You and your siblings will be safe if I have anything to do with it. I swear I won't let them do that to her. I will do everything to get your sister back, even if it means sacrificing my own life."

"You'd do that for us?" I ask, not entirely surprised. After all, he needs my help just as much as I need his.

"Well, yeah," he says matter-of-factly. "I'd do it for any Lost Kid."

I drop my gaze to the ground. "I'm not a Lost Kid," I say. My voice echoes through the cavern. *Not a Lost Kid. Not a Lost Kid. Not a Lost Kid.*

Pete tilts my chin up. The lantern lights his handsome face and green eyes that remind me of the color of lucky clovers. "You are a Lost Girl."

Something crumbles inside of me and like Everland's cityscape, the raw supports that barely hold me up feel exposed. Relieved to have someone other than myself to count on, I wrap my arms around his neck. He hesitates, but eventually returns the hug. It's the first time since my parents disappeared that someone else comforts me instead of the other way around.

"Thank you," I whisper, feeling his soft hair beneath my fingers.

"Anytime, Gwen," he murmurs into the curve of my ear.

I pull back and suddenly feel my cheeks flush. "You called me by my name."

Pete blushes. "Immune doesn't suit you." He takes my hand, a burst of energy gracing his expression. His hand doesn't let go of mine. A crooked grin grows on his face as our eyes meet. Beneath his stare, I shift uncomfortably and gently pull my hand from his. Having attended a girls' private school, my interactions with boys were limited. I'm unsure how to react. Pete's grin fades as he shoves his hands into his pockets.

"We should go. It's time for you to meet Doc. He'll know what to do," Pete says, nudging me forward, and we descend into the dark, stale tunnel.

· H O O K ·

Two steel cannons protrude over my shoulders as I lean against the front of the insectile military vehicle. The tank hisses as steam rises from the boiler. Carefully, I polish the metal barrel of my modified Gatling arm gun, taking special care to clean the grease from in between the teeth of every cog, wheel, and spring. Smeeth runs toward me, stops, and salutes.

"Captain," the soldier says.

"At ease, Mr. Smeeth," I answer, not bothering to look up at him. I tuck the polishing cloth into the front pocket of my coat. Squinting, I scrutinize the weapon, inspecting every bit of the surface for smudges.

Smeeth's shoulders relax as he tilts his chin, his neck giving an audible crack. It's an annoying habit of his. I imagine the same sound emitting from his thick throat as I wrap my hands around it. *Snap!*

"No luck. The girl and Pete are nowhere to be found." Lifting his mirrored goggles from his eyes, he places them on the brim of his military cap. He fusses nervously with his gloved hands. He's a fidget, not a good trait for someone who bears a weapon, but I've equipped his Gatling gun with blanks. As dumb as the boy is, he doesn't know any better. How he managed to become a soldier in the Royal Guard, I'll never know.

I scan the blackened and worn rooftops of the nearly demolished suburban neighborhood. "And what about Bella and the boy?" I ask, clenching my fists. Each knuckle pops beneath my gloves.

"We lost them." Smeeth drops his gaze to the ground, unwilling to meet my eyes.

"You lost them?" I growl. "How can a little girl and an even littler boy get away from my army?"

"I don't know, Captain," Smeeth says, shifting from one foot to another. "One minute they were there, the next minute they were gone. There was nowhere for them to go. No buildings or alleys. They just vanished."

I rocket from my seated position, halting in front of Smeeth. "Vanished? What do you mean *vanished*?" I say, spittle raining down on his face. Spinning, I punch the front grille, leaving four scratches in the metal where my brass rings strike.

Smeeth shudders but doesn't make eye contact.

Leaning against the Steam Crawler, I snatch my revolver from my hip and methodically spin the cylinder, removing each bullet. "I'm beginning to have my doubts about you, Mr. Smeeth. Maybe I should have let you perish with the rest of your English countrymen." I pocket the ammunition, leaving only one bullet in the chamber. I knew Smeeth's days were numbered, but I had hoped to keep him around for just a while longer so that he could be of some further use to me. "I thought I saw something unique in you. It's not often you find a soldier who will betray his queen. Perhaps I was wrong about you."

The hammer snaps in place and I lift the barrel of the gun, its aim set on the small spot between Mr. Smeeth's dark eyes. He gasps as I squeeze the trigger. As the hammer slams back in place, the copper cylinder spins.

Click!

"I'm growing weary of your incompetence. We need those girls now!" I shout.

Smeeth trembles beyond the gun's barrel.

"You *will* find them. I will not return to Germany empty-handed. Trust me, you wouldn't want to disappoint my mother, or worse, me!"

Sweat drips from Smeeth's forehead. "It is my fault we lost them. It won't happen again."

Click!

Again the cylinder of the revolver spins.

"I'm certain my reptilian pets would relish fresh meat instead of the rotting corpses that inhabit the sewers," I say, pulling the hammer back again.

Smeeth's face blanches as he gives a quick nod. "I understand, Captain."

Again I pull the trigger.

Click!

The gun doesn't discharge. "Do you realize how valuable those girls are? They may be the last and are our only ticket out of here."

Smeeth trembles as he wipes the sweat from his head. "I'll find them today. I swear!"

Click!

"I cannot, will not, go back to Lohr Castle without a cure. And I refuse to stay in this rotten place any longer. Do you understand me, Mr. Smeeth?" I ask.

"I do, Captain," Smeeth whispers with the little breath he can take in.

Click!

Smeeth winces as I pull the hammer back.

"Only one chamber left," I say.

"Wait! Captain, there's something else!" Smeeth says, shrinking to his knees beneath the gun's barrel with hands lifted in surrender. "We've got another girl. It's not Bella or the young lass traveling with Pete, but still a girl."

Surprised, I sit back, keeping my aim on Smeeth. "Another girl?"

"Yes, sir. Found on the outskirts of Everland. She's on her way to the lab right now."

I drop the barrel from Smeeth's head. "Interesting. That's two girls other than Bella in a few hours. There have been so few of them left, but perhaps I was wrong. Maybe there are other girls. The girls are all but extinct. But I wonder . . ."

"Wonder what, sir?"

"How many more girls are out there? What if Pete is hiding them? What if he's being more than just chivalrous, but is protecting the girls because he also knows that one of them is the Immune?" I say as more questions than answers tumble through my thoughts.

"It's possible," Smeeth says.

"What sort of condition is she in?" I ask.

Smeeth sighs and stands. "Sick, but better than most. I'd say early stages of the virus based on the information I have received. We won't know until the Professor has a look at her."

As if tied to a stone and thrown into the ocean, my hope sinks. She can't possibly be the girl the Professor is looking for. I rally from my disappointment, reminding myself that sick isn't dead and there's still a chance she could be useful. I reach in my pocket, pull the rest of the bullets out, and refill the revolver's cylinder. "Well done, Smeeth. You're not completely useless. Do you or your men have any inkling of where Pete, Bella, and the others might be hiding?"

Smeeth's chest heaves as he breathes a relieved sigh. "Not yet."

"Find them!"

Smeeth spins, ready to bolt.

"One more thing, soldier," I say.

He stops and hesitantly turns. "Yes, Captain?"

I stand and slide the door of the Steam Crawler open. Its hinges wail in protest. "Release the crocs."

Smeeth's face pales before he nods and hurries off, shouting orders at several soldiers.

My single eye takes in the view, searching for something, some clue I know I must be missing, before I climb into the Steam Crawler. When both doors close, the internal air is drawn out by the engine's fans. When the whooshing sound dies down, alerting the driver that we are safely within the airtight vehicle, I snatch up a bottle of rum from the center console. Taking a long pull from the bottle, I welcome the warmth as it soothes my temper.

Looking through the windows beyond the gleaming chrome legs of the Steam Crawler, I scan the skeletal remains of homes and businesses. "Where are you, Pete? Where are you hiding those girls?"

The dark cityscape responds in silence, like whispers from lost souls forever trapped in the ruins of London.

· GWEN ·

Broken shadows dance on the cracked concrete walls as light flickers from the gas lanterns strung along the ceiling. The rumbling sounds of machinery and the ping of tools upon metal echoes through the small cavern. Pete leads me through the damp, dark channel. The tunnel descends into a rock and dirt passageway, leaving the cement walls and warped metal track behind. As we round one last corner, my breath catches.

The narrow corridor opens up into a vast, well-lit chamber the size of a small town and rises nearly four stories high. Copper pipes zigzag along the ceiling, steam billowing from some of the gears rotating at the joints. Other lines feed water into an underground river that flows into a large turbine. Buildings made of wood, stone, and brick line the circumference of the city's center. Hanging from each crudely built structure is a wooden sign with words scrawled across it designating its purpose: STOCK ROOM, KITCHEN, APOTHECARY, and numerous others. Along one side of the cavern, dozens of caves, each large enough to fit a person, are carved into the dirt walls. Pulleys bolted to the ceiling are threaded with thick ropes attached to rickety lifts, which sit below the cave openings. At least seven other tunnels, not unlike the one we have traveled, are visible from where I stand. In the center of the city, a silver statue of a winged man with a bow is mounted on a large fountain. It takes me a moment to recognize the famous statue of Eros, which once stood in the center of Piccadilly Circus.

The entire city grumbles with machinery, steam hissing from boilers and pipes. In the gas lamplight, the copper and bronze tubes, wheels, and gears glitter, giving the impression of a city made of gold.

Most impressive are the young boys running about their business, repairing boilers, filling carts with supplies, and loading some sort of digging machine with coal. A child no older than ten, wearing a tan aviator hat and goggles, pedals past me on a wobbly tricycle. Attached to the bike is a wooden wagon with mismatched wheels. Tins of food and bags of rice threaten to topple the cart. Two boys hang precariously from ropes attached to the copper pipes as they swing from one gas lamp to the next, refueling as they go. In one corner, a bonfire roars beneath an enormous pot. Above it, pipes spill water into the container until a kid standing at the top of a staircase spins a wheel, shutting off the water supply. As the town buzzes with activity, each child appears to have his own job. The number of children gathered in this small underground city awes me. The last time I saw this many children was the final day of school when the first bombs dropped.

I take in the scene before me, drowning in a cacophony of hissing, grinding, and squealing machine parts. Bella sits on a copper pipe that spans the entire city. She reaches inside her satchel and withdraws a bag of chocolate chip cookies. Using her slingshot, she flings them down to a crowd of small kids, each child waving their hands in the air. "Bella, pick me! I want one!" they shout. My stomach clenches jealously.

Mikey rushes from the city center, his eyes bright with wonder. "Can you believe it, Gwen?" he asks, tugging my hand. "There's so many of them."

He's right. There must be a hundred or more boys. The older boys tote peculiar gadgets on tool belts while the littler children do simpler tasks.

Two boys burst from an adjacent tunnel, not unlike the one we've just traveled. Sweat laces their brows while they gasp for breath, as if they've just outrun a monster or, worse yet, a Marauder. They drop their rucksacks to the ground and grip their hands awkwardly in what appears to be a secret handshake.

"Scavengers," Pete whispers, leaning in close to me. "That's Pickpocket in the waistcoat and Pyro in the jacket. Judging by their rucksacks, they've been out for a few days, scavenging beyond Everland's borders."

Smaller boys notice their arrival and surround them, mimicking the hand gestures and giddy with excitement. Pyro hefts the bulging rucksacks over his muscular shoulders and heads toward a building with STOCK ROOM scribbled in red paint on the piece of wood. The smaller boys squeal with delight as Pickpocket reaches into his pockets and hands out brightly colored marbles.

"Pickpocket!" His name echoes off the stone and concrete walls, drawing the attention of every boy. Another boy, with shoulder-length hair as black as ebony, storms from the stock room. He tosses a lit cigarette into the water at the base of the fountain as he picks up his pace, shoving past Pyro and sprinting toward Pickpocket.

"Uh-oh," Pete says. "This can't be good."

"What's happening?" I ask.

"I don't know, but Jack's the last person you want to piss off around here," Pete says, starting toward the boys.

Bella watches with wide eyes from her perch, unmoving. Scout leans against the fountain, arms folded and head shaking.

Pickpocket's smile fades as the little boys scatter.

"Thief!" Jack says before punching Pickpocket square in the jaw.

Pickpocket stumbles back, gripping his chin in his hand. Blood drips from a cut on his chin, leaving a crimson trail on his dark bronze skin. Shock fades to anger on his face. It only takes a second before Pickpocket tackles Jack and they are rolling on the floor, grunting and throwing punches. Pyro drops the rucksacks and attempts to pull Pickpocket off of Jack.

"Cool it, you two!" Pete yells as he bolts toward the boys.

Jack swings a fist and Pickpocket ducks. Pyro doesn't see the punch coming until Jack's fist connects with his nose, sending a gush of blood down his mouth and chin.

"Bloody idiot!" Pyro growls, holding his nose.

The altercation takes all of five seconds, but in that short time all three of the boys are bleeding.

Mikey grips my hand tightly as I follow behind at a distance.

"Enough!" Pete yells, trying to wrench Jack from Pickpocket.

Older kids join in the brawl, trying to pry the seething Lost Kids off one another. It eventually takes four boys to separate Pickpocket and Jack.

Pete breathes heavily as he stands between them. "The next person who throws a punch is banished from the Lost City!"

Jack wrests free from the two boys holding him back. His lip is split. He wipes at it with the back of his hand, inspects the bloodred streak, and spits on the ground. He points a finger at

Pickpocket. "You stole an extra ration, Pickpocket," he growls. "The punishment for theft is three days in the stockade."

Pickpocket rubs his jaw, the open gash marking where Jack's fist made contact. "I took what I was allotted. Two sets of rations for each day I was gone."

"You left midday the day before last. You should've only had three rations!" Jack juts a finger in Pickpocket's chest.

Pickpocket swipes Jack's hand from him. "You're kidding me? And what were we supposed to eat today? It's nearly suppertime as it is."

"And with all of the running we do, it isn't enough," Pyro interjects, wiping blood off his face with a handkerchief.

"Oh, give me a break. We all know you Scavengers eat more than your share of the plunder while you're out. If I were in charge, none of you would receive rations!"

"And that's exactly why you are only second-in-command. If you were leader, we'd all starve," Pickpocket says through gritted teeth. He backs up and throws his hands out flippantly. "Checks and balances, Jack. You"—he points at the dark-haired boy— "need to be kept in check."

Jack balls his hand and lifts it, ready to pummel the boy.

"I said enough!" Pete yells. "I'm in charge. I make the rules. If any of you have a problem with them, you can take it up with me."

Jack lifts his hands as if in surrender and takes a step back. "You're the boss."

"Glad we have an understanding," Pete says, glaring at Jack as if challenging him to argue. Jack says nothing and instead heads toward a gathering of boys congregated by the statue in the city's center.

Pickpocket rubs his jaw again. "Thanks, Pete. He's getting worse."

Pete nods. "We've lost three Scavengers in the last month, and the ones that are still running are bringing back less and less each scavenge. He's not coping with the dwindling supplies very well. I'll talk to him."

"You'd better do it sooner than later. The Littles are frightened of him and the Biggers are about to string him up by his boot-straps," Pyro says.

"I'll take care of it today. Go have Doc take a look at that," Pete says, pointing at the gash on Pickpocket's chin.

Pickpocket rubs his sleeve across the open wound. "Nah, it's just a paper cut."

Pete grins and shakes his head. He cups his hands to his mouth and crows like a rooster. His voice reverberates off the metal pipes. Children spill from the buildings and tunnels.

"Listen up, Lost Boys! We have guests," Pete says.

With wide eyes and gaping mouths, the children stare at me. "It's a girl," the younger ones whisper to one another, pointing in my direction.

"Oh, here we go again with the 'it's a girl,'" Bella says, rolling her eyes. She deploys her wings and flutters to the ground, landing on the dirt floor with a thud. "What do you numskulls think I am?"

"She's so . . . so huge," a young boy says. Approaching with caution, he tips his head to the side and raises an eyebrow. "You're not from Everland, are you? Are you one of those pirates?"

"Of course not. Do you think I would bring a Marauder down here?" Pete asks.

The boys train their eyes on me, but say nothing. I fidget and try not to meet their gaze. Mikey shifts closer to me, clearly uncomfortable.

Shaking his head and rubbing his face with one hand, Pete mumbles, "I'm going to have to have Cogs check the air intake. You Littles must be oxygen deprived."

He marches to the city center, leaving me feeling vulnerable as the group of gawking boys surrounds me. Pete climbs the fountain, stands on the statue, curls in his bottom lip, and blows out a shrill whistle.

"Lost Boys!" he announces. "This is Gwen. You will treat her with the same respect you would treat any other Lost Boy. Is this clear?"

"Or Lost Girl," Bella adds in a disgruntled tone.

The boys murmur their reply, but their words are muddled.

"I said, is that clear?" Pete shouts.

The boys reply, "Yes, sir!" Some grunt but say nothing.

"Wait!" a teenage boy calls, peering through goggles with thick lenses. His eyes appear larger than they should behind the glass. "She isn't a Lost Kid unless there's a vote. That's what the rules say." His tone is authoritative, but still has a hint of hesitancy.

"Justice's gotta point," Scout says, and spits on the ground.

Justice twists a knob on the side of his goggles. The lenses move forward, protruding from his face like two telescopes. He pulls a spiral notebook from his shirt pocket, flips a few pages, and clears his throat.

"According to the Statutes of the City of Lost Kids, section fifteen, article five, subarticle A-3, 'No Lost Boy shall bring outsiders within the city limits without prior consent and two-thirds vote of the Lost citizens,'" the boy says, holding up the notebook. "Rules are rules."

Bella marches up to Justice and swats the paper pad out of his hand. A few loose pages slip from the metal spiral spine as the notebook flutters to the floor. The boy frowns at Bella as his lips press into a thin line.

"Do that again, princess, and I'll dip your wings in candle wax. You'll be grounded for at least a day or more," Justice says, glaring at Bella.

Bella is unfazed and only smirks. "You and your book of stupid rules! I'm tired of them."

Justice grimaces. "You do know what the statutes say about retaliating against another Lost Boy, don't you, Bella?"

"I'm not a Lost Boy—the rules don't apply to me." She crosses her arms, almost as if she is expecting the boy to challenge her.

"We're going to have to call an emergency council meeting and make an amendment to include Lost Girls," he growls.

Justice bends to pick up his notebook, but Bella steps on it. She leans in close so that she is only centimeters from his face. "Are you sure you really want to do that?" she says. "Remember what happened the last time you called an emergency council meeting? How did that work out for you?"

Justice releases the notebook, leaving it under Bella's boot. He stands, rolls his shoulders back, and straightens his waistcoat. "I was cleaning glue from the gears of my spectacles for weeks," Justice mutters.

Bella stands on her tiptoes so she's close to Justice's ear. "Pete and I found firecrackers on our last scavenge. It'd be a shame if they found their way into your sleeping quarters."

"Bella, that's enough," Pete says, the tone of his voice indicating a stern warning.

"Fine!" Bella says. But she leans close one more time and whispers, "I still wouldn't advise any emergency council meetings if I were you." She winks, spins on the heels of her boots, stomps to the center of the city, and stands in front of the statue.

Pete rolls his eyes. "Did you have to do that?" he says.

Bella cocks her weight to one hip and grins.

"But the rules state we must vote first. You have no idea if these two are associated with the Marauders," Justice says, picking up his notebook and flipping through the pages.

"Gwen and Mikey are *my* guests. They're staying," Pete says, dismissing the altercation between Bella and Justice. He strides toward Mikey and me. "I declare you, Gwen . . . What did you say your last name was?" he asks.

"I didn't say what it was. It's Darling, Gwen Darling," I mumble.

"Hmm, not as bad as Gwen the Immune, but you might consider taking a new name now that you're a Lost Kid," Pete says. "All the smart kids do. You could go with Stubbornly. Feisty. How about Cheeky?"

The boys erupt in laughter.

I scowl. "Thanks for the advice, Prince Charming."

"So is that a no?"

I give him a light smack on his chest and narrow my eyes.

Pete winks. "I'm only kidding." He throws his arms in the air in a dramatic display. "Gwen Darling, do you promise to protect all of those smaller than you, even the Lost Bugs, except when Sous the Chef serves them for dinner because there is nothing else to eat?" Pete asks a little too loudly.

The littlest of the Lost Boys giggle, some of them scrunching up their noses at the suggestion of eating bugs.

"I guess so," I say.

Pete turns to Justice. "Are you satisfied now?"

Justice's telescope eyes scrutinize me before he gives a quick nod.

"Excellent! Gwen Darling, I declare you a Lost Kid. You will all regard her with the same dignity as you would any other Lost Kid. Anyone who treats her otherwise will have to report to me, and I assure you the Plungers have an endless amount of drains to snake. I'm sure they'd be thrilled with an extra hand or two," Pete says.

A hush blankets the gathering of boys, but no one challenges Pete.

He points at Mikey. "And he's a Lost Boy, too. No questions asked."

A melodious cheer erupts from the crowd. Bella claps with an expression of boredom on her face. "Huzzah," she says with sarcasm.

Mikey smiles a muddy grin, still dirty from his earthy disguise. Justice studies my brother with a pinched expression but says nothing. An East Asian boy Mikey's age raises his hand and bounces on the balls of his feet. "Pete! Hey, Pete! Right here!" the boy shouts.

The crowd parts as the young boy steps forward.

Pete rolls his eyes. "Yes, Gabs?"

"Does she like to tell stories? I mean like real stories. Not the stories you tell because they're way too short, and I don't think you really like telling stories anyway. Stories like my mum used to tell about warriors and battles and even fire-breathing dragons that roar so loud it shakes the ground like an earthquake. That's really where earthquakes come from, you know. It's dragons who are really, really, really mad. The kind of mad your mum gets because you drew on the walls when you know you shouldn't. And the dragon mums, they're mad because someone stole their dragon eggs and the mum dragons are trying to find their babies. Sometimes they dive into mountains and make volcanoes. That's not really lava, you know. It's dragon spit that will burn you up and then you'll know better not to touch the dragon spit because . . . well, I guess you won't because then you'd be all burned up. Anyway . . . does she tell stories?"

"And that is why we call him Gabs," Pete says through the side of his mouth.

The boy peers at me with obsidian-colored eyes hidden beneath overgrown, jet-black hair. He waits for my response, an eager, wide-eyed expression spanning his face. Immediately, I like Gabs, and from the crooked smile on Mikey's face, I can tell he likes him, too.

"Well, I don't know about that. I . . ." My gaze catches the hint of disappointment in Gabs. When I glance back at Mikey, he's fidgeting with the arm of his teddy bear. Because he was only five when the war started, hardly old enough for primary school, I realize he doesn't know how to make friends. He pulls his bear in tighter before he speaks.

"She tells great stories," Mikey says shyly, but a frown forms. "Well, she used to when she was just my sister and not my mum."

Confused, I glance down at Mikey. "Mikey, I'm not your . . ."

Gabs wraps his arms around my waist. "Oh! You're a mother? Will you be my mother, too? I've missed my own mum so much."

I look at Pete, surprised. He gives me a lopsided smile and shrugs.

Mikey tugs at my shirt. "Are you really his mother now, too? That would make him my brother. I've always wanted a brother."

Gabs peers at me and I search for words, but they jumble with my conflicted thoughts. Overwhelmed, I look to Pete for help. He approaches, wiggling an eyebrow at me. Wrapping both arms around my neck, he presses his warm face against mine.

"I could use a mum as well," he says, planting a wet kiss on my cheek.

"Eww, gross!" I say as I wipe the remnants of his slobbery kiss off with the sleeve of my coat. The warmth of his lips on my face brings a rush of heat to my cheeks. I jab an elbow into his ribs, giving him a disgusted look, and try not to let him see the blush I feel growing hot on my skin.

Pete chuckles. "Well, there you have it. I think this calls for a celebration. Gabs, tell Stock to pull the brew and pop from storage. Take Mikey with you to help carry the tins," Pete says.

"Got it!" Gabs says, wrapping a thin arm around my brother's shoulder. "Come on, Mikey. You're really going to like Stock. He's tall and skinny, sort of like the Jolly Green Giant, but he's not so green. He's more of a chocolaty color if you ask me. Speaking of chocolate, are you hungry? I'm starving. I'll take you to meet Sous the Chef, which is spelled S-O-U-S. Not Sue like the girl's name."

Gabs grips Mikey by the hand, but my brother pulls from the boy.

"Well, what's wrong?" Gabs asks. "You're not scared, are you?"

My brother shrugs and peers at me with an uneasy glance.

"There's nothing to be scared of. Here, you can play with this." Gabs pulls out a rusty soup can from the pocket of his oversize coat and hands it to my brother. Gold wire spirals from the top, giving it the impression of having hair. Arms and legs made of clock scraps are bolted onto the tin. An antique key protrudes from the back of the can.

Mikey shrinks behind me.

"It's okay. It's Clink the Robotock. Watch this," Gabs says, twisting the key. He sets the can on the ground and it hobbles on clumsy legs. "Pete made it for me."

Mikey hands his bear to Gabs before picking up the toy and twisting the key. He smiles when the arms and legs swivel.

"A teddy bear!" Gabs exclaims. "You're so lucky. I left mine in my bedroom when the house got all smoky."

"You can borrow it," Mikey says. His voice is timid.

Gabs pats my brother's back. "Really? Wow, thanks! Come on. I'll show you around the Lost City first." The boys walk off with Gabs still chatting, the brown bear tucked under his arm.

"Well, well," Pete says, watching them disappear into the crowd of kids. "Someone who actually likes to hear Gabs talk. There's always a first time for everything."

"You made him a toy?" I ask, surprised.

Pete stares into my eyes and smiles. "We may have been robbed of our childhoods, but they still have theirs. This here and now is their childhood. It isn't much, but it's better than nothing."

My heart swells with a mixture of emotions for this boy. In just a short time I have regarded him with fear, anger, curiosity, wonder, gratitude, respect, and now something new: affection? My cheeks flush with embarrassment at the thought.

"What about Joanna? When are we going after her?" I ask, changing the subject.

"We'll leave once we gather supplies, but first I have to convince our rescue team."

Pete points to a crowd of boys near the statue. Jack stands barechested, his fists raised in front of him. Scout spits on the ground and mirrors his stance. A crowd of kids exchanges small trinkets, as if placing bets. Pickpocket leans against the base of the statue, his arms folded in front of him as he shakes his head.

"Convince them?" I ask, cringing as I watch Jack's fist connect with his competition's cheek. Scout takes the punch with hardly a flinch.

"It'll take a lot to persuade them," he says, scratching his head. "We don't do rescues."

"Not even for a Lost Kid?" I ask, shocked that they would abandon one of their own.

"Once those pirates have you, you don't come back. We can't risk the lives of other children for one careless child," Pete says. "We have strict rules about venturing into Everland. If you go, we won't come after you. That's why we pick the fastest runners, the most agile of the Lost Boys to be Scavengers. The bottom line is, once you leave the Lost City, your neck is on the line, and we're not coming to save you. If you can't handle Everland and what lies beyond it, you don't belong there. Joanna will be our first rescue."

My heart skips several beats. An uneasy feeling creeps up my spine, settling over my limbs.

"How will you convince them to come with us? Why would they risk their lives for me? For Joanna?" I ask, watching the boys cheer as Jack kicks Scout's legs from beneath him, sending him sprawling to the ground.

"They won't do it for you or Joanna. But they'll do it for her." He turns and nods toward Bella. A group of kids tag behind her, hanging on to her every word as she waves her hands in the air with excitement. When she reaches the lift, she blows a kiss to the boys before hoisting the platform to the highest opening along the wall.

"Until you came along, she was all they had as far as a sister. If they know you hold the key to her survival, they'll do just about anything," Pete says.

I don't know what to say. My heart shreds, a tiny fiber for each Lost Boy, for Bella, and for Pete. Worry lines crease his forehead, making him appear much older than he really is.

"I should go talk to Blade about preparing our weapons. Why don't you go introduce yourself to Doc? You'll find him in the apothecary building." Pete points to a brick structure. Burgundy curtains hang in the windowless frame.

"You're not coming with me?" I ask.

Pete shakes his head. "Let's just say Doc and I are not the greatest of friends. He stays out of my business and I stay out of his. It's probably best if you introduce yourself on your own. I'll come find you later."

"I think I'll look in on Bella first, if you don't mind," I say, glancing up at the ballet of shadows in the cave opening.

"Suit yourself." Pete shrugs. "If you're hungry, stop by the kitchen. And if you get tired, you and Mikey can use my sleeping quarters. Mine is to the right of Bella's."

"Thank you," I say, not feeling tired, but definitely feeling hungry.

He offers a quick nod and shoves his hands into his pockets before joining a group of boys pouring what looks like beer from an amber bottle into tin cans and clinking them with one another.

I turn toward the sleeping quarters and climb onto the lift. Gripping the rope, I raise the platform to Bella's cave. As I reach Bella's room, quiet sobs rebound through the entrance. I secure the rope on a hook and peer around the cave wall, careful not to be seen. Other than the little bit of light sputtering from a single candle, the room is relatively dark.

Bella wipes the cascade of tears from her face as she stares at her boots. She slips her thin arms from the straps of her metal wings and leans them against a wall. Finally, she takes a breath and pulls the leather boots off her feet. With each tug, a whimper escapes through her gritted teeth. Every slight movement appears to cause her excruciating pain until her foot is free.

Dark red stains blot the toes of her thick socks. She rolls them to her ankles and removes them from her feet with extra care. Her toes are bloody and blistered. The nails on her feet are broken and black. She dips her feet into a clay pot filled with a murky brown liquid. Her face crinkles into a painful wince before her expression relaxes into one of relief. She lies back on a ragged pillow, pulls a tattered blanket over herself, and with her feet still in the pot, she sighs.

My body aches as I suck in a breath. I didn't realize how bad it was until now.

"Bella? Can I come in?" I ask.

She bolts upright, her feet tipping the pot and flooding the bottom of her bedroll with muddy water. She rips her slingshot from her belt and aims at me quicker than I can blink. It takes her only a second to recognize me and she lowers her weapon. "What are you doing here?" she asks.

"I came to check on you," I say. My eyes flash to the ulcers on her tiny toes. "I had no idea."

Bella sets her slingshot on a ledge and thrusts the frayed quilt over her feet. "Why would you? It's not your business anyway," she says, lying back down with her back to me.

"But . . ."

"Just go away." Her words tumble out, quiet but razor-sharp.

Shrinking back, I'm unsure how to respond to her hostility. "I only wanted to help," I say, surprised by the sound of hurt in my own voice.

"I didn't ask for your help," Bella snaps as she sits up. Her eyes shimmer with unshed tears. "Why did you come here, anyway? Are you trying to hook up with Pete? Because if you are, you might as well give up. He doesn't have time for a girl like you."

Shaking my head, I hold up my palms and step back. "That's not it at all. I'm here because you invited me. You said you'd help get Joanna back."

"I didn't invite you; Pete did," Bella says haughtily. Then she turns her back to me, extinguishes the candle, and wraps the quilt around her. A small toe peeks from beneath the blanket and lies in the pool of water at the end of her bed.

I should be offended, but I recognize the ferocity the war has instilled in all of us.

Below, in the city center, the boys roar as another competitor steps up, challenging Jack. Scout holds a kerchief to a cut above his brow. I wonder if any of them knows how much Bella is really suffering. Beyond the crowd of children, a window in the brick apothecary building is lit by a single lantern on its sill.

I lower the lift to the dirt floor and sneak past the crowd of Lost Boys. I climb the wobbly wooden steps up to the apothecary, knock, and open the door.

The pungent smell of alcohol stings my nose. Textbooks lie strewn across the wood floor and fill numerous bookshelves in the room. A half-dozen cots align on one side of the room and they, too, are covered with books. A lopsided desk made from scrap lumber sits in one corner. Threadbare burgundy Victorian curtains droop from a rusted copper pipe crudely made into a curtain rod.

On the far side of the room, crickets sing from two tanks

placed near gas lanterns. Dozens of different lizards bask on sticks in the lamps' heat. Other containers line the shelves filled with insects, rodents, and more reptiles.

I step into the space and glance at the open pages of the manuals. They are filled with diagrams, charts, and terms I do not understand. Notes scrawl along the margins of the pages in nearly illegible handwriting. A doctor's script, I realize. A thick textbook titled *The Anatomy of Infectious Diseases* lies on one cot, along with other medical journals, their pages open to information regarding the Horologia virus.

From the back of the building, someone clears his throat. I look up to find a broad-shouldered, blond teenage boy staring at me with eyes as blue as sapphires. At first, an expression of shock crosses his face, but he shakes it off, replacing it with an uneasy smile.

"Um, well, this is quite unexpected," he says, tugging on his waistcoat and brushing his fingers through his thick hair. "I haven't had a lady visitor in my office for quite some time. Can I help you . . . um, miss?" he asks.

"I'm looking for Doc," I say, fiddling with the bottom button on my jacket.

He squints. "May I ask who might be looking for him?"

"I'm Gwen. Gwen Darling."

He approaches me and holds a hand out. "Well, if you're looking for Doc, you've found him," the boy says with a giant grin.

· GWEN ·

Doc watches me as I avert my gaze to a nearby textbook, picking it up and pretending to thumb through it. I have never considered myself shy, but for the second time in less than a day, my cheeks flush under a boy's stare.

"Pardon me," Doc says, moving books off a chair. "It's been so long since I've seen a girl, I have forgotten my manners. Please, have a seat. How can I be of assistance to you today?"

"Thank you," I say as the rusted metal folding chair gives an audible squeak when I sit. "Actually, I came to introduce myself and . . ."

Doc sweeps his arm across the seat of another chair, sending books tumbling to the floor like dominoes. He pulls the chair up so close to mine that when he sits our knees almost touch. Leaning forward, elbows propped on his long legs, he watches me with an intense gaze.

Nervous, I shift in my seat and glance at the front door, wondering if I should excuse myself and leave.

"Your complexion is remarkable. Flawless, in fact," Doc interrupts, tapping his chin with a finger. "The whites of your eyes are so clear. No yellowing in them." He clutches my right hand and inspects it. "No discoloration, no ulcers on your fingers. It is absolutely incredible."

I jerk my hand from his and scoot my chair back.

Doc pulls the medispectacles perched on top of his head over his eyes and twists knobs on either side of them. Several lenses of different shapes and sizes shift, clicking into place and magnifying his blue eyes. As with Justice's spectacles, the lenses give him a bug-eyed appearance. He moves his face close to mine. "Stick out your tongue."

Wiggling free from the little space between us, I stand and back up toward the door. "I think this might have been a mistake. Perhaps I'll come back later." Eager to leave, I hurry to the entrance.

"Wait!" he says as I touch the doorknob. He walks toward me, slowly removing the medispectacles from his face and placing them back on top of his head. The lenses, still protruding from the frames, give the illusion of two horns poking from his skull. "I'm sorry. I didn't mean to startle you. The only female I've seen in months is Bella. Then you show up completely healthy. It's a miracle. How have you done it? How have you survived?"

I say nothing, gripping the doorknob tightly.

"I've spent months scouring every book, magazine, journal, and old newspaper article searching for anything to find a cure, but have had no success. The best I have been able to do is to slow the progression, but I haven't found an antidote. Bella, the only surviving girl, gets worse every day, which led me to believe there was no hope for your gender."

His attentive stare gives me butterflies. I pick up one of the textbooks, pretending to read it, hoping to break his stare.

Someone knocks, interrupting the awkwardness. "Doc, I see you've met Gwen," Pete says, striding into the room.

"I have," Doc says, still staring at me, not meeting Pete's gaze. "She's incredible."

There is an unnerving air between them: Pete's fixed stare and Doc's refusal to meet it.

"Do you think she's immune?" Pete asks, his words pointed like the tip of a dagger. "Can she help Bella?"

"It's hard to say. I'd need to draw blood, separate out the white blood cells, and combine it with Bella's medication. But it would be Gwen's decision to make. I wouldn't experiment without her permission."

Experiment—a word almost as vile as *immune*. I shudder, imagining myself lying on one of Doc's cots with needles, tubes, and the whirring of equipment around me. Everything would be done by hand, slowly and painfully.

"Right," Pete says. He gazes at me with concerned eyes. "Of course it would be her decision."

I drop my chin to my chest and plop onto the closest cot. "I've already agreed to help. Let's just get this over with so we can go get Joanna."

"Who's Joanna?" Doc asks.

"Joanna's my sister. Hook has her," I say. "Pete agreed to help me get her back and in exchange I agreed to helping you find an antidote for Bella."

"He did what?" Doc asks, glaring at Pete. "Pete, do you know the risks you're taking? There is no way you and Gwen will make it past Hook's men alone. You might as well march right up to the palace doors and surrender."

"You're right," Pete says. "Alone we wouldn't get within a kilometer of Hook's bunkers without being caught. That's why I'm taking a team."

"A team? You can't be serious," Doc says. He places his fists on his hips and watches Pete with a stone-cold stare.

Pete crosses his arms, undaunted by Doc's rebuttal. "Sous is packing rations for us, and Blade is preparing our weapons."

"Pete, you of all people know how dangerous this ludicrous plan is. No one has ever come back from Everland. Ever! They always end up in Hook's lab. It's one thing when you put your own life at risk, but are you really willing to risk the lives of other Lost Boys? Or Gwen's? She's the first healthy girl we've seen."

The impact of his words strikes me hard, and the guilt is overwhelming. How could I endanger the lives of any of the Lost Boys for a problem that is all my own? It is my fault. I should never have left Joanna and Mikey alone with the Marauders so close to our hideout.

"Lost Kids," Pete says smugly.

"What do mean, Lost Kids?" Doc asks, eyeing Pete.

"Bella is coming with us," Pete says.

"Bella?" Shocked, I shake my head. "No, Pete, she's much too sick to come with us. She should stay here where Doc can continue to treat her."

"If I leave without her, she'll just follow us anyway," Pete says, sighing as he sits on the cot next to me. The springs creak in protest. He leans his elbows on his knees and gazes down at his calloused hands. "We're family; we saved each other. She lost everything, everyone important to her, and I lost the only person important to me. Bella means everything to me. She's my little sister. There's no way she'd let me leave her behind." Pete shoots Doc a glare. Doc looks away, unwilling to meet his gaze.

I'm surprised by this display of raw emotion but decide not to press him further.

"It's true. She can be stubborn," Doc says, rubbing his chin. "All right, I guess that means I'm coming with you. I'll pack up my medical kit and stock up on her medicines."

"No way," Pete says, sitting straighter.

Doc scowls at Pete. "You think you can go gallivanting into Everland with a handful of kids and still care for Bella? She's my patient. If she goes, I go. Someone needs to give her medications to her. I'm not going through the trouble of trying to find a cure for her only to have her die on a crazy mission with you."

"You were not invited," Pete says through gritted teeth. "You haven't been outside of the Lost City in months. You have no idea what lies out there."

Doc kicks a chair, sending it crashing to the floor. I jump, startled by the sudden outburst. He marches up to Pete and shoves him. "Blast it, Pete! Do you think I don't know what's out there? Do you know how many bullets I have pulled from those boys? How many wounds I have stitched up from the Marauders? Have you any idea how many boys have exhaled their last breath here in this very office? Don't you dare tell me that I don't know what lies beyond the walls of the Lost City!" Doc turns and opens a medicine bag, shoving supplies into it.

An awkward silence hangs heavy in the air.

"Look, just take your sample of Gwen's blood and work on

the cure while we're gone. We'll be back soon enough," Pete finally says.

"Pete!" Doc roars. "A cure is no good if Bella dies."

Pete grimaces, as if talk of Bella's survival, or lack thereof, sears every cell within. "Then you should prepare a new medication for Bella before we leave." When their eyes meet, Pete nods toward me.

Doc grunts. "I suppose you're right," he says. "That is, if Gwen is up for it."

My hands shake. I sit on them, hoping to hide my terror. "I have to warn you, I am not fond of needles. My mother was a doctor, and she was always obsessed with vaccinating my siblings and me."

"Vaccinating?" Doc runs a frustrated hand through his hair. "That could be why you're not showing any indication of being infected with the virus."

"That doesn't explain why her sister is showing symptoms. If both of them were vaccinated, why is Joanna sick?" Pete asks.

"Your sister is showing symptoms? That doesn't make sense." Doc taps the glass lenses on his goggles. "Unless . . ."

"Unless what?" I ask.

Doc turns to me. "When was the last time she vaccinated you?"

"I don't know," I say. "She was giving us shots all the time. I guess the last one was just before the war started, right before my fifteenth birthday."

Doc searches through a stack of books before picking up a navy-blue one with silver lettering. He shuffles through the pages and stops about a quarter into the book. He mumbles as his finger skims across the page. "Here, read this." He hands the book to me.

I take the book and he taps on a passage. I read it aloud for Pete to hear.

" 'It's not entirely understood why the length of acquired immunity varies with vaccines. While many offer lifelong immunity with a single dose, others require boosters in order to maintain immunity.' "

"A booster? But it still doesn't make sense. My mother vaccinated all of us, not just me," I say, rereading the passage. "She would've given us all boosters. Why would Joanna show symptoms and not me?"

"And that doesn't explain why males are immune and females are not," Pete says.

Doc sighs and sinks back into a chair with resolve. "That's where you're wrong. Males are not immune either."

"What?" Pete and I both say at the same time, loudly.

"Males are not immune," Doc repeats, sounding deflated. "There is something specific, unique, within the Y chromosome which makes boys more tolerant of the virus. In fact, it seems that the Horologia virus is activated depending on the biochemistry of the person. Things like growth hormones, genetics, and other biological aspects determine who lives and who dies. It's almost as if it was developed to decimate everyone except those who could be taken in and trained to be soldiers. Survival of the fittest. While the stronger live, the weaker, which in this case means the oldest and youngest, die, along with girls." Doc shoots me a glance. "No offense to you."

"None taken," I say.

"However, it turns out that while those of us who have the Y chromosome seem to be more resilient, we're not immune," Doc continues.

"How can that be right?" I ask. "Look at all those boys out there who have managed to survive. Boys must have some, if not complete, immunity."

"You're right, but if it was entirely based on genetics, if the Y chromosome alone determined immunity, the adult males would have survived. The only reason those boys survived was simply because they are children, not adults. They not only have their gender going for them but are brimming with growth hormone." Doc shuts the book and sets it back on the stack. "Adults have less growth hormone and babies are, well . . . incapable of caring for themselves. Without someone to provide them with fluids and nutrition, most of them died off within the first week. We have a few younger boys who were rescued, but not many."

"So if what you're saying is true, what is the prognosis for the Lost Boys?" Pete asks. Worry lines wrinkle his forehead.

Doc drops his head, runs his hand across the back of his neck, and grimaces. "To be truthful, I don't know. Since Hook's Marauders continue patrolling with masks, they must suspect that the virus is still airborne. While the boys will produce some of their own antibodies, being exposed to the virus, there is no telling how effective they will be, or for how long. If this virus is strong enough to take down a grown man, who knows what it is capable of after years of exposure. Some of the boys are already showing symptoms."

"What? Who?" Pete says in almost a shout.

"That information is confidential. The boys who have come in with symptoms are afraid of becoming outcasts once the others discover they are carriers. Not only that, if the others learn that some of the kids are infected, it may produce panic. I have promised to keep their identities private. However . . . it doesn't take a genius to figure it out," Doc says. He points to the window.

I walk to the paneless opening. The Lost City shines under the gas lanterns' luminescence. Clusters of boys gather, laughing and chasing one another in a friendly game of tag. Another group kicks a football around. It is then that I see it, the one thing that identifies the sick from the healthy.

"The gloves," I say. At least a third of the boys wear one glove; some wear two.

Doc smiles. "The Immune is quite perceptive."

For the first time, the nickname strikes me as almost a compliment. I may have failed as a sister, breaking promises to never grow up, and I may have failed as a guardian, but this new identity— this is something I can only fail by refusing to help.

Pete scans the crowd of boys. "There's so many. How come I never noticed?"

"Perhaps intelligence is also a trait of being an Immune," Doc says, smugly.

Pete whirls and grabs Doc's shirt, pulling him close to his face. "I am the leader of the Lost City. Why didn't you tell me that the boys were suffering, too? First my sister. Now this family? You continue to let the people I care about die!"

"You know that wasn't my fault. Gabrielle was beyond my

help," Doc says. "I loved her and did everything I could to save her. Everything!"

"Stop it!" I yell. I try to pull Pete off Doc, but he refuses to release his grip.

"You should have told me about the Lost Boys!" Pete says with a sneer.

"I tried. You wouldn't listen to me. You're so blinded with bitterness about what happened to your sister, you wouldn't have seen their decaying bodies even if I'd pointed them out to you," Doc spits.

"I ought to dismember you, wrap your body parts in a rubbish bag, and personally deliver you on Hook's doorstep to feed to his pet crocodiles," Pete says, his voice seething with fury.

"Enough!" I shout. "Can you two knock it off for just a minute so we can figure out what to do?"

Pete loosens his grip on Doc and gives him a shove. Doc straightens his shirt and waistcoat, not taking his glowering eyes off Pete. I stand in between the boys, hoping they don't resort to throwing punches.

"Do you really think everyone could die?" I ask.

"Yes, everyone but you," Doc says. "That's where this virus appears to be heading."

"If I am the only Immune, then my antibodies could potentially help not only Bella but all of the Lost Boys."

"That is correct," Doc says with a nod. "At least that's my theory."

"Let's get on with it, then," I say with a sigh. Removing a stack of books from a cot, I rest my head on the pillow. "Take as much as you need. How much is that? A pint?" I ask, trying my best to be brave, but the quiver in my voice betrays me. I close my eyes tight.

"A pint is hardly anything, but that amount won't be necessary," Doc says, digging through his medicine bag. "I won't be taking much of your blood. Right now Bella is the worst of the sick. She will be the one receiving treatment. If the treatment proves successful, we will take care of the others. For now, we need to test you to see if you do carry the antibodies to cure the virus."

Doc rummages through his medicine bag again, turning from us, but I see the tightness in his jaw. "Besides, you will need your strength to travel to Everland. No sense in draining all of your blood and weakening you right before your journey, especially when we have no idea if you even carry the cure. Since I will be joining you, we will need only a small sample. Just enough to start Bella's treatment. If we need more, we'll deal with it later."

"I've already told you that you're not coming with us," Pete growls.

"Is that so?" Doc says. "So tell me this, who will be giving Bella her injections? Certainly not you? While I think it's fantastic you've so generously offered your own antibodies to help Bella up until this point, let me remind you, fearless leader, you faint at the sight of needles." Doc pulls out a long needle from his bag. My heart quickens and I feel a little dizzy. I have never seen a needle so large.

"Now, I'm guessing you have some things to do before venturing into Everland?" Doc says with a wide smirk.

Pete's face turns pale and he averts his gaze. "I have to check on Blade and Stock to see if they've got our stuff together anyway." He turns to me; his hardened expression fades. "Thank you, Gwen. You don't know how much this means to me."

He faces Doc. "Make it quick. We're leaving before sunset." Pete marches to the door and slams it behind him, rattling the glass jars lined on the shelves.

"I thought you said you didn't need much blood," I say, eyeing the large needle.

Doc snickers as he puts the needle back in his bag. "Don't worry. This needle is not for you. I took it out to spook Pete. Gets him every time. One of the Scavengers brought this needle back from a farm thinking I could use it. It is a horse's needle, but I like to keep it as a souvenir. Also, it keeps blokes like him out of my hair."

Relieved, my shoulders relax and I melt into the cot, suddenly exhausted.

Doc digs through his bag again. "Just lie back. This will feel no worse than the prick of a sewing needle."

Closing my eyes, I turn my wrists, exposing the inside of my forearms. I wait for the sharp stab to sting the flesh in the crease of my arm. Instead, Doc lifts my hand from the cot and takes hold of my index finger. I open my eyes in time to see him puncture the tip with a tiny needle. A crimson-red bead flows onto the pad of my finger. Doc grabs a small tube from his bag. He squeezes, collecting the blood as it starts to drip.

"That's it?" I ask, surprised.

"Did you want me to take more?" he says through a chuckle.

"Well, no, but I assumed . . ."

Doc wipes my finger with an alcohol swab. "You've got quite the imagination, don't you?"

I sigh. "What I wouldn't give for that to be my biggest problem."

"That makes two of us." Doc puts a bandage on the puncture. "There we go. Just like new."

I feel the corners of my mouth draw up in a smile.

"Are you sure that will be enough?" I ask, examining the small vial of red liquid. "It doesn't seem like much."

"It's plenty. I can get at least two doses out of this sample. Judging Bella's height and weight, one injection should be enough to begin with."

"Two doses?" I ask, looking at the vial hardly filled with blood. "How is that possible?"

"Someday I'll show you how it all works, but for now, you'll have to accept it as fact," Doc says with a grin. "Now, I've got work to do, but it's been a great pleasure meeting you." Doc extends his hand.

"It's been nice meeting you, too," I say, shaking his hand.

Doc nods at me before positioning his medispectacles on his face. He takes the small vial of blood, puts it in some sort of contraption, and begins churning at a handle. The circular container holding the sample spins quickly. At the door, I take one last look at Doc.

"I hope I really am what you think I am," I say, but the doctor does not hear me.

· HOOK ·

With my army swarming Everland and its outskirts in search of orphaned girls, I return to Buckingham Palace, intrigued by the prospect of our newest prisoner. The Professor has known all along that any hope for a cure could be found in a girl. I can't help but wonder what else she has failed to tell me. While I know providing her with the knowledge of our latest prisoner is exactly what she wants, even needs, to progress, I decide to hold my cards close. After all, that's what *she's* done this whole time, isn't it?

When I enter the lab, the Professor is peering into a microscope. I clear my throat. She holds one finger up and scribbles something in a notebook. When she's done, she turns to me, giving me the blank expression I've become so accustomed to. It wasn't always this way, at least not at first. Initially, her eyes shone with nothing but hatred for me. But as the weeks dragged into months, the fire left, leaving a shell of the defiant woman I first rescued from the rubble. If it weren't for the hazmat suit she wore and my help, she'd have died right there. She ought to be grateful, if not downright indebted, to me. Instead, she addresses me with scorn, nothing like the fondness she shows the children. I loathe it.

"Have you made any progress?" I ask.

"Of course not! I need the girl," she says as if reprimanding me.

I ball my fists but bite my words. I need her on my side . . . for now.

"Is there anything more I can do?" I ask through clenched teeth.

Leaning against the counter, she drops her chin to her chest and shakes her head. "No, there's nothing more I can do without the girl. We are all lost." She slams her hands on the countertop and lets out an exaggerated sigh.

I shift from one foot to the other, searching for words. It's my fault that it has come to this, the lives of everyone, of all of humankind, hanging on a single girl. But I don't have time for regrets. I chase the gut-wrenching guilt away with a question that has nagged me since we arrived in Everland. "Do you know why the virus is so lethal?"

"The virus's virulence is due to a plant. A tree that isn't indigenous anywhere in Europe."

"A tree? What kind of tree?" I ask.

The Professor returns to her microscope and removes a slide, replacing it with another. "The plant is known as pwazon pòm. It's native to the tropics. It is thought to have been eradicated years ago due to its effects on humans, but apparently that isn't the case. Take a look." She gestures toward the microscope.

I peer into the scope. A group of what appear to be cells lies on the slide. "What am I looking at?" I ask.

"Those are epithelial cells, basic skin cells. Now watch this," she says. She picks up a vial from the counter and places a drop of the red liquid on the slide.

Immediately, tiny dark red spots surround the cells and devour them. Within a few seconds there is nothing left of the cluster. I look back up at the Professor, my breath hitching. "What was that?"

"That sample was simple dead skin cells. Epithelial tissue lines the cavities and surfaces of structures throughout the body. We're talking your skin, lungs, heart, blood vessels . . . just about everything. That liquid is a blood sample infected with the Horologia virus. Now imagine if the virus had access to an entire human body. Once in contact, especially in airborne samples, it wouldn't take long to ravage a person's organs. That is why, when the virus became airborne, so many died quickly. I believe the base was made from the sap of the plant."

Thoughtfully, I rub my chin, staring at her. "How is it that the virus annihilated the adults, but the children survived?"

"I'm not entirely sure I have an answer to that. The children you've brought in all show signs of infection, but not nearly as bad as the adults in the early days after the war started," she says, her eyes flicking up to mine and back to her paper.

"But even they succumb to the virus," I say.

The Professor drops her gaze before turning back toward the microscope. "Yes, and once I've determined they're infected and unable to contribute to finding a cure, I dispose of them as you have requested."

"Cremation?" I ask, watching every one of her moves. She doesn't meet my eyes.

"Of course," she says, peering into the microscope again.

I clutch my hands behind me and pace. She's hiding something. I'm sure of it. "I've been told the Marauders have captured another child," I say finally, watching for her reaction.

The Professor continues to stare into the microscope while

writing down notes. "Oh, really? I'll prepare a bed for him as soon as I'm done with this."

"It's a *her*," I say, stopping just behind her and folding my arms.

The Professor spins. Her eyes grow wide. "That's great. I should see her right away," she says with enthusiasm.

"You will. But unfortunately, she is not the one you're looking for. She shows signs of being infected. I'll have my men put her in confinement until you're ready," I say, marching toward the lab door.

The Professor rushes toward me and grips my arms. "Captain Kretschmer, you will let me examine her immediately."

I flinch beneath her grasp, feeling as if bugs were crawling over my entire body. I detest being touched. When her scarred hands fall away, I am grateful.

She bites her bottom lip and for the first time since I've walked in she meets my gaze, searching my face for . . . what? Understanding? Compassion?

"Please, let me see her." This time her tone lacks admonishment, but instead sounds as if she's pleading.

Something catches my eye. A glint of gold shimmers beneath a cot. I walk toward it, but the Professor shoves her way between me and the cot. She stares at me with intent, dark eyes.

"That little girl may be sick, but she still might be useful."

"I don't follow you," I say, scrutinizing her delicate features. She's quite pretty . . . for an older woman. She's practically my own mother's age, but there's something about her. Something my mother never had. A beauty that lies deeper than her appearance. There's a fondness I have for her, but not in the romantic sense. I can't quite put my finger on it.

The Professor continues talking, but I'm distracted by the shimmering item on the floor. I kneel to pick up the gold object. It is a link from a chain belt or piece of jewelry, but as I scan the room, there is nothing that matches it. The Professor notices the chain link in between my gloved fingers and her eyes widen, stopping midsentence. "I . . . I've been looking for that," she says, reaching for the gold metal.

I wrap my gloved fingers tightly around the link. Again she's hiding something from me. After months of working with her, I've begun to recognize her slight idiosyncrasies. She's a terrible liar. With a sigh she prattles on. I am lost in my own thoughts, inspecting the piece of metal and wondering of its origin. I miss everything she says to me except the last words.

". . . if she dies, we all die."

· GWEN ·

Shouts erupt from an angry crowd gathered at the statue of Eros as I slip into the city square. Pete stands at the base of the fountain, surrounded by dozens of other boys. With a stern expression on his face, Pete sifts through an onslaught of questions.

"Are you bloody mad?" shouts Pyro. The muscles in his neck cord beneath his dark skin. "No one gets rescued from Everland."

"Pyro's right. Why would we risk four of our own for one measly little girl?" Pickpocket says, fidgeting with the brass buttons on his waistcoat.

"Measly girl? Is that what Bella is to you, Pickpocket? That girl is worth more than twenty of you boys," Pete says hotly.

"We're not talking about Bella, we're talking about some girl who may or may not even be alive," Pickpocket says. "For all we know Hook's already dissected her or whatever that madman does to kids."

Mikey, his face cleaned of the mud stains from earlier, hides behind a wooden barrel a short distance from the disgruntled group. I crouch down beside him.

"What's going on? They all seem so angry," I whisper.

He wraps his arms around my neck. "They don't want to help get Joanna back."

"Don't worry. Pete will convince them," I say. "And if he doesn't, I will."

"This isn't going to work," Pyro says. "No one ever comes back from Everland. You know the rules! If you get caught, you're on your own."

"No one's returned because no one has tried," Pete says.

The gathering of boys say nothing, but pass worried glances among themselves.

"I am going, whether you choose to come or not," Pete says, resting his hands on the hilts of his daggers. "I've given Gwen my word and I intend to keep it. On my own, there's no guarantee the mission will be successful. But if you come with me, if I can count on you, I *know* we'll get Joanna back."

"Why us?" a stout boy says, his hands twisting the fabric of his oversize brown trench coat. His milky eyes stare past Pete. "What do you need us for?"

"Mole, who is a better tracker than you?" Pete asks.

"Nobody. I can smell a Marauder several blocks away," Mole says, wrinkling his nose. "Among other foul things."

"And you, Pickpocket, there isn't a Lost Boy who can crack locks like you can," Pete says, pointing at the muscular boy.

"That is true," Pickpocket says gruffly. The Lost Boys nod in agreement.

"And you, Pyro, you know everything there is to know about explosives," Pete says.

Pyro removes his derby hat and scratches his closely shaven head. "True enough. I could blow a hole a meter wide into a steel door with just a stick of dynamite."

"So let me get this straight—we're putting our necks on the

line for her?" Pickpocket says, pointing to me. "Even she knows how crazy this is. Look at her! She's cowering behind a barrel."

"Stay here, Mikey," I whisper as I creep from behind the drum.

"We're putting our necks on the line for her sister, to be accurate," Pete says.

"Please!" I say, addressing the boys. "I need your help to get her back. If Pete says you're the best, then you have to help."

"I'm not risking my life for your sister. Count me out," Pickpocket says, storming past me. "You're on your own, Immune."

"Lost Girl," Pete corrects, his expression serious. "She's one of us now."

I gaze at the green-eyed boy, my chest swelling at his words. Lost Girl. They settle over me and I realize for the first time that I am a part of their group. Their family.

Pickpocket halts but doesn't turn around.

"Please, just listen to me for one minute," I say, placing a hand on Pickpocket's shoulder.

He turns, folds his arms, and frowns. It is then I notice them, the gloves that cover both of his hands.

"Joanna and Mikey are the only family I have, at least until now," I say, glancing at Pete. He nods, encouraging me to continue. "Surely you had a sister, a brother, parents, someone you've lost. You'd want someone to help you rescue them if you had the chance, wouldn't you?"

Pickpocket leans close to me, his hot breath whispering against my cheeks. "My family is dead. I am my own family now." He shoves me aside, his leather-gloved hand brushing against my arm.

Impulsively, I grab his hand, curl my fingers under the leather edge, and rip it off. The Lost Boys gasp.

"What are you doing?" he yells, protectively pulling his fist into his chest.

I throw his glove to the ground. "Show me your fingers."

"What are you talking about?" he says. His eyes dart from me to the other boys. He tucks his naked fist into the crook of his arm, hiding it from view.

"Show me your hand," I demand, reaching for him.

Pickpocket doesn't budge.

"Do it!" Pete says in an authoritative tone.

Pickpocket glares at Pete but reluctantly holds his hand out. His fingers are covered in boils. The skin on his palms is flaky and the backs have spots of raw flesh. He winces as my fingers barely graze his hand.

"You're not immune," I say.

More boys join us, erupting in a flurry of whispers. Pickpocket reaches for his glove. He shifts uncomfortably, noticing the shocked expressions on Mole's and Pyro's faces. "It's only a few sores. What's it to you?" he says, growling.

"I can help you." I show him my hands. "I am immune. The only Immune. My body contains the cure—the antidote or whatever. I am resistant to the virus. Or at least that's what Doc seems to think."

Immune. I inhale deeply as the term spills from my lips. As if uttering those two syllables breathes life, truth, and hope into a word that once tasted bitter on my tongue. *Immune*: a word that once was degrading, but now encompasses the fate of this boy, the fate of all of the Lost Boys, and possibly the rest of humankind.

Pickpocket gazes at my unblemished hands, turning them over and inspecting them as if they were a priceless work of art, a Degas in the midst of nursery-school finger paintings.

"I can help you," I say, with a confidence bubbling in my voice that surprises me. "But I need your help, too. Together we can find a cure, for you, for Bella, and for any other sick Lost Kid."

"You're really an Immune?" he asks. His voice is flat, devoid of emotion.

"That's what Doc says," Pete interjects as he leans against the fountain.

I place a hand on Pickpocket's arm. "Look, I know what it's like to lose family. I've lost my father and mother to the war, and now I've lost Joanna not only to Hook but, if I don't get her back soon, to the virus. We don't have to lose anyone else." I point to a group of kids playing a game with Bella. Her wings flutter and the boys mimic her, waving their arms in the air. "*You* don't have to lose any more family."

Pickpocket watches Bella float above the Lost Kids, a pained expression crossing his face. He glances down at his blistered hands.

Taking his hand gently, I peer into his dark eyes. "You have my word. I will help you."

Pickpocket pauses, peering at his fingers and then at Bella. "I'll help you find your sister, but not for me. For Bella."

"Me too," says Mole. "I'd do just about anything for Bella."

"I suppose I'm in as well," Pyro says. "I don't want to be the only prat who says no."

The smaller boys cheer and break into imaginary sword fights. "Take that, Hook!" Gabs shouts, jabbing another boy with an invisible knife. The other boy dramatically feigns death, grunting as he collapses on the ground.

"Then it's decided," Pete says, raising his voice above the chatter. "You guys head over to Blade's place. Arm yourselves with the best weapons Blade has."

"You comin', too?" Pickpocket asks, jerking his glove onto his hand, seemingly still annoyed with me.

"We'll be along shortly," Pete says, his face emotionless.

"Suit yourself. Let's go, Lost Boys," Pickpocket says, leading Mole and Pyro toward the weapons armory.

Enthusiastic, I turn to Pete. His grin is wide as he walks toward me. "They're going to help!" I say with excitement.

"Nice job, Immune," he says, giving me a fist bump. "I couldn't have done it better myself. Well, I probably could have, but batting my eyelashes like you did wouldn't have worked as well for me as it did for you."

"I didn't bat my eyelashes!" I protest.

"Hey, Pete, is Jack going to be the leader while you're gone?" Gabs asks, fidgeting with the ends of the dirty scarf wrapped around his neck. He leans in and whispers, "He can be awfully bossy when you're not here."

Pete's face twists into a grimace and quickly fades into a reassuring smile. "Jack is complicated. He's a good guy. Troubled, but good nonetheless. Don't you worry, Gabs. I've got it covered."

Pete ruffles Gabs's hair and the anxiety slips from Gabs's expression.

"Lost Boys, line up!" Pete shouts.

Chattering with excitement, the boys queue up in two straight lines, jockeying for position according to their height. Mikey sneaks from his hiding spot and sidles in between two kids. I join him, taking him by his small hand. Pete strides between the two rows, scrutinizing each boy.

Jack, suddenly noticing the crowd of boys, joins Pete in the center. "What's this about?"

"You're getting your wish," Pete mutters.

Jack squints, confusion marking the sharp angles of his cheeks and jaw.

Pete holds his hands up, grabbing the attention of the hundred or so boys.

"Lost Boys, today has been an eventful day, with the recruitment of Gwen and Mikey to the Lost City." Pete clutches his hands behind his back, pacing as he speaks. "And it's no secret that girls are scarce and an important part of our society. Integral to our survival. They are more rare, more valuable than any other item we can scavenge."

I wince, listening to him speak about girls as if we were objects, priceless treasures.

The older boys elbow one another, raising their eyebrows. I roll my eyes, imagining what shallow comments the older boys are making to one another.

"Today I will be taking a team of our best Scavengers with me on an important task in order to recover something stolen from our newest citizen, Gwen." Pete gestures toward me. "My team is with Blade as we speak, arming themselves for the battle that lies ahead. This will be the most dangerous scavenge we've done yet."

"Pete, what are you doing?" Jack grumbles.

Pete ignores the question. "While I'm away, Jack will be the primary leader and Justice the second-in-command."

A groan rumbles through the crowd. Justice beams. Scout rolls his eyes, turns, and walks away, adjusting his weapon at his hip as he travels down a darkened tunnel.

Jack faces Pete, eyeing him sternly. "What's this about, Pete? You can't just take off with our best Scavengers. Do you know how long that will set us back? We're already running low on supplies."

Pete steps toward Jack so that they're nearly nose to nose. "We're going to Everland."

A collective gasp echoes through the cavern.

"You're kidding me," Jack says, folding his arms. "This is a joke, right?"

Pete stares him down. "Do I look like I'm joking?"

Jack shifts uncomfortably. "You're scavenging in Everland? That's against the bylaws. Do you know how dangerous that is? No one *ever* makes it back from Everland."

Pete doesn't break his stare. "We *will* make it back."

"You're a fool!" Jack says, stabbing a finger toward Pete.

"Some things are worth risking everything for," Pete replies, unflinching.

Jack throws his hands in the air and takes two steps back. "Whatever. You're the leader. Completely mad, but still the leader."

Jack spins on his heels and starts back to the stock room, cursing under his breath.

"I'm going after Hook," Pete announces.

A hush falls over the boys.

Jack abruptly stops. Slowly he turns. "Hook?"

Pete's grin grows wide. "Hook has Gwen's sister. We're breaking into Buckingham Palace to get her back."

The corner of Jack's mouth twitches into a lopsided smirk. He pushes either side of his coat back, revealing a belt with an array of tools, buttons, and switches on it. "You're right, Pete. Some things are worth risking everything for. I'm coming with you. I've got my own bone to pick with Hook."

Pete nods, gesturing at Jack's tool belt. "And that is why we call you the Jack of All Trades. Every great adventure could use a Lost Boy like you. Glad to have you along."

Jack clasps Pete's hand and gives it a firm shake. "I wouldn't have it any other way. I'll go check and see how the boys are getting on with Blade."

"Thanks!" Pete says, and pats him on the shoulder as Jack heads toward the weaponeer building.

Pete faces the rest of the Lost Boys. "Justice will be your interim leader while we're away. I know you boys will show him the respect you show me."

The boys cheer and slap Justice on the back.

"I won't let you down, Pete," Justice says, adjusting his goggles.

"I can't think of a better suited Lost Boy than you," Pete says. He leans in close to Justice's ear. "Try to go with your gut, kid. Not by the rules." Pete snatches the spiral notebook from Justice's shirt pocket and stuffs it inside his own coat. Justice's mouth gapes open, but he says nothing.

"Gabs, take Justice to the map room and give him a rundown on his duties. Everyone else, clear out! The party is over. Get back to work," shouts Pete. The boys scatter, taking up their work posts.

"Sure thing, Pete," Gabs says, tugging on Justice's arm. "Come on, Justice. You're gonna like the map room. It's got this ginormous map that sort of looks like a treasure map only not really. Instead of where a treasure might be, X marks the spot where the Scavengers have been. He's got a fan that spins when you pedal the footplates, but you have to pedal really fast or otherwise it doesn't cool you off. And there's an inkwell, which holds three different color inks, if you had ink to put in it. I like to squeeze my beets in there since I don't like beets all that much. There's also a . . ." Gabs stops and twists back toward my brother. "Well, aren't you coming, Mikey?"

Mikey tugs at my shirtsleeve. "Can I go with Gabs and Justice? I want to see the map room, too."

"Go ahead," I tell Mikey, giving him a reassuring nudge.

Pete pulls something out of his coat pocket and hands it to my brother. "Here, take this."

Mikey takes the object: a red hard candy. "Wow, thanks a lot. I can't remember when I had candy last."

"The Lost City is your home now. We are your new family," Pete says, kneeling to Mikey's eye level. He juts a hand out and shakes Mikey's tiny one.

Mikey drops Pete's hand and throws both of his arms around his neck. "Thanks, Pete!"

My chest swells at the exchange, and for the first time in a year, I really believe my brother will be safe. Perhaps safer than when he was in my care.

Pete hands a candy to the other two boys. Justice unwraps his with enthusiasm and pops the green ball in his mouth. Gabs sniffs his own yellow candy and holds it out to Mikey.

"Trade?" Gabs asks.

"Sure!" Mikey says, swapping treats with him.

"Pete says too much sugar makes me hyper. I don't know what he's talking about, but lemon isn't my favorite flavor anyhow. It's sour and makes me pucker like this." Gabs's eyes cross as he puckers his lips. "My big sister used to tell me if I made this face and someone hit me in the back of the head it'd be permanent. I just can't take that risk."

The boys' voices fade in the pinging of tools and whirring of machines.

I smile at the boys' exchange. It is heartwarming to see Mikey with a friend. I spin toward Pete. His goggles reflect my grin, a mirror of his own smile. I slip the spectacles off his head. "You, dear sir, can be awfully sweet when you want to be," I say.

He grabs for the goggles but misses as I hold them out of reach. "I'd give those back if I were you, Immune," he says teasingly.

"Not until you stop calling me Immune," I say, twirling the goggles on a finger.

"What should I call you?" he asks. "You still haven't picked a Lost Girl name."

"What's wrong with just calling me Gwen?"

"It doesn't suit you," he says. "Gwen seems like the name of a proper English woman, one who wears hoopskirts, carries a parasol, and is on the arm of a gentleman."

"And I don't seem 'proper' to you?" I say, poking a finger into his chest.

"Hardly," Pete says with a snort.

I pretend to be offended. "Oh, really?"

"Of course not. Have you looked in the mirror?" he asks.

Taken aback by the insult, I suck in my bottom lip and pretend to be interested in his goggles. What was I thinking? Of course I don't appear proper to him. I can only guess how disheveled I appear. By instinct, I reach to comb my fingers through my hair, hoping that it isn't sticking out in every direction.

"Aww, Gwen, I didn't mean it like it sounded," he says, rubbing a hand over his eyes. "I just meant that you're not all weak and damsel-in-distress-like."

The ache of the insult slips away, but it still takes me a moment to lift my eyes to his. I'm terrified that he's covering up, making something up to placate me, and I know it's his stunning eyes that will give it away. He reaches for me and tilts my chin up so that I have nowhere to look but into those eyes.

"Gwen, it's your strength and determination that set you apart. You are by no means a frail Englishwoman," he says, his gaze unwavering.

I instantly feel better and wrap my arms around his neck. He smells of sweat mingled with fresh rain.

"Yes, but I wouldn't be here without your help. Thank you, for everything," I whisper. My heart slams against my ribs. I wonder if he can hear it.

"Don't mention it," he says.

Just as I pull away, my ponytail is violently yanked. I am ripped from Pete's embrace and stumble backward, almost losing my balance. Turning to see who my assailant is, I am shocked to see Bella glaring at me.

"Bella, what'd you do that for?" Pete says, sounding surprised.

Bella folds her arms and tilts her head to the side. "Really? You two can thank me later for saving you from doing the kissy face in front of all of these kids."

Snickers erupt around me as the Lost Boys stare, having paused from their duties to watch us. Heat prickles my cheeks, neck, and ears. I hide my eyes behind a trembling hand. I wasn't being kissy face with him—or was I? I'm not sure. Aside from his good looks, there's nothing about him I'd be remotely attracted to.

"Back to work!" Pete hollers. The kids continue to giggle as they pull their goggles over their eyes, pick up their tools, and return to their duties.

Silently, I berate myself and wrap my arms around my body tightly. I wish I could wind back the clocks and wipe this embarrassing moment from my thoughts.

"And you," Pete says, spinning toward Bella, "what's up with attacking Gwen?"

She shrugs. "I wasn't attacking her; I was trying to get her attention," she says in an innocent tone. She bats her long, dark lashes.

"Next time, a 'hey, Gwen' will suffice," Pete says.

"Fine," Bella says in a snarky tone while rolling her eyes.

"I mean it, Bella. There's no place for your childishness here."

"Or what?" she retorts. "You'll ground me? Take away my toys? You might be the leader, but I'm not just some random girl you picked up on the street and declared a Lost Kid." Bella flicks her hand toward me.

Pete stands a little taller, his face flushed with anger. "Random Lost Kid or not, she's one of us now. And if I see you so much as scowl at Gwen, you *will* be banished."

"Pete!" His name tumbles from my lips loudly, drawing the attention of the other boys.

Despite the flash of defiance in Bella's eyes, I also see tears well up. "You wouldn't dare."

Pete presses his lips together and turns his back to Bella. "It's the same as I'd do for any other Lost Kid. If I have to, I'll personally escort you from the Lost City, and that's a promise."

"Pete, stop it!" I say, positioning myself between Bella and him. I lay a hand on his arm. "That's enough. You're being too harsh on her."

Bella shoves me away from Pete. A tear slides down her pink cheek. Her eyes shift from me to Pete and back to me. She points a finger at me, her hand trembling. "I hate you! I wish you never came here!"

My breath catches as I gaze into her angry blue eyes, a fury in her expression so similar to Joanna's the last time I saw her.

"Bella, I . . ." Before I can finish my sentence, she sprints away, her blond hair fading into the bustle of working boys. "Bella!" I call after her.

"Let her go," Pete says. "She just needs to cool off."

I whirl and grab him by the shoulder, spinning him to face me. "How could you talk to her like that? She's just a kid and you aren't her dad." I give him a slight shove.

"I *am* her guardian." Pete turns and storms through the city center. I follow behind. "And I was defending you. You ought to be grateful," he says over his shoulder.

"What guardian threatens banishment? And *I* should be grateful? For what?" I step in front of him, forcing him to stop abruptly. I wave a hand in the direction Bella has disappeared. "Protecting me from her?"

"She attacked you. I wasn't about to let her get away with that."

I roll my eyes. "She pulled my hair. Besides, what happened to 'you're no damsel in distress'? You don't think I can hold my own against a twelve-year-old girl?"

"Look, I was bluffing about exiling her to Everland, but we have rules and I can't have discord among the kids. The last thing I need is an uprising or, worse, anarchy."

"She's a child, Pete! They're all children, not a bunch of rebels trying to dethrone you." Incredulous, I stomp off in the direction of the building with a sign that reads WEAPONEER.

"Gwen, wait!" Pete shouts, hurrying after me.

Ignoring him, I dash up the steps, taking two at a time, and shove the door open. Inside, Pickpocket is testing out the scope on a rifle before placing it in the scabbard on his back. Mole holds a medieval-looking staff with spikes. Pyro attaches several grenades to a pouch on his hip. A string of firecrackers loops around his derby hat. Next to him, Jack clips random tools to his belt. Each weapon and tool that the boys hold is decorated with brass engravings and embellishments that reflect the flicker of an overhead lamp.

A boy with spiky black hair steps into the room from a closet in the back of the building. Leather and copper pistols are strapped to each of his wrists. Daggers and guns hang from his weapons belt.

"Hi, guys," he says with caution as Pete follows me. His gaze darts between Pete and me. "What's going on?"

"Gwen, this is the way things are run around here," Pete says. "Don't be mad at me because I'm doing my job. I have to do what I have to do to keep the peace."

Ignoring him, I walk up to the spiky-haired boy. I pull my daggers from their sheaths and slam them on a table. "Are you Blade?"

"Yes," he says hesitantly.

"I need replacements for these. Apparently, they are about as good as butter knives, at least according to that dolt you call a leader."

Blade gives a sideways glance toward Pete before replying. "Sure, I'll be right back," he says. He hurries to the closet and pulls aside the sheet covering the doorway.

"Gwen, talk to me." Pete places a hand on my elbow.

I jerk my arm away. "You know what? You are nothing but a bully. What you did to her was far worse than what she would do to me or anyone else."

"What's going on?" Pickpocket asks, placing his revolver in its holster on his back.

"What do you want me to do?" Pete says, frustrated.

I cock my weight to one hip. "You can start with an apology."

"Apologize? Fine! I'm sorry!" Pete holds his hands up defensively.

He sounds insincere, although I'm not surprised. He doesn't strike me as someone who would readily admit fault to anything.

"It's not me you owe an apology to," I say.

Blade walks into the room and places two matching knives on the counter. Brass trim wraps around the grips. They are the most impressive daggers I've ever seen. I snatch the blades from the counter and, without further inspection, I thrust them into the sheaths attached to my hips.

"I guess that means those will do?" Blade asks, picking up my old daggers and tossing them in a wooden crate.

"They're perfect," I say. I push Pete out of my way as I head to the door.

"What's going on?" Blade whispers to Mole.

"Lovers' quarrel?" Mole says. The other boys snicker.

Pete bolts to the door, blocking it before I can go through. "You're right. Maybe I was too harsh on her," he says. "I'll talk to her about it the next time I see her."

"Do it now," I insist. "Did you see the look on her face? She was devastated."

The door bursts open, nearly knocking Pete over, and Gabs rushes in, breathless. "Pete, you have to come. You have to come right now. It's a 'mergency and a really big, ginormous one. Well, maybe not that big or ginormous because she isn't that big of a person . . ."

"What's going on?" Pete asks, alarm evident in his voice.

"I tried to stop her. I really did try, but she's so much bigger than me so I guess that would make it a big problem. I said to her, 'Bella, I don't think this is such a fantastic idea,' and she wouldn't listen to me. Oh no. I knew it was a bad idea right from the start, or at least I wouldn't do it, well, not until I was big and brave like you, but definitely not now and not even if I was as big as Bella."

"Gabs, what's wrong with Bella?" asks Pete, placing both hands on Gabs's shoulders and giving him a slight shake.

"She's gone," the little boy says with wide eyes. "She's in Everland!"

· GWEN ·

W hat do you mean Bella's gone?" I ask.

"Like gone-gone. She left the Lost City," says Gabs. "Disappeared. Ran away."

"Why would she do that?" Pickpocket asks.

Gabs puts one hand on a hip as he pitches his voice in a higher octave, mimicking Bella. "She's all, 'No one treats me like a real Lost Kid,' and 'I'm going to prove that I'm as good as any of you boys.'" He throws his hands in the air. "Seriously, I've never thought she was less important than any of us and I tried to tell her so, but she wouldn't listen. She just packed her bag of gold dust, put on her wings, and left. I have no clue what she's yammering about, all this talk about her not being a Lost Kid."

"This is bad," Jack says, his eyes darting to the other Lost Boys.

"Did she say where she was going?" I ask, kneeling in front of the small boy.

"She said she's going after Hook." Gabs's eyes grow wide with fear.

"What is she thinking? She can't take on Hook alone!" Pete exclaims.

Gabs mimics Bella again, waving a hand around. "She says, 'I'm going to get Gwen's sister by myself and then that girl can go back to her dump of a house.' I don't think she likes you much, Gwen. No offense."

"Did you see which direction she went?" Pete asks.

"She left through the western tunnel," Gabs says, pointing to his left.

I shove past Pete toward the door. "Nice job, idiot. So much for being Bella's guardian."

"We'll get her back before she reaches Hook's palace," Pete says. His voice is less confident than usual.

Spinning, I scowl at Pete. "This wouldn't have happened if you hadn't thrown your authority around and acted like . . . like . . ."

"Like what, a leader? Which is precisely what I am." Pete's brows narrow.

"No," I whisper, "like her father, and a very poor one I might add." My stomach drops as I recall again my last conversation with Joanna. *You were a much better sister than you are a mother,* she said, and here I am repeating her statement. I wish I could take back everything I said to Joanna. I wish she were here, safe with Mikey and me. I gulp the stale air, trying to shake the weight of blame. Turning, I open the door and burst out, nearly crashing into Doc as he runs up the steps with his medical bag in hand.

"I just heard about Bella," Doc says, brushing by me. "How long has she been gone?"

"Maybe ten or fifteen minutes," Gabs answers. "But I wouldn't know for sure because I still haven't earned a watch yet even though I've cleaned the privies out at least a dozen times."

"She can't leave. We've got to stop her." Worry lines crease Doc's brow.

"I'm already on it," Pete says, pushing past Doc. "I'll get our supplies. Meet me at the western tunnel in five minutes, Lost Boys."

"We need to find her right away," Doc replies with urgency. "Bella sees me twice a day for medication. She's already overdue for her second dose."

"I only see you once a week," Pickpocket says. "If she's receiving medication twice daily, she should be fine for a while, shouldn't she?"

"No, the virus progresses slower in males, but in Bella's case it is extremely aggressive. You might experience mild symptoms a week after your injection, but she will show severe symptoms within twelve hours after her last dose if she's not treated right away."

"What are you saying, Doc?" I ask, feeling a growing sense of anxiety.

"I'm saying if we don't get her back soon, she'll be dead in a day. Two days at best."

Pete's expression goes slack with alarm. "Jack, Pickpocket, get our supply packs from Stock. The rest of us will meet you at the entrance of the western tunnel. Gabs, where's Justice?"

"He's already at the tunnel entrance. He tried to stop her, too," Gabs says, bouncing on his toes. "He tried to stop Bella, but she was in turbo mode and flew out like a rocket ship. Cogs really ought to tinker with her wings and make a 'mergency shutoff button or something."

"Take me to Justice. I need to make sure he's all set to be in charge of the Lost City," Pete says, bursting out the door. "We're leaving now!"

Within minutes, we are traveling through a dirt passageway. The western tunnel is crudely constructed and not very well lit. Without the overhead gas lanterns to light the way, we depend on our guide's single lamp. Dozer, a boy whose skin is as brown as his eyes from the layer of dirt coating his body, leads us through a recently dug passage. Wooden beams crisscross along the tunnel, supporting the low ceiling.

"Watch your step," Dozer says through a yawn. "My crew and I haven't completed this channel yet."

"Thanks for helping us out. I know you have your rules about non-Diggers in the unfinished tunnels," Pete says, stepping over a plank of timber.

"It's your neck," Dozer grumbles, rubbing the sleep out of his eyes. "You blokes take five while I go make sure the support joists ahead are secure."

"We're going with you," Pete insists.

Dozer holds up his miner's pick and looks Pete in the eye. "You'll do no such thing. These tunnels are incomplete and my responsibility. You'll be staying here or you won't be going anywhere at all."

Pete looks at the boy, his face pinched. "You have five minutes. After that, if you're not back, we're going ahead."

"Correction," Dozer retorts. "You woke me from my nap. You'll follow *my* rules. I'll be back when I'm good and ready and when I'm sure the lot of you aren't going to lose a few more brain cells when the ceiling caves in on you."

Shuffling toward me, he mumbles, "Not that it would do much damage to those thick skulls. Fools must have a screw or two loose to go into Everland." He pulls a candle from his pocket, lights it, and hands the lantern to me. "Hold this. I'll be back." He disappears into the tunnel, still murmuring to himself.

"He doesn't seem particularly happy about us being here," I whisper to Doc.

"Can't say I blame him," he says. "I wouldn't be happy if a bunch of kids were tromping through the infirmary. Haven't you had a space that was all your own? A place where everything had its special place and every place had its special thing?"

"I suppose it would be my room at home," I say. Memories of the pale aqua room lined with posters of horses come back to me: my equestrian trophies stacked two deep on a simple shelf, a closet full of school uniforms, and a family photo on my writing desk. My mother resting her forehead against my father's as they peer at each other in a romantic gaze. In front of them, I sit with my arms around Joanna and Mikey with the picturesque, lush fields of Scotland in the background. Sorrow and loss threaten to choke me, but Doc speaks again.

"How would you feel if those twits were strolling through your bedroom?" he says, gesturing toward the Lost Boys.

Jack chuckles as he places a hand on Mole's head, keeping him at arm's distance. Mole swings blindly, landing a few weak punches. Leaning up against the dirt wall, Pete, Pyro, and Pickpocket laugh at the boys' antics. Mole grabs the staff strapped to his back. He swings it just above the ground, making contact with Jack's calves, knocking him on his hindquarters with a heavy thud.

"Never underestimate a short, blind boy," Pete says, laughing. "Mole might seem like an easy target, but he has keen spatial awareness and great aim."

The corners of Mole's mouth twitch into a smirk.

"He might have 'keen spatial awareness' and 'great aim,'" Pickpocket says, gesturing quotes in the air, "but I'll bet he can't beat me at wrestling."

"Is that a challenge?" Mole asks.

Pete whistles and cringes. "Buddy, you're asking for trouble. My money is on Mole."

"Bring it," Pickpocket says, lacing his fingers together and popping his knuckles.

Pyro digs trinkets out of the silk lining of his derby hat. "I'll get in on this wager."

Pyro, Jack, and Pete pull small trinkets from their pockets.

"A stick of gum, a screwdriver, and handful of bolts says Pickpocket will win," Jack challenges. "What do you got?"

Pyro throws down the contents of his hat. "A book of matches, a flint, and a firecracker on Pickpocket. How about you, Pete?"

"A chocolate, a thimble, and a broken watch," Pete says, laying out his wager.

"You're going down, Pan," Jack says.

Pete's brows lift. "Oh, this is serious, isn't it? Resorting to surnames, are we, Mr. White?"

Pickpocket and Mole fling their arms around each other, grunting as Jack and Pete cheer.

"Blimey, you see what I've got to work with?" Doc says. "A court jester and his bumbling fools. It's a miracle the Lost City was built with that boy in charge." He nods toward Pete.

"Pete built the Lost City?" I ask, surprised.

"Who else would build it?"

"I don't know. I guess if anyone seemed capable of building a city for a bunch of orphaned boys, it would be the engineers, or maybe you."

"The Tinkers helped with the logistics. But me? No way. If it doesn't bleed, I don't know what to do with it," Doc says, his brows lifting. "What would make you think that I could build the Lost City?"

"You seem smart, and more, how should I say it? Mature, at least more than them," I say, glancing at the entire group of boys now dog-piling on Pickpocket. Mole sits on the top of the pyramid with a triumphant grin. Pete howls with laughter, begging Mole to get off him.

Doc laughs. "Trust me, I know Pete. He might appear to be immature and carefree right now, but it's all a ruse for the sake of the Lost Boys. He's worried about Bella, but he knows he has to keep it together. The boys look up to him. If he shows a hint of anxiety, then they'll worry, too."

Pete glances at me, an insincere smile spreading across his face.

"Besides," Doc continues, "intelligence and maturity cannot build a city. It's true, I might be smart, but I could never have done the things Pete has done. It takes heart and strength, overcoming tragedy, to have the will to build something as fantastic as the Lost City."

"Tragedy?" I ask, watching the boys wrestle. Pete has pinned Jack to the floor. He tilts his head toward me and winks before proclaiming his victory, crowing like a rooster.

"Didn't he tell you?" Doc asks. I shake my head. Doc sighs and continues, "Pete has been an orphan since he was seven. His parents were killed in a car accident."

"That's terrible," I say as a familiar heartache grips me, the same one that so often creeps up when memories of my own parents come to my mind.

"I met him before the war," Doc continues. "I finished secondary school by the time I was twelve and went on to study medicine. I was interning at North West London Hospital. Pete came in with a large gash on his cheek, an apparent 'bicycle accident.' When his visits became a weekly occurrence, I confronted him, worried he was suffering some sort of abuse. Turned out he was earning money by competing in underground boxing matches." Doc laughs heartily. "Pete would come in at midnight every Wednesday night with something needing to be stitched up. We became fast friends."

"So what happened to you two?" I ask. "That fight I witnessed earlier was hardly evidence of a good friendship."

Doc sighs. "Pete wasn't the only survivor in the accident. He had a sister, Gabrielle. The accident left her in a wheelchair. The other children at the orphanage teased her, but Pete wouldn't tolerate it. After years of defending his sister, he decided to use his skill to make money so he could get his sister out of the orphanage and into a place of their own." He drops his gaze, kicks at a stone lying in front of him, and hesitates. "She was beautiful. One of the most beautiful girls I've ever met."

"What happened to her?" I ask.

"The same thing that happened to all the girls after the outbreak. Pete brought her to me. She was in bad shape. I did everything I could to save her, but it wasn't enough." Tears brim at the corners of his eyes. "I cared for her, and when she took her last breath, a part of me died with her."

"I'm so sorry," I say, resting a hand on his arm.

Doc nods, acknowledging my gesture of sympathy, and turns his eyes toward Pete. "He's never been the same and hasn't forgiven me."

"But it wasn't your fault she died. You said you did everything you could for her."

"I know it and you know it, but him?" Doc says, waving toward Pete. "It's neither here nor there. Two weeks went by and I hadn't seen him. By then the Marauders had gained control of the city. Then one day he comes storming into the hospital. He tells me there's a bunch of orphaned kids holed up in the tunnels, many who are badly hurt, and if I am worth a sack of beans, I will come with him to save the children." Doc shrugs. "I went with him. We worked around the clock. I treated patients and he rescued kids. Many died, especially the girls, but the survivors are what make up the Lost City now."

"Why only the kids?" I ask. "If he had saved the adults, too, you might have extra help."

"Two reasons. First, the virus killed the adults so quick they couldn't be saved. Second, only an orphan knows what it is like to be an orphan. After the bombing of London and the viral outbreak, the city was swarming with orphaned kids. Pete couldn't save his sister, but he could save the other parentless children."

"Along with your help," I remind him.

"Yes, along with my help."

"But if you've helped so many, why is he still angry with you?"

"My debt isn't paid, and it'll never be paid until I figure out how to rescue the one person who means the most to him. Bella,"

Doc says, frowning. "It is the only reason he is allowing me to come along on this rescue mission. He knows that without me, Bella will die, and he can't bear to lose another."

I'm about to ask why Bella is so special when Dozer emerges from the dark tunnel and stops at the heap of boys, all tangled up with arms and legs in wrestling maneuvers.

"You're kidding me," he says. "I leave you nitwits for five minutes and I come back to find you acting like savages. You city boys are a curious bunch."

"City boys?" I ask.

"Dozer is a Digger. He and about five other boys are in charge of creating new tunnels in and out of Everland," Doc says. "They don't hang out in the Lost City much. I really only see the Diggers when one of them is injured in the tunnels and I have to go patch them up."

Dozer gives an unattractive grunt. "And you, Mole, I thought I taught you better than that. You boys," he says before casting his gaze on me, "and girl, follow me." He yawns, stretching his arms, and turns to proceed down the dark passage.

Mole struggles to his feet, brushes the dirt from his clothes, and reaches his hands out in search of his weapon. Pete hops up from the ground with ease and grabs the metal staff.

"Here you go, kid," he says, handing it to Mole.

"Thanks," Mole says. His shoulders slump and he frowns.

"Chin up. Don't let him get to you," Pete says, patting the boy's shoulder. "Remember, I chose *you* to come on this adventure."

Mole's lips stretch into a wide grin. I watch the entire interaction, uncertain of what just happened but touched by his compassion toward the blind boy.

"Dozer is Mole's older brother," Doc says. "He's bitter about having to be Mole's eyes his whole life, but since their folks have perished, he's taken on the role of Mole's guardian."

As the boys gather their packs and weapons, I watch Pete take special care to make sure Mole is set to travel the tunnels. I can't help but smile at his kindness, a stark difference from his reprimand of Bella earlier.

"Well, well, why didn't I see it sooner?" Doc says, grinning wide.

"What?" I ask, confused.

Doc picks up his own pack and medicine bag as he shakes his head. "I should've known."

"What are you talking about?" I ask, pulling my rucksack onto my shoulders.

He turns and faces me. "You fancy him, don't you?"

"Who? Pete?" I whisper, not wanting the other boys to hear the conversation.

Doc rolls his eyes. "No. I meant the twelve-year-old blind boy. Of course Pete," he says, too loudly.

We walk through the dirt tunnel as the other boys lead the way, peering over their shoulders at us. I return their puzzled expressions with a weak smile.

"Pete?" I scoff. "He's rude and conceited and . . . and . . ." I try to come up with other flaws, but they are lost beyond my flustered thoughts and the heat prickling at my cheeks.

"Yes, but you still fancy him," Doc says, teasing.

"Do not," I say with insistence. "Why would I fancy anyone like him?"

Doc shrugs. "Your guess is as good as mine, but I saw that glint in your eye."

I'm starting to protest when Pete joins us. "May I have a word with Gwen in private?" he asks.

"Don't let me stop you." Doc grasps the brim of his aviator cap and tips his head toward me. "Nice chatting with you."

Doc jogs ahead and joins the other Lost Boys.

"Um, you were . . . well, you were right about Bella," Pete says with some reluctance.

I raise an eyebrow. "Am I hearing you correctly? The leader of the Lost Boys is admitting he's wrong?"

Pete stares at the ground. "I just wanted you to feel welcome. Everyone had been staring at you since you got here and Bella was being a brat. I, uh, I lost my temper. Now she's gone and . . . and it's my fault."

"Yes, it is," I say matter-of-factly.

Pete looks at me with surprised, wide eyes as my words settle over him. He drops his gaze back to the ground and frowns. "We have to get her back. I've already failed my sister. When Gabrielle died . . . she . . . Gabrielle was all that was left of my family, and then she was gone. I've lost everyone I ever cared for—that is, until I found Bella." Pete's glassy eyes meet mine. "I can't fail her, too."

The grief in his expression mirrors the ache in my own heart. While I grapple with the sting of my failed attempt to protect my sister, I can only imagine the anguish he must feel, being the daunt-less leader of so many but having lost the most precious of them all.

I lift his chin with my hand. "We will find her. We'll bring both of them back, Bella and Joanna. We'll rescue them and be back to the Lost City in no time."

Pete glances at me. "We? Does that mean you'll stay with us?"

An awkward energy fills the space between us. "I mean you and Bella will be back at home in the Lost City." I spin and quicken my pace, trying to catch up to the other Lost Boys.

Pete takes my arm in a gentle grasp. "You know, Gwen, you're welcome to live in the Lost City as long as you like—you and your siblings. You're as much an orphan as any of us."

I flick my eyes to him and back to the ground, unwilling to meet his gaze. *Orphan.* The word stings. I never considered myself an orphan, even though I know my parents are gone. My head jumbles with words, looking for a response, but none come to me. Fortunately, Dozer's deep voice bellows from the tunnel ahead. We join him where the other boys have gathered.

"This is as far as I go," Dozer says. "About ten meters ahead, the tunnel ends at a hatch that leads into the city's sewage system. Follow the right wall about a kilometer until you come to a ladder. From there, you'll be about a half block from St. Paul's Cathedral. Once you're out on the streets, head south to the Thames. Follow the water's edge until Big Ben, at least what is left of it, comes into view. Once you see it, the palace is about one and a half kilometers northwest of the river's edge."

"Great job," Pete says, slapping Dozer on the shoulder.

"Sorry I couldn't get you closer. We've been working on expanding the tunnel into the palace courtyard in hopes of tapping into some of their resources, but these things take time, and we've been short on supplies to stabilize the passageways."

"You did well, Dozer," Pete says. He takes the lead, with Doc, Pickpocket, Pyro, and Jack following behind. Mole steps behind Jack, but Dozer stops him.

"Take care of yourself, kid," he says. "Stay close to Pete."

Mole frowns. Dozer pulls his brother into him, wrapping his arms around him. "See you soon," Mole says. He releases his brother and joins the other Lost Boys.

As I walk past him, Dozer asks, "Is she worth it?" I stop in my tracks. "I mean is one girl worth the lives of seven other people—eight, if you count Bella?"

"Let me ask you: If it was Mole who was taken, how many other lives would you risk getting him back?"

Dozer considers this for a moment before responding. "I'd risk the lives of every Lost Boy to get him back."

"Me too," I reply.

"Just make sure he comes back safe," he says before walking away.

I move to join the other boys.

"Hey, Immune," he says. I turn to him. His back faces me. "His real name is Michael."

"Michael? That's my brother's name, too," I say.

"I know. You look after my brother, and I'll keep my eye on yours," Dozer replies. I nod, but Dozer doesn't see the gesture. He quickly disappears into the darkness.

Farther up the tunnel, I see Pete spin the wheel to the hatch leading to the sewer. The hinges squeal sharply and the boys duck as they step through the opening.

Pete pokes his head out from the opening. "Gwen, you coming?"

As I start to walk down the passageway, a loud crack to my left draws my attention. Dirt sprinkles down on me from the ceiling. My pulse quickens as another snap erupts to my right. I spin toward the noise. This time I see a fissure grow through one of the support beams.

Dozer reappears, sprinting back into the tunnel. He scans the support beams over my head and he blanches. "Run!" Dozer screams. He turns and runs in the opposite direction. "Get out of there, now!"

"Come on, Gwen," Pete says, waving me toward him. "Hurry!"

A plank of wood falls from the ceiling, narrowly missing me as I dash toward him. The sound of lumber, mud, and metal crashing to the ground follows me. Dirt showers down on me, stinging my eyes. I know I have only seconds before the entire tunnel caves in. I leap in the air, grasping for Pete's waiting hands.

· HOOK ·

The Steam Crawler rumbles down the crumbled remains of St. Margaret Street, followed by two dozen duplicate vehicles and fifty soldiers on foot. The long steel legs of the machines punch gaping holes into the street as they advance east, leaving behind a cloud of dust and tar pebbles in their wake. The few unbroken shop windows shatter and crumble to the concrete in a puddle of shards.

"Any word on the girl the soldiers found this morning?" I ask my driver.

"She's on her way to the palace as we speak," he says in clipped words that echo within his helmet.

"Good. Turn here," I instruct. "Toward the bridge."

"You mean what's left of the bridge?" the driver says with a snicker. I glare at him, seeing only my own reflection in his dented helmet. I wish he didn't have to wear the mask so that I could strike him. His laugh grates on every nerve, sending tingling sensations up my spine and down to the tips of my fingers and toes. This isn't funny. There's nothing amusing about the destruction and loss of life we are responsible for. Not *we . . . me! I* am responsible for the carnage before my eyes. It wasn't supposed to happen like this. Drop a few bombs on key sites in London. That was all that I was directed to do. So what if a few buildings would be damaged; the point was to come in demanding the Queen of England hand over her crown. I had no idea what the targets were, just that my mother insisted on taking out specific ones. My fingers graze my eye patch, reminding me that I had no choice. I never have.

The Crawler turns south on Bridge Street, toward the ruins of the Palace of Westminster. Ahead, Westminster Bridge juts into the murky Thames water before severing off in broken fragments. As the military vehicles advance, a faint ping ricochets from the roof of my tank. I tilt my ear toward the steel ceiling. Again another ping rings off the top.

"Stop!" I shout, tipping my view toward the bulletproof window. The Steam Crawler comes to a halt, blocking the way of the other tanks. Another quiet ping pierces the night air.

"What is that?" I ask, sliding my door open. I stand on the frame of the Crawler, scanning the rubble scattered throughout the street.

Big Ben looms over the ruins, illuminated by a nearly full moon peeking through fragmented clouds. Remarkably, the tower remains relatively unscathed. Both hands point toward midnight, frozen in time, a reminder of when the first bombs fell on the sleeping residents of London, plummeting them into a nightmare and facing demons that I brought to the once-bustling town. My stomach lurches, but I clench my teeth, refusing to give in to the guilt festering within me. I did what I was commanded to do. I followed orders. Had I known the biological weapons lab was the Bloodred Queen's intended target, perhaps I wouldn't have dropped the bombs.

My targets. The ones my mother designated to be destroyed. I have only the briefest moment to wonder if my mother knew what would happen if she destroyed the weapons lab, and if so, why she would send me. Something whirs past my head, startling me from my thoughts.

The face of the clock is pocked with holes, but otherwise is intact. I squint, focusing on the subtle movement from the bell's keep. A blond girl lifts a slingshot and aims. She leans against the frame of the belfry, teetering on the edge.

"Bella!" I grumble beneath my breath. I inhale, taking in the night air, and remind myself of the Professor's words. How very few girls have survived. That the human race depends on their existence.

What a grim outcome.

The Professor is right, though. Other than the girl my men found earlier, Bella, and the girl with the heart-shaped face with Pete, there are no girls left, at least none that I know of. I breathe in the sour smell wafting from the Thames and shudder. After all this girl and Pete have put me through, it grinds every nerve fiber in my being to be nice, but I dig deep, recalling the kindness the help at Lohr Castle once showed me when I was just a boy not much older than Bella is now.

"Bella," I shout again, this time echoing the tone of those who truly loved me. "Let's be reasonable. Come down from there so we can talk."

Bella releases the elastic with a snap, and I duck as a steel ball skips across the top of the Crawler, barely missing my head. Gritting my teeth, I remind myself to keep my temper intact. I need her to trust me.

The soldiers direct their weapons to the bell tower.

"Fire at—" an officer yells.

"No! Hold your fire!" I shout, still ducking from Bella's aim. "Hold your fire!"

Taking cover behind the vehicle, I wait for another shot from the belfry, but none comes. "Let's be sensible, Bella. You're completely surrounded. You can't possibly think you're going to get away," I reason, struggling with words. Reaching back in my memories to rediscover some soothing word said to me, something to convince this little girl she needs me as much as I need her. "How about you put your weapon down so no one gets hurt? Perhaps we can negotiate an agreeable outcome."

Bella pulls another steel shot from her pouch and places it in the pocket of the slingshot. "The only agreeable outcome is a hole in your skull," she shouts. "It's just you and me, Hook. I'm done running from you. You wanted me, now you have me." She pulls back on her slingshot, aiming right at me.

"It's not you I'm after!" I holler, hoping she believes my pretense.

Bella lowers her slingshot warily.

I steal a glance over the roof of the tank, my hands raised. "All I want is the girl with Pete! Nothing else. Just tell me where I can find her."

"Gwen? What do you want with her?" Bella yells. Her hair flutters in the wind as a gust nearly sends her off balance.

"What does it matter? Tell me where she is and I'll leave you alone, forever," I say a little too flippantly. I've got to pull it together. Convince her that *she* needs *me*, not the other way around. "I'll leave Everland to you *and* Pete."

Another gust whips through the night air. Bella crouches,

trying to maintain her balance. When she regains her footing, she raises her slingshot, but even from this far I can see her tremble. She's angry with me, and I don't know why. I'm failing. If I ever want to get near her, to take her to the Professor, I need to tap into what's important to her.

"By the way, where is your sidekick? You and Pete are inseparable. Yet here you are alone," I call up to her.

She furiously wipes at her face with her arm—tears, I have to assume—and she readjusts her slingshot.

"She's come between you two, hasn't she?" I ask, trying for sympathy while shouting.

As if to answer me, Bella buries her face in her hands.

Stepping out from behind the tank, I fold my hands behind my back. "Poor, poor Bella. So unappreciated. So unloved. I can see the pain she's brought."

She peers at me and wipes her nose on her sleeve.

"Tell me where she is, Bella, and I'll leave Everland for good. No more hiding, no more running from me. Everland will be yours. And as an added bonus, I'll take the little vixen with me. She'll never come between you and Pete again."

Bella brushes another tear from her cheek. She stands at the edge of the tower and takes aim. "I'll never, ever side with you, Hook!" She pulls the elastic of the slingshot back as a gust of wind ruffles her shirt. She staggers and drops her slingshot, sending it hurling ninety meters to the ground. Screaming, she sways forward once more, her knees collapsing underneath her. She reaches for a lever on her rocket pack, but misses. Another gust rolls over her tiny body, sending her over the edge. Her copper wings clip the ledge hard, shooting springs and cogs in every direction and shattering the iridescent film. Bella grips the edge of the bell tower just in time, her small feet kicking beneath her.

My chest clenches, my breath catches, and adrenaline courses through me. She's going to die right here in front of me. *If she dies, we all die.* The Professor's words echo in my mind. What if Bella is the Immune?

I take several steps toward the tower, determined to save her, to catch her before her body splinters into pieces on the ground below. I know I'll never make it in time, but I must try. I bolt for the fence, throwing myself over it. I land hard on the concrete and look up.

As Bella's about to plummet, two hands reach for her from the dim shadows of the bell tower, grabbing her by her wrists. A moment later she is pulled inside the belfry. I breathe a sigh of relief, but the respite doesn't last.

"Someone else is in there!" I shout. "Surround the building, secure every exit, and someone get up to the tower. If Pete's in there with her, bring him back alive."

The soldiers race toward the tower, climbing the wrought-iron fence like a tidal wave cresting a levee wall. The masked men surge forward over debris and shattered glass. There's nowhere for her to go. She's as good as mine.

"Two girls down, one to go," I say.

· GWEN ·

A curl of dirt and dust rises through the opening. My lungs seize, leaving me in a fit of coughs. Multiple hands grab my arms and hurl me through the entrance of the sewer. The crash of wooden beams, rock, and metal scaffolding erupts behind me. I crouch, gasping for air and brushing the dirt from my clothes.

"That was close. Are you all right?" Mole asks, placing a gentle hand on my arm.

"I'm okay," I say, running my fingers through my kinky curls, pulling out pebbles.

"Well, I guess we're not going back that way," Pickpocket says, peering at the wreckage beyond the sewer opening.

Mole bites his lip. "How are we going to get back to the Lost City?"

"There's another entrance about three kilometers from here," Jack says. "It's a little narrow, but we can get through it."

Pete slams the metal hatch and spins the wheel, locking the entrance shut. I'm about to ask him why the hatch is even there when a hiss slithers through the tunnels of the dark sewer system and answers my question. The wide-eyed expressions on all of the boys' faces lets me know that I'm not the only one who heard the noise.

"What was that?" Mole says, biting at the frayed cuff of his coat.

"This isn't good," Pete says. "We need to get out of here."

He leads the way, splashing through foul, murky water. I take Mole by the hand to ensure he doesn't fall behind. The knee-high muck seeps into my boots as I follow. From a nearby tunnel, something growls and then splashes into the water. My pulse quickens.

"What is that?" I ask.

Pickpocket places a hand on my back and urges me on. "Trust me, you don't want to find out. Keep moving."

I trudge forward in the sludge, taking two thick steps, but halt when a reptilian hiss travels up the brick tunnel.

"They're getting closer!" Doc says, looking over his shoulder, his face white with panic.

"They? There's more than one?" I shift uncomfortably. "And who exactly are they?"

"We've got to pick up the pace," Jack says, passing Pete.

Taking Jack's lead, the group starts to jog, grunting as they struggle to lift their water-soaked boots. I glance behind me, making sure that Mole and Pyro are still close. While Mole is right on my heels, Pyro stops at a brick archway and rips a stick of dynamite from his belt.

"We're not going to make it. We've got to blockade them," Pyro says. He runs his fingers across the stones until he finds a crevice in the archway.

"Pyro! Get back here!" Pete shouts.

Pyro ignores him and pulls out a box of matches. "Give me thirty seconds!"

Doc holds a hand up. "Do you hear that?"

The sewer is eerily quiet. Even the rats seem to have gone into hiding, sensing danger.

"I don't think they're gone," Mole whispers.

Pete takes Jack's lantern and sidles through our group, taking a few steps toward Pyro. "Pyro, I command you to rejoin the group. That's an order!"

Pyro nods. "Ten more seconds. That's all I need!" As Pyro lights the fuse of the dynamite, something slithers in the dark, cloudy water behind him.

"Pyro, run!" Pete shouts.

It's too late. Sharp, serrated teeth clamp down on Pyro's leg. His bloodcurdling scream shatters the silence as the crocodile drags him under the water. A second reptile, larger than the other, snaps down on Pyro's arm as he reaches out toward us, pleading for help.

"No!" Pete screams. He starts to run through the water as the crocodiles drag Pyro farther down the tunnel. Pickpocket holds him back.

"It's too late! We have to go!" Pickpocket says, staring at the dwindling fuse. "Go! Go! Go!"

We rush forward, our waterlogged boots splashing through the murky sludge. Pete struggles in Pickpocket's grip, fighting to break free. Jack takes Pete's other arm, and the two Lost Boys drag Pete away as he screams for Pyro.

"No! We can't leave him!" Pete yells. "Pyro! Come back!"

"He's gone, Pete. We have to get out of here," Jack says.

Pete refuses to look away from the crimson-tinted water and thrashing reptiles as the Lost Boys encourage him to duck around a corner.

"Hurry, take cover," Doc says, pushing everyone ahead, into another passageway.

Pickpocket and Jack shove Pete to safety, and he collapses onto the ground. He leans up against the wall, his expression contorted into grief-stricken agony. Pete snatches up a stone and hurls it across the tunnel. As an explosion rocks the tunnel, sending shards of brick and plumes of dust hurtling through the tunnel opening, Pete hardly flinches. When the dust settles, I bolt to the entrance and look back at where Pyro had lit the stick of dynamite. All that's left is a pile of rubble. Stone, brick, and dirt pile neck-high, blocking the archway.

Pete maneuvers around me. He races toward the rubble and places a hand on the pile of rocks. He drops his chin to his chest, giving a slight shake of his head.

Mole sniffles next to me as Pickpocket joins Pete, throwing an arm around him.

"You okay?" Pickpocket asks.

"He was a good Scavenger. The best of the best of all of us Lost Boys," Pete says weakly. He picks up Pyro's derby hat from the debris and brushes off the dirt. He places the hat on top of the pile of rocks. "Godspeed, Lost Boy."

"Come on," Pickpocket says, gripping his shoulder. "That won't hold them back for long. We need to get out of here and into Everland."

Pickpocket leads Pete back to our group. The sorrow in Pete's expression is overwhelming. It's the same expression my brother and sister had when they realized our parents weren't ever returning home. As Pete passes by me, I reach out a hand to him.

"Pete?" I say, his name catching in the lump within my throat. I want to take his hand, to hold him and absorb even a little bit of the pain etched in his face.

Pete peers up at me with glassy eyes before he drops his gaze back down to the brackish water below him. He takes the lead, not acknowledging me as he continues ahead. My heart snaps in two, but I press my lips together. I won't let him, any of them, see me cry.

We travel for half an hour in an uncomfortable silence. The only sound is the sloshing of our feet as we travel through the water. A ladder attached to a brick wall appears ahead of us.

"This is it," Pickpocket says.

One by one, we climb through the manhole. Pete takes my hand as I reach street level. As his fingers touch mine, relief washes over me, but it is only brief.

"Welcome back to Everland," Pete says, frowning.

The city is nothing like I remember. The street is littered with debris and broken concrete, evidence of the magnificent structures that once stood here. Thick cracks weave through the fragmented street of St. Paul's churchyard like a web with rubble from nearby buildings caught in its snare. Wagons lie in tangled heaps on their sides.

St. Paul's Cathedral looms a short distance away, its domed roof now a crown of charcoal-colored, jagged spikes. Hurrying up the street, the Lost Boys, Pete, and I pass by the remains of the church's majestic columns and parapet. I avert my gaze as we walk past the severed head of the saint's statue, which had stood on top of the building.

Mole sniffs the air and shakes his head. "Bella was here, but the rain has washed away most of her scent. It's going to be tough to find her."

"Bella has a scent?" I ask, curious what she might smell like. Or what I might smell like, for that matter. Having not bathed in weeks, I can only imagine it isn't anything pleasant.

"Sure," Pete replies. "We all do. Why do you think I brought Mole along?"

"Mole says I smell like the forest," Jack says. "Pickpocket smells like grease, Doc smells like ammonia, and Pete smells like . . ."

"A rooster," Mole interjects, wrinkling his nose.

"That's gross, but it explains the cock-a-doodle-doo you do," I say, elbowing Pete.

Pete gives a lopsided grin. "If the stink fits."

"Shh," Mole whispers with a wave, "we're not alone. What is that sound?"

In the distance, the faint sound of machines, metal scraping against metal, fills the early evening air. The ground vibrates as the noise draws closer, shaking loose debris from the structures around us.

"Watch out!" Pete tackles me as concrete stones break off the face of the building and plummet to the ground. We fall hard onto the pavement. Pete shelters me from the falling rock, his hands wrapped tightly over his own dark hair. His breath is hot and rapid against my cheek. When the spray of pebbles stops, he lifts his head, watching me with worry. Bright sunlight shimmers in my vision. I blink and shield my eyes from the sun. When I look back at him, the only light that remains is the one that sparkles in his eyes.

"Are you okay?" he asks, his lips close to mine.

I struggle to find words, but they catch in my throat. Instead I nod.

Pete rolls off me and extends a hand, helping me to my feet.

Doc stands from his crouched position, coughing. "Is anyone hurt?"

The rest of the boys mumble as they shake the dust off. The ground trembles again, shaking loose more debris.

"Come on," Pete says. "We need to find cover."

"What is that?" Jack asks, steadying himself.

The color in Mole's face drains. "We need to hide! Now!"

Pete brushes dust from his green coat. "What do you smell?" he asks urgently.

"It smells like a graveyard. Death," Mole squeaks. "It's Marauders, and a lot of them. I'd say at least a few dozen, maybe more."

"Let's get out of here," Pickpocket says.

Pete sprints into a nearby building. We follow, climbing through the empty windows of the ground-floor shop of the now five-and-a-half-story building. The other half lies in pieces on the street, along with most of the face of the structure. We push aside the toppled café tables and chairs while broken panes of glass crunch beneath our boots. Pete helps me climb over the counter. The other Lost Boys follow behind, knocking a stack of Café Rouge menus to the floor.

Hiding, we listen as the high shrill of rusty gears pierces through the hammering of something heavy on the street. As the noise draws nearer, the building shudders violently, showering us with ceiling tiles as the ground quakes. Pete peeks over the counter.

His mouth drops open. "I've never seen so many soldiers in one place."

I glance through the vacant windows. A dozen machines held together with bronze-colored bolts, cogs, and wheels crawl down the street like an army of spiders. Spirals of steam rise from pipes on the back of the vehicles like wisps of phantom energy. Marauders flank either side of the tanks, searching the buildings through goggled face masks and scoped weapons, their guns engaged in ready position. Some soldiers enter the other buildings, breaking windows and tossing pieces of furniture as if they were made of children's blocks.

"This isn't good," Pickpocket says. "What are we going to do?"

"We better think of something before they decide to search in here," Doc says.

"We should split up," Jack suggests, fussing with the gadgets on his belt. "We have a better chance of reaching the palace if we aren't traveling in a large group."

Pickpocket glances around the counter at the open window. "I don't know if that's such a great idea."

"Look," Jack says, "there are dozens of Marauders out there. If Doc, Pickpocket, Mole, and I distract them, you two can slip by them unnoticed. Pete, you have to get Gwen to the palace."

"No!" I protest. "It's too dangerous. We should stay together."

"I don't think I like your idea either," Mole says. "I'm not very good at distracting."

Doc's brows furrow. "Do you understand the implications of what you're saying? If we run out there, we'll be caught for sure, and then what?"

"Now I'm really, really not happy with this plan," Mole says.

"We won't be caught," Jack insists. "I know this city like the back of my hand."

"I don't know, Jack," Pickpocket says. "It sounds risky."

"No, Jack's right. We should split up," Pete interrupts. "It's the only way. They'll find us if we stay here, but if we run, we can split them up and maybe get away."

"Have you gone mad?" Doc says indignantly. "What you're suggesting is suicide."

"I don't like the idea either, but I don't see any other way, do you?" Pete retorts.

"We had better make a decision," I say, listening to the machine draw nearer. "They're getting close."

"I'll take Pickpocket, Mole, and Doc. Pete and Gwen, you run for the other door," Jack says. There's a glint in his eye, a spark that I don't trust, but no one else questions him.

"Mole stays with us," I say. "I promised Dozer I'd look after him."

Mole's shoulders relax and he sighs. Jack starts to say something but stops himself.

"Doc goes with Gwen and Mole," Pete says, sounding somewhat reluctant. "The other boys and I are experienced runners. We will distract them while you get away. We'll meet up at the National Gallery. Keep your eyes open for Bella."

Doc opens his bag, pulls out a needle filled with a milky liquid, and hands it to Pete.

"What is this for?" he asks, inspecting the contents within the glass.

"Bella's treatment is overdue. If you find her, she'll be in a lot of pain. Give her this. I know you don't like needles, but you know how to administer it, right?" Doc asks with urgency, glancing toward the advancing soldiers.

Pete glares and snatches the needle, placing it in the side pocket of his rucksack. "Of course I know how to administer it."

"Don't lose it," Doc warns. "I added Gwen's white blood cells to the serum. I didn't have time to make a big batch, just enough to find Bella and get her back to the Lost City."

"What if you find Bella first?" Pete asks, buttoning the pocket of his pack closed.

Doc pulls out a second needle from his medical bag. "I brought two doses, enough medicine to give us just a day or two. Since it's a tweaked version of what she usually gets, I have no idea how effective this will be. She may need more, so if you do find her, it's important I see her as soon as possible."

The clanking of metal draws closer. Mole fidgets with the hem of his black coat. "We really ought to go," he mumbles.

"Which direction did Bella go, Mole?" Pete asks.

Mole sniffs the air. "She went toward the Thames." He frowns and sniffs again. "I don't think she's alone, though. I smell something else. Licorice, perhaps?"

"What do you mean?" Pete asks, worry wrinkling his face. "Who is she with?"

"I don't know, but it's not a Marauder," Mole says, inhaling. "I think it's another girl."

"A girl?" Pickpocket and Jack say at the same time.

"What girl?" Pete says. His shoulders stiffen.

"Not to interrupt you guys, but . . ." Doc points to soldiers less than a half a block from the café. "Shall we get on with the plan?"

"We'll see you at the gallery in an hour," Pete says.

"See you there," Doc says, extending a hand. "And don't get caught."

Pete hesitates but doesn't take Doc's hand. "Never."

Doc frowns.

The Lost Boys exchange a round of fist-bumping. Finally, Pete turns to me, holding his hand up as if waiting for me to knuckle-bump him. I lift my fist, but instead of repeating the gesture he exchanged with the other boys, he takes my hand and kisses the top of it. My heartbeat doubles as I feel his lips touch my skin. With a smile, he releases my still-clenched fist and crawls toward the far end of the counter. Pickpocket and Jack follow him.

Staying low, I wait for a sign to run as Jack climbs on top of the counter and hits a switch on his tool belt. Two copper barrels flip up from either side of the belt. "Argh," he yells, sounding more like a pirate than a Lost Boy. Pete and Pickpocket glance at each other before following his lead. They throw themselves over the counter-top. Pickpocket pulls his revolver from his holster as Pete slips a dagger from his hip. I am not sure if I should laugh, cry, or be worried about their valiant attempt to draw attention to themselves. Instead, I join Doc and Mole as they crawl toward the door.

At first, the soldiers don't notice the boys jumping through the empty window frame. Finally, Pete, Jack, and Pickpocket dash into the street and stand in front of the army, which has made its way to the front of the café.

Smeeth marches through the ranks of Marauders, stopping in front of the café window. He crosses his arms as an amused look grows on his face.

"Hey, Pickpocket, do you smell that?" Pete says in a loud voice, holding his daggers in front of him. The soldiers turn toward the boys. "It smells like fish—codfish, to be precise."

"Only one Marauder smells that funny," Pickpocket says, holding out his gun.

"Let's get this over with," Jack growls, his eyes fixated on the soldiers. From this distance, I can see the perspiration on his face, sparkling like raindrops under the street lanterns.

"Well, you're not exactly who I'm looking for, but I can work with that," Smeeth sneers.

"Wrong answer," Pete says. "Speaking of codfish, where is your odorous leader?"

Jack shifts, the scowl on his face deepening.

Smeeth grits his teeth and points the barrel of his gun at the boys. "I'll make this easy on you. Tell me where your little girlfriend and Bella are, and I'll put a good word in with the Captain."

I breathe a sigh of relief. If the Marauders are still looking for Bella, she must be safe, at least for now. Pete seems to make the same assumption, as I notice his shoulders relax.

"A girl? What girl? How about you, Pickpocket? Do you know about a girl?" Pete asks.

"The only girl I know is Smeeth's ugly bulldog," Pickpocket says. "Oh wait, that was your mother, wasn't it, Mr. Smeeth? Mistaken identity."

Mole snickers next to me. "That was a good one," he whispers.

"Very funny," Smeeth says. "Tell me where she is now, or you'll be tonight's gruel for the Captain's crocs. I normally don't feed them such filth because it upsets their delicate digestive systems, but I'll make a special exception in this case."

"What do you think, Lost Boys? Should we become crocodile chow?" Pete asks. "I've seen others die under worse conditions, I suppose."

"This is ridiculous! Enough!" Jack shouts as he reaches for a lever on his belt.

Pete lunges for him. "No, Jack! Not yet!"

It's too late. Jack flicks the switch. Dozens of small trajectories burst from the miniature guns. Each ball bearing bursts, crackling as it hits the street, creating a thick smoke screen.

Pete releases his dagger. It flies through the air and lands in the thick, meaty leg of a soldier. Blood bursts from the guard's thigh as he crumples to the ground with an agonizing scream. Jack pulls a small knife from its sheath on his belt and plunges it into the left shoulder of another soldier, sending the man to the street howling in pain. Snatching his revolver from its holster, Pickpocket fires several rounds into a group of Marauders. They run for cover as they return fire. The blast of gunfire and the ping of metal weapons rings through the evening air echoing off the tall buildings.

Smeeth fires three shots into the cloud of smoke. The boys dodge his bullets. Pickpocket dives to the ground, firing a shot at Smeeth. The Marauder falters but doesn't fall. He lets loose a manic laugh and rips the brass buttons open on his black leather jacket, revealing a bulletproof armor.

"Run!" Pete yells. The boys stumble to their feet and sprint away. Jack whirls around and starts to run. Smeeth raises his gun and fires. As Jack steps forward, his back arches and he falls to his knees, collapsing on the wet pavement. He clutches his side, curling in on himself in a fetal position as agony grows on his expression.

"Jack," I say with quiet urgency, stifling back a scream with my hand.

"Let's go!" Doc says, climbing over the countertop.

Mole follows, holding on to Doc's waistcoat. I swing myself over the counter behind him. Something catches on the cash register, but I tug until I break free. There is a metallic clink behind me. It isn't until I have climbed through the empty window frame and started to sprint down the street that I realize what the sound was. I clamp my hand on my chest, searching for my father's military tags, but they are no longer there. I spin, rushing back to the café.

"Gwen!" Doc yells. He chases me down and grabs me by the back of my jacket as I throw a leg through the window.

"My dad's tags," I say, trying desperately to pull myself from Doc's grasp.

The silver chain lies on the floor, the tags scattered among the menus. From the corner of my eye, I see Jack writhing in pain on the street. Soldiers whip their heads our way. My mind swims in a whirlwind of choices, but none of them seems right. My instinct is to run to him, but I know that I'll be caught if I do.

"It's the girl!" Smeeth yells, pointing straight at me. "Get her!" Every soldier abandons his place and runs toward us.

"There's no time," Doc says, pulling my arm. "We have to go!"

Mole's voice quivers as he shouts, "Gwen. Doc. Hurry!"

I struggle in Doc's grip, trying once more to retrieve my father's tags. As I scramble through the empty frame, I misjudge the size of the entrance and slam my head against the brick just above the window's opening. Pain ricochets through my skull as stars bloom in my vision.

"It's too late," Doc pleads, pulling me from the window. "You have to let them go."

My eyes blur with warm tears and my heartbeat pulses in my ears, its rapid cadence competing with the shouts of the soldiers and Doc's voice begging me to come with him. I stumble, my hand in Doc's, as my surroundings spin. Every beat of my heart aches, taking my breath away. A gentle breeze drifts in the air, carrying with it the sulfuric scent of gunfire and the metallic odor of blood, but all I can think about are my father's precious tags, the only thing I have left of him. My legs go weak and my ears ring before I plunge into a midnight-black chasm.

· HOOK ·

W hat do you mean Bella's gone?" I scream, fury seething so intensely that I can feel every capillary in my face burst red. This isn't possible. "There was nowhere for her to go. She must be here!"

The officer fidgets with the grip of his gun in his holster. "We've spent over an hour checking everywhere she could possibly hide. She's just disappeared."

Strolling down the center aisle of the chamber of the House of Lords, I take in the ashen and splintered furniture. The glimmer of the lanterns held by the Marauders casts a golden radiance on the red upholstered wooden benches on either side. "Search the grounds outside. She can't be far."

"Yes, sir," the soldier says. He shouts orders, sending a group of guards to the courtyard, but I know he won't find her. Like always, she'll have ducked away unnoticed.

"And you, Mr. Smeeth," I say, glaring at my right-hand man. "You lost the girl again?"

"They split up," Smeeth says with a quiver in his voice. "My men went after them, but they vanished. They turned a corner and when we pursued, they were gone."

Poking a finger into Smeeth's chest, I loom over the burly officer, peering into his glassy dark eyes. "You incompetent, insignificant, worthless excuse for a soldier. How many times have you let them get away? If I didn't know any better, I'd think you're working with Pete. Or maybe you're still in allegiance with the Crown of England?"

I grip Smeeth's throat. My grasp tightens around the soldier's flesh until the muscles in his neck grow taut beneath my fingertips and his face pales. "Mr. Smeeth, I showed you preference over your fellow Englishmen," I say, glaring at him. "While the lords and ladies of Buckingham Palace were disposed of, I granted you favor, although right now the reason seems to escape me."

Smeeth tries to speak, grasping at my hands, but only manages some small gasps.

"Ah, now I remember," I say, lifting Smeeth by his neck. His boots kick wildly as they rise off the ground. He struggles against my clutched hand, his pink complexion paling to white. "You looked pathetic in your red coat and silly bearskin hat. Some Royal Guard you were, cowering beneath a table in the Queen's formal dining room. When you begged me to spare you, I realized then how useful you could be. Any English brat would know the ins and outs of the city, but what better one than a soldier. Perhaps I was wrong about you?"

Smeeth's face turns blue as the blood drains from his cheeks. His eyes turn up, disappearing behind his lids. As he quivers in my grip, I release him, sending him crashing to the floor like a rag doll, wheezing on the blue-and-green carpet. He coughs, sputters indecipherable words, and finally his gaze meets mine. I recognize that expression, and I reel back in horror as the man in front of me transforms into a younger version of myself, trembling at the feet of my mother. Burning embers flare within my gut and I can't look at him. I can't face that expression of terror on his face. I spin, ready to bolt for the door, when his voice stops me.

"Captain?" he chokes. I turn toward him, keeping my eye shut. When I open it, Smeeth's trembling hand reaches into a pocket on his jacket and pulls out a silver chain. Two military tags dangle from the necklace. I snatch it, inspecting the rectangular metal pieces. My finger runs along the engraved name.

"G. Darling," I read aloud. "Where did you find this?"

"It was the girl's," Smeeth says through coughs, the tint of pink returning to his lips. He points to the entryway. "A prisoner," he gasps.

At the entryway, two soldiers lead the tall boy into the room. His long, dark hair hangs in his face, curtaining his glaring eyes, an expression I've become all too familiar with. Bright red blood stains the side of his shirt and waistcoat.

I can't help the wicked grin that grows on my face. It wasn't a matter of *if* but *when* I'd see him again. "So good to see you, Jack," I say, regarding the Lost Boy.

"Wish the feeling was mutual, brother," Jack sneers, holding a hand over his wound. Blood seeps between his fingers, but it isn't the worst injury I've seen him endure. While my mother was cruel to me, she was monstrous toward Jack, especially after his father met an unfortunate end. It's a wonder Jack lived to see his last birthday.

With his hand still clasped at his throat, Smeeth peers up at me, confusion lacing his peaked complexion. "He's your brother?"

"Stepbrother and traitor," I say with disdain. I stride over to a nearby officer, seize the lantern from his hand, and smash it against one of the long couch-like benches, setting the red upholstery ablaze. Immediately, the acrid fumes fill the room. The fire catches on nearby curtains and races toward the ceiling.

"Change of plans, boys," I say, before storming out of the room.

· GWEN ·

I s she dead?" Mole's voice cuts through the thick fog in my head. Stubby little fingers poke my ribs and cheeks. "Blimey, Doc, I think we might have killed her."

I swat the prodding hand away, my thoughts muddled and disoriented.

"She's alive!" Mole exclaims.

"Of course she's alive," Doc says.

I blink, trying to focus on the dark shapes in the narrow room. The subtle smell of smoldering wood draws my attention to the figure kneeling in the corner. The flames of a small fire built in a metal rubbish bin dance wildly, casting bright yellow light on Doc's face.

"Where are we?" I ask, rubbing my throbbing head.

"The National Gallery," Doc says, breaking down the remains of a wooden bench and feeding the pieces into the fire. "That's where we said we'd meet everyone."

Priceless paintings hang on the walls; disapproving eyes stare down at me. I prop myself on my elbows and rub my head, wincing. "How'd I get here?"

"Doc carried you," Mole says. "Man, oh, man. What I wouldn't give to have two good eyes to have seen the whole thing. I'd even take one good eye. Can you imagine? Doc threw you over his shoulder while he was dragging me behind him. The soldiers shot bullets at us. Lucky for us they want you alive or they wouldn't have aimed at our feet. I am glad I was on your team. Otherwise I might look like Swiss cheese if I had gone with the other Lost Kids."

"You carried me?" I ask, grimacing as I sit up.

"You wouldn't be the first patient I've had to carry," Doc says, still feeding the fire.

A dull ache throbs from my forehead. I run my hand through my disheveled hair, which is sticky and matted. When my fingers graze a golf ball–size lump, I wince.

"Careful," Doc says. "It took a while to stop the bleeding. I wouldn't be surprised if you had a slight concussion."

"I fainted?" I ask, trying to recall my last memory.

"Yep," Mole says. "Good thing Pickpocket fired on those awful soldiers or we'd have never gotten away."

The last moments prior to blacking out flood back to me: the standoff with the Lost Boys, gunfire, and running. "What about the other Lost Boys? Did they get away?" I ask.

"I believe so, but I don't know for sure," Doc says, brushing my hair over my shoulder. "Since we split up, the Marauders were confused, hopefully for long enough to let them run."

"And Jack?" I ask, thinking of the boy on the street.

Doc frowns and shakes his head.

My heart sinks and I place my hand on my chest, stilling the ache. "My father's tags," I whisper, grasping for the chain that had been around my neck. My hand touches the collar of my shirt but comes up empty.

"They're gone," Doc says, scooting next to me. "I'm sorry."

I feel a hot tear slide down my cheek. "They were the only thing I had left of him."

Doc rubs his thumb over my cheek, wiping away the tear. "Let me see your head wound," he says.

I lean forward while Doc inspects my injury, his touch gentle.

"Those Lost Boys are brave," Mole mumbles while poking at the fire with a piece of wood. "I wish I could be like them."

"What are you talking about?" Doc says. "You could have stayed behind in the Lost City where it's safe, but instead you've chosen to be here with us. I think that's extremely brave."

Mole smiles meekly, appearing unconvinced.

Doc pulls a canteen from his rucksack. "Lean over. I'm going to wash the blood out of your hair."

"No," I protest. "That's your water. You need it."

"We'll get more. Now quit arguing and lean your head over," he says.

I remove my jacket and drop my head. The cool water brings goose bumps to the skin on the back of my neck as it streams through my hair and pools on the floor in front of me. In the dull light, I can see the red tint to the liquid.

"How bad is it?" I ask, worried by the amount of blood washed from my hair.

"A concussion is not great, but you'll live," Doc says.

"Isn't that the truth," Mole interjects. "I was always banging my head on stuff when I was little, especially when I was tall enough to whack my head on the kitchen counter. I cannot tell you how many bumps and cuts my mother patched up. She used to say it was a rite of passage, that when I was tall enough to hit my head on the counter instead of running right underneath it, I was officially a big kid." Mole sighs and frowns. "I miss her."

I place my hand on his leg. "I miss my mother, too."

"There you go. It won't take away the pain, but at least it's clean." Doc caps the canteen and returns the container to his rucksack, this time pulling out a package of biscuits. He offers me one, but my stomach churns at the smell of them. I turn away and hold my breath.

"The nausea will pass eventually," Doc says, offering the biscuits to Mole, who eagerly takes a handful.

I run my fingers through my hair before squeezing the excess water from it. When I look back up, Doc's stare is fixed on me, and one corner of his mouth is turned up in a lopsided grin.

"What is it?"

He shakes his head and drops his gaze to the fire. "It's nothing."

"Tell me what you were thinking."

In the orange gleam of the fire, I see his cheeks flush. He pokes at the embers. "I was just thinking that I can see what Pete sees in you," he says. "You're a brave girl trying to go back for your dad's tags. Mad in the head, but still brave. You two are a lot like each other, maybe even more than you think."

"You're just now figuring that out?" Mole guffaws. "I knew she was brave when I first met her. I'd wager she's more brave than Pete, but don't tell him I said so. She's pretty, too."

"Pretty? How do you know she's pretty?" Doc asks, staring at Mole with a puzzled expression. "You can't even see her."

Mole shakes his head. "You don't have to see someone to know they're pretty. She could be uglier than a croc and still be pretty. She's nice, she smells of vanilla, and her voice is soothing. I think she's beautiful."

My face flushes under their compliments.

"Pete's a lucky guy," Mole says with a sigh.

"Pete? Pete and I are not . . . we're not . . . ," I say, stumbling over my words.

Mole snorts. "I might be blind, but I know when someone's in love." He draws out the last word in a singsong tone. Pointing to his nose, he continues, "This sniffer can smell lovey-dovey phero- mones from a mile away."

Fiddling with the brass buttons on my jacket, I try to restrain the grin growing on my face. Feeling light-headed, I brush my hair from my face, occupying my hands to keep them from trembling. No one says anything for several moments, until an odd expression grows on Mole's face as he sniffs.

"Someone's coming," Mole says, worry creasing a wrinkle between his brows.

Broken glass crunches beneath boots in the next room. A deep grunt followed by soft whispering comes from the room adjacent to the hallway. Doc snatches up a splintered wooden board. "Stay behind me," he whispers.

Mole sniffs the air and his face softens. "Thank goodness," he says.

"Who is it?" Doc asks. "What do you smell?"

"Greasy rooster," Mole replies, chuckling and shuffling ahead of Doc.

Two boys appear in the doorway, out of breath and completely wet from head to toe. "You guys made it," Pete says through chat- tering teeth as he brushes his wet hair out of his face.

I push past Doc. "What happened to you?"

Pete rushes by me toward the fire. Pickpocket follows. "We hid under a bridge in the Thames. That water is cold even during the summer."

"At least you're okay," I say with a relieved sigh. It's then I notice the dark stain on the arm of his forest-green coat. "You're hurt!"

Pete huddles near the fire, holding his hands over the flames. "It's just a scratch," he says, his tone somber.

I inspect the sleeve further. Blood gushes through a gaping hole.

"You've been shot! We have to stop the bleeding," I say. Doc reaches for his bag, but I snatch it out of his hand, rip it open, and grab scraps of fabric from inside. Slipping my fingers through the tear in Pete's jacket, I rip his sleeve off. Although my heart is racing already, it skips a beat as my gaze falls on his tattooed arm. The inked wheels, cogs, and chains almost seem lifelike. Resisting the temptation to run my fingers over them, I wrap a bandage around the wound instead.

"It's not that big of a deal," Pete says gruffly as he watches me tie a knot in the fabric.

"Where's Jack?" Mole asks, sniffing the air. "He isn't with you."

Pickpocket and Pete glance at each other before looking back at us. "He took a shot and fell. The Marauders have him," Pickpocket says with an exasperated sigh.

"You didn't go after him?" Doc asks.

"We ran after the gunfire started," Pickpocket says. "When he went down, we tried to carry him, but he insisted that we run and he'd cover for us. I would have argued with him, but we were taking fire and there was no time. It took a while to get here with the Marauders out on the streets as it is. They're everywhere!"

"When was the last time you saw him?" Doc asks.

"I don't know," Pickpocket says, shrugging. "Maybe an hour ago."

"We have to go back and find Jack," I insist.

No one speaks. They exchange worried glances with one another and then fix their gazes on Pete, waiting for him to make the final call.

"He's a brave Lost Boy. One of the finest we have. But he's made a sacrifice for all of us," Pete says, throwing his rucksack to the ground.

Pickpocket and Doc stare uneasily at Pete. Mole shuffles. I feel his small hand on my arm as he hides behind me. Their silence is palpable, leaving only the sound of the crackling fire.

Pete kicks at the pile of wood, sending boards scattering across the room. "Hook, that bloody codfish! I'm going to kill him. First Pyro. Now Jack."

Pickpocket cautiously steps toward Pete and rests a hand on his shoulder. "You doing okay, Pete?"

"Blimey, it's freezing in here," Pete grumbles, sounding irritated as he brushes Pickpocket's hand away. He steps into an adjoining room and rustles around in it. When he returns, he is carrying a large framed painting. Before I can object, he throws it onto the flames.

"What are you doing?" I ask with outrage. "Those paintings are irreplaceable."

He runs into the other room again, ignoring me, and returns with another piece of art.

"Stop it!" I say, trying to take the artwork from his hands. He tugs it from my grip and tosses it into the flames.

"That was van Gogh's *Sunflowers* painting," Doc says, incredulous.

"Who's van Gogh?" Pete asks, warming his hands in the fire, ignoring our indignation.

"Who's van Gogh?" Mole asks, a renewed boldness in the tone of his voice. "I can't see, but even *I* know who he is."

"He's only one of the most inspirational nineteenth-century painters in the whole world. The picture you burned is a priceless work of art!" Doc exclaims.

Pete chuckles under his breath. "Yeah, it sure is priceless. Not sure if you've noticed, but there is no one around to buy it!"

"So that's it?" Doc says, his voice rising. "We lose a couple of Lost Boys and you're going to destroy valuable art in a temper tantrum? What are you, two years old?"

Pete's face creases into a snarl. "Don't you dare talk about them as if they were nothing! Pyro was one of the best Scavengers we had. And Jack . . . Jack's not just any Lost Boy. He knew every entrance into the palace. He understood the ins and outs of those Marauders better than any of us. You've seen what those Marauders do with kids. Once they go into the palace, they never come out. Hook won't have an ounce of mercy on him, *especially* because he's a Lost Boy. And without him, we're not getting into Hook's headquarters, we're not saving Joanna, and more than likely, if Bella made it to the palace, we'll never see her again either. They're all as good as dead," he says, pulling another painting from the wall and throwing it across the room.

Pete grabs another picture, but before he can hurl it into the fire, Doc snatches it from his hands and sets it against the wall.

Pete's anger fades as suddenly as it arrived. "I should have gone back for him," he says quietly.

I take a step toward him, but he sees me and takes a step back, keeping the distance. His lips press into a thin line before he speaks. "It's freezing in here. Pickpocket and I are soaked to the bone. If you don't mind, I'd like to sit by this fire and warm up before we return to the Lost City."

My heart skips a beat and I can't breathe. Return to the Lost City? Pete stares down his nose at Doc. Doc returns his gaze, expressionless and unflinching.

"That's it? You're giving up?" Doc accuses. "Coward!" He shoves Pete hard, sending him crashing to the ground. Shock blooms in Pete's eyes before he rockets from the floor and launches himself at Doc.

Pickpocket bolts toward the boys as profanity bursts from their lips. Mole cowers close and I pull him into a tight hug, shielding him from the violent brawl. Pete throws a punch, connecting with Doc's chin just as Pickpocket steps between the boys.

"Enough already!" Pickpocket says, blocking Pete as he flails, trying to land another punch. Pickpocket corrals Pete in the opposite corner of the room.

"I am not giving up," Pete shouts, shaking his clenched fist. "I'm sending the rest of you back to the Lost City and I'm going after all of them myself, Jack included."

Doc's fiery eyes bore into Pete. He licks a bead of blood from his bottom lip and spits on the floor. "You're a fool."

Mole lifts his head, his arms still clinging to my waist.

"You're right, Doc. For once you're actually right," Pete says, shoving his hands into his coat pockets. "I am a fool. I was foolish to bring a team into Everland with me. It was stupid to risk your lives, to risk Pyro's and Jack's lives. I should've just gone after Joanna myself."

Doc wipes his mouth with the back of his arm, leaving a scarlet smudge on his disheveled white shirt. "No. You're foolish to think you can save them alone."

Pete's eyes flash with fury.

I give Mole a reassuring pat on his shoulder and step over to Pete, placing a hand on his arm. "Come on, let's get you warm," I say, trying to defuse the situation.

Pete lets me guide him to the fire, where he squats and balances himself on the backs of his heels. His eyes fix on the dancing flames and glowing embers. "What are we doing? There's nobody left but us kids and the Marauders."

I crouch beside him, warming my chilled hands. "You don't really think this is all that is left, do you? Hook, his army, and the Lost Kids?"

"Umm, guys," Mole says. I glance toward him, noticing that he has moved to the doorway and is standing next to Pickpocket. Doc leans against a wall, rubbing his jaw.

"And you don't?" Pete asks, wringing out his shirt. A pool of river water spills at his feet.

"No, I don't. And frankly, even if I thought we were the last ones, I wouldn't just give up on humanity," I say.

"That makes two of us," Doc mutters.

"Pete?" Mole interrupts.

Pete pays no attention to him. "Who else do you think is out there, Gwen? Our allies are gone. No one is left. If they were going to come to help us, they would have come by now. Everland *is* all that's left." The tone of his voice rises with each word, harsh and angry. "The only hope left for humankind is you, your sister, and Bella. That's it. You are the last girls in the entire world."

The last girls in the entire world. The reminder makes the back of my throat burn.

"Guys, we're not alone," Mole says, tilting his nose up in the air. "Someone else is near. Actually, there's a lot of someone elses near."

"Who's coming?" Pickpocket says with worry in his expression.

"Death!" Mole squeals before covering his face with his hands. He squeezes his eyes shut as if closing them will make the terrifying images in his head disappear.

Doc pulls out two containers of water from his pack. "Hurry, put the fire out!"

The other boys reach for their packs and pour their water over the fire, sending it hissing in the humid, cramped room. They knock the rubbish bin over and stamp the leftover flames out.

The hallway grows darker as the last few flames dim before extinguishing, leaving a few red-hot coals behind. We are plunged into blackness. Pete lights a small emergency candle, shedding minimal light into the room. The entry door of the building bursts open with a loud explosion, sending Mole into a fit of tremors. Distant voices echo in another room; their familiar robotic dialect through their heavy masks sends chills through me.

"It's Hook's men," Pickpocket says. "But how? How do they know we're here?"

"I have no idea. They must have followed us or something," Pete says. In the dark, I hear him fidget with his daggers.

Mole moves closer to me and twists the hem of his sleeve on his trench coat. "Anyone have a plan?"

"Unless there is an emergency exit in the back of the building, we're going to have to fight our way out," Pickpocket says. He pulls his revolver from the holster on his back.

Bouncing on his feet, Mole bites his lip. "Okay, I'm not liking this plan so much. Anybody else?"

"There's no way the five of us are going to take out Hook's army," I say. "Someone better offer some ideas or we'll all be his latest trophies."

Pete runs a jerky hand through his hair. "Doc, you take Gwen and see if you can find another exit. Shout if you find anything. Pickpocket and Mole, you stay with me and we'll hold them off."

Taking a deep breath, Mole draws his spiked staff. "If I'm going to die, I will die with dignity. That's what Dozer would want."

Pickpocket glances at Mole and back to Pete. "You sure about this, Pete?"

Pete rolls his shoulders back and lifts his chin. "It's been a pleasure leading you boys." He snatches both daggers from their sheaths.

"No, wait!" I say, stealing a glance at the entry to the hall as the voices draw closer. "They don't need you boys. They need me." I bite back the dread threatening to scream from my throat. "They have to know by now that I am the cure. All these months with sick or dead girls, they must have figured out there is something different about me. They may be thugs, but I hope they aren't blithering idiots." I take in a breath, swallowing my fear. "You boys go and get out. I'll turn myself over to them."

Mole stifles a small whimper. "I was afraid she was going to say that."

"That's mad. Do you know what they'll do to you?" Pickpocket says.

"They won't hurt me. They need me alive, and it may be the only way to get to Joanna. If we are lucky, they have Bella, too. If they take me to the palace, I can rescue both girls and Jack," I say.

"No!" Pete says, his fingers twitching around the hilt of his blades. "I won't allow it."

"She's right," Doc whispers, his voice wavering. "If we stay, we'll be captured, if not killed. There is no reason Hook needs any of us boys. And Gwen will be caught and taken to the palace anyway. How long can we run and hide? At least this way we have a fighting chance to reorganize and save all three girls."

I do not allow them time to protest. "Go," I say, nudging Pickpocket to the back of the building. "Get them out of here."

None of the Lost Boys move. Instead, they glance at one another, waiting for someone to argue, to come up with an alternative plan.

"Didn't you hear me?" I shove Pete. "I said, get out of here! Now! They're going to be here any minute. Save yourselves!"

The boys still don't budge. Furniture clatters in the lobby of the building, ripping me from my racing thoughts. I grab Pete's wrist, prepared to lead him toward the back of the building to find an exit, when something slides behind me. I turn toward the sound, whipping my daggers from their sheaths, but in the dark, I can't make out anything. A light appears from behind a panel in the wall, which has been pushed to the side. In the glimmer of a lamp, a teenage girl with long, raven-colored hair holds a finger to her lips, warning us to keep quiet. The lantern's glow lights her flawless bronze skin and dark eyes, the trim on her black sari and chain belt glimmering like polished coins. Her forehead is adorned with a red bindi, and a jeweled hoop gleams in her pierced nose. Chrome-tinted cogs interlink in a long chain that wraps around her neck in a decorative collar necklace and drapes down each of her shoulders. The bronze hilt of a sword glitters from its sheath at her hip in the lantern's glow. She waves a petite hand, beckoning us to come with her.

Glancing over my shoulder, I catch the glint of lamplight off Pete's blades, Pickpocket's rifle, and Mole's spiked staff, all aimed at the girl. "Who are you?" Pete demands in a harsh whisper.

"There isn't time for explanations. Are you coming or not?" she says, her eyes darting toward the entrance of the museum.

The soldiers' angry voices move nearer, and among them, I can now distinguish Hook's deep growl shouting orders.

"I think we should go with her," Pickpocket says, shifting from one foot to the other. He keeps the gun aimed at her.

Mole sniffs the air and loosens his grip on his mace. "She smells like licorice."

"The same as you smelled with Bella?" Pete asks, eyeing the girl warily.

Mole nods.

"What about Jack?" I ask. "What if he was able to get away and comes here looking for us?"

"If he's not here by now, he's been caught and probably imprisoned at Buckingham Palace. This is the only way any of us are getting out of here unscathed, and if Mole is right, she knows where Bella is," Pete says with reluctance. He sheathes a dagger and sighs. "We're going with her. It's better than you turning yourself over to Hook. "

We dash to the open panel in the wall. Doc, Pickpocket, and Pete hurry through the opening while Mole hangs on to Pete's sleeve. I am the last to step through the gap.

"Who are you? How did you get here?" I ask as she hands her lantern to me to hold.

"My name is Lily," the girl says with a sly smile.

With that, she closes the panel behind us.

· HOOK ·

With my black buckled boot I kick a scrap of what is left of a van Gogh painting from the burning embers. The rubbish bin lies sideways on the floor, its contents spilled in a pile next to it. I pick up the small, charred fragment, the petals in the picture appearing as limp as the canvas itself. With my night-vision goggles perched on top of my head, I squint at the art.

"What a shame," I say, addressing the soldiers. "One thing more valuable than gold or jewels is history." I release the piece of canvas and it flutters to the floor. I turn my gaze to the shielded faces of my soldiers. They look more like automatons than people.

"But there's no room for sentimentality. London's rooftops burned a year ago. Today, her reincarnation, Everland, will face the same demise."

The soldiers shift uncomfortably, flicking their goggled gazes to one another.

"Burn it down!" I shout. "Burn it all down until there is nowhere else for them to hide." I fix my glare on Jack and clench my jaw. "And get rid of my traitorous stepbrother."

The uniform-clad men shout orders, their voices sounding as mechanical as robots when I push past them.

"Wait!" Jack says. He struggles in the grip of an officer, his wrists bound tightly behind him. "That wasn't the deal!"

I whirl on my heels and march close enough that Jack falters backward. "You're right, Lost Boy: It wasn't the deal we agreed upon. I should've killed you the moment Smeeth brought you to me. But no, instead I spared your life. We made a deal: You give me Gwen and I leave Everland forever. But the girl is not here, thus our agreement is null and void. Good-bye, dear brother."

As I storm toward the entrance of the building, Jack lashes out with pathetic pleas. His words fall away, lost as my boots pound on the floor.

"What if I can offer you a better deal?" Jack shouts.

I stop, shadowed in the dark room, but don't turn around. "What sort of deal?"

"What if I could tell you a sure way to catch the girl?"

"Why should I invest any more of my time in you? We've made agreements and your end of the bargain has fallen through, *twice*," I say, taking another step toward the exit. "You were supposed to infiltrate the Lost Boys. Instead, you joined them and never reported back. This time you promised me Gwen. She's not here. Why should I believe anything you say?"

"I know where Pete and Gwen are going next," Jack says. "And it doesn't matter if you burn all of Everland down—you'll never find them. Not without my information."

Intrigued, I march back up to the boy. "What is in it for you?"

Jack grimaces, holds his breath, and turns his head away, unwilling to meet my eyes.

"Those boys are more than just a bunch of orphaned kids," Jack says quietly. He turns his eyes back to me and his glare is murderous. "They're my family, which is more than I can say about you and your mother."

Amused, I grin as memories of our childhood resurface in my mind. With nothing to eat but leftover scraps from supper, Jack was always a scrawny kid. While I was allowed to live within Lohr Castle, Jack was forced to sleep in a dilapidated delver's cottage that served as a den to the forest rats. Jack joined my crusade to England in order to escape the Bloodred Queen's wrath in exchange for labor. But I can live without him.

Cocking my head to one side, I take in the disheveled boy. "Naïve little stepbrother. Our parents' marriage had nothing to do with being family. My mother wanted the crown, and after your father's unfortunate 'accident' "—I gesture quotation marks in the air—"you were just extra baggage."

Scowling, Jack spits. "She murdered him and you know it!"

"*Murdered* is such a harsh word," I say, circling Jack.

Jack's face flares red with fury. "Katherina has no right to the throne!"

Laughter bubbles deep within me and erupts in a thunderous roar, echoing off the museum walls. "Now stop wasting my time. What is it you want in exchange for Gwen's location?"

"Because of you, the Lost Boys have *nothing* left," Jack says, narrowing his eyes. "They have no families, no homes, and now they're going to lose their lives. They are showing symptoms of the virus. They need the antidote and for you and the Marauders to leave. Forever! If we can negotiate a deal to guarantee that, I'll do whatever I can to get you the girl."

I stop pacing in front of Jack and hesitate, knowing that it's torture for him to wait for my response. As kids, he always hated it when he knew I held a secret. At first it was all in fun, but as we got older I knew he'd do just about anything I asked in exchange for information regarding his father's death. Information I never had, but he didn't know that.

"Interesting proposition," I say. "I'll tell you what, Jack. I can be reasonable. I will give you what you're asking for, in exchange for information on where they are headed next *and* the Lost Boys' hideout."

"The Lost Boys?" Jack says in an uncertain tone. "What do you want with them?"

"Collateral," I say, pacing the dark room. "Tell me where the Lost Boys are and give me the girl's whereabouts, or I will tear Everland apart bit by bit, piece by piece, and without mercy to anyone I come across, starting with you."

"No, I swore on my life never to reveal the Lost Boys' hiding place," Jack says, shaking his head. "I will tell you where to find Gwen, but I won't reveal the location of the Lost City."

I straighten, inspecting my Gatling gun and purposely aiming it in Jack's direction. "It seems water is thicker than blood, step-brother. Then again, we were never blood, were we?" My brother and I exchange hardened glares, but neither of us budges. Disgust gurgles up within me. "Kill him."

I rocket toward the doorway, expecting, waiting for my step-brother to cave. Glancing back at Jack, I recognize the familiar grimace.

A Marauder aims his weapon at Jack's forehead, while another shoves him to the ground. He falls hard onto his knees. The gun gives an audible click as the soldier pulls back the hammer. Jack's gaze darts from me to the gun.

"Fine!" Jack shouts. "I'll tell you, but promise me that you will not harm them."

"I promise I will not lay a single finger on any of them," I say, waggling my gloved fingers in the air.

"And you will provide them with the antidote once you have it," Jack says.

"Deal." I spin so he can't see the smirk I feel tickling the corners of my mouth.

"One more thing," Jack says.

Aggravated, I steal a passing glance over my shoulder. "What now?"

Jack lifts his chin and swallows hard. "When you and your men leave Everland, I'm coming with you."

After his betrayal, the fact that he abandoned the Marauders, I had no intention of bringing him with me. Caught off guard, I stumble through my words. "You want to come back? What happened to all that nonsense about the Lost Boys being your family?"

Jack spits and snarls. "Once I give you the location of the Lost City, I can never go back to the Lost Boys. I'm as good as dead if I stay with them."

Flicking my stare to the officers, I guffaw, trying to cover up the uncertainty brewing within me. I'm not sure that my stepbrother can be trusted. The soldiers join in the laughter, while

Jack averts his gaze. I pat Jack's shoulder, still laughing along with my men.

"Gentlemen, we have a martyr on our hands. Very well, it's a deal." I give Jack a brisk slap on the cheek. "I knew you'd make a fine Marauder, Jack. Our mother would be proud."

The Marauders chuckle among themselves.

"Smeeth, take him outside. Find out where those kids are. Send half of your men to the Lost City and the other half to the girl's location."

"Yes, Captain!" Smeeth says, shoving Jack out the door.

I pull a book of matches from the pocket of my black coat. Striking the matches, I drop them on a pile of artwork, lighting it into a bonfire. The fire grows, licking the nearby walls and ceiling.

As the building burns, we move outside. Flames reach toward the night sky from the roof of the National Gallery and ash rains onto the street, blanketing it like powdery gray snow. Soldiers dart between buildings, dousing the structures with kerosene, lighting them all ablaze.

Jack's eyes shimmer with fear, the orange fire reflecting in their dark, muddy pigment.

"This is it," I say, excitement evident in my tone. Everland glows, leaving me with a quiet satisfaction, relief washing away the endless months of misery. "A year in this wasteland and tonight it will all come to an end. By the time the sun rises, there will be nothing left, nowhere for Pete and the Lost Boys to hide. We will take the girls and leave Everland forever!"

"It's been a long time, Captain," Smeeth says, holding a gun to Jack's back. "I shall be glad to leave this place."

I grunt approvingly. With the cure in my hands, I am certain my return to Lohr Castle will not only be welcome, but lauded as heroic. The prize of England is only a grain of sand compared with the vast glory the cure will bring. If the world is in the condition that I expect it's in, millions will be grateful for my gift. Considering the Professor's suggestion that girls are on the brink of extinction, I'll be a world hero and I'll rule it, starting with the German crown.

I turn to Smeeth. "Did you get the locations?"

"Yes, sir. Girl's heading to the palace, and you won't believe it, Captain, but the others have been hiding in the Underground this whole time," Smeeth says.

Disgusted, I grab Jack's shirt and shake him.

"This whole time? All this time you've been right under my feet?" I give him a hard shove. He stumbles, but regains his balance.

I take in my younger brother, my fists clenching. "Before you take us to the Lost City, there is one more item we must take care of. One last thing to be sure neither you nor anyone else questions where you belong."

Jack steps back, bumping into Smeeth's gun. "What more could you possibly want from me?"

I stride toward the burning gallery and pick up a piece of wood. A flame dances wildly on the end. I hold the torch close to my gloved left hand, careful not to burn myself but close enough to make the ring on my middle finger glow red in the heat.

Smeeth shoves Jack to his knees. The boy grunts as he hits the ground hard. He sits back on his heels, his head bowed. Smeeth's fingers wrap around Jack's ebony hair and yank his head up.

I stoop, my gaze meeting the Lost Boy's glare. Jack clenches his teeth together defiantly.

I press the red-hot ring behind Jack's right ear, relishing his violent screams as they rise above the sizzling of fiery metal against his skin. The putrid smell of burning flesh fills the smoky air. Jack's face grows pale with a hint of green as he crouches and vomits. The insignia of the Marauders, a skull and crossbones, marks the skin behind his ear, angry and raw. Jack spits and stares up at me, his nostrils flaring.

"Welcome back to the Marauders, little brother," I say in a guttural growl.

· GWEN ·

Traveling the narrow passageway, I shiver and wipe away the tickle of spiderwebs from my face and hair. Lily leads, holding the lantern to light the dark shadows ahead of us. A wave of claustrophobia washes over me as thick black smoke and the smell of something burning makes the air feel thinner in the small space.

"We must hurry," Lily says, holding the fabric of her sari to her nose and mouth. "It is just a bit farther ahead."

"Where are you taking us?" I ask, distracting myself from the anxiety that mounts within me, my breaths becoming more shallow and rapid.

She answers without turning. "Eventually, as far from Everland as possible, but for now, somewhere safe."

"We're looking for our friend Bella," Pete says, crinkling his brow. "She's about this tall, with blond hair and mechanical wings. Have you seen her?"

Lily keeps moving forward. "Not now. I will explain everything once we are safe."

We travel a few moments more and stop at a hole in the ground. Lily holds her lamp over the opening, but it sheds very little light into the gaping, dark chasm.

"Take this," she says, handing me the lamp. She sits on the edge of the gap, her legs dangling over the side. Her foot finds a step and she slides in, disappearing into the thick blackness.

Doc reaches for the lantern. "You're next," he says.

"No, you go," I say. "Pete's injured. He'll need you and Pickpocket to help him down."

Pete shoots his gaze toward Doc and frowns, seeming ruffled by the comment, but he doesn't say anything. He holds his injured arm with his good hand and gives Doc a tired expression. Doc shifts past me toward the hole in the ground. Lily's hand pokes through the darkness and her gloved fingers wrap around his hand as she helps him climb down the steps.

"Now you," Lily says, motioning to Pickpocket.

He glances at me with a wary expression but swings his legs into the gap and carefully lowers himself into the hole. Mole follows without hesitation.

Unable to control my cough, I crouch toward the ground, where the smoke isn't as thick. Pete drops to his knees, covering his mouth and nose.

"You're hurt. You go next," I say to Pete, nudging him toward the opening.

"No, Gwen . . . ," he begins to protest.

"No time to argue. Just go," I say, choking on my words.

He glances at me with some hesitancy but sits on the edge of the opening and drops into the dark abyss. My lungs burn and my vision spins. Lying on the dirt ground, I pass the lantern down into the hole. Almost tumbling in and gasping for air, I roll into two waiting hands.

"I got you!" Pete says, cradling me with a wince. I know he's in a lot of pain, but he tries to hide it. He gently places me on the ground.

"I told you you should've gone first," he says, patting my back.

"Because it would've been better if I caught you instead?" I ask, wheezing.

Pete laughs. "Spoken like a true Lost Girl."

My faces flushes and I elbow him. "I learned from the best."

"Let's get you up," Pete says, helping me to my feet. His hand lingers a little too long on my elbow, sending a renewed energy through my limbs. Too soon, he releases his grip.

The click of a latch shutting draws my attention. Lily stands on the top step of a crudely made wooden staircase and closes a trapdoor, blocking the smoke from entering the passage. Her face brightens in the lamplight, revealing dark eyes, warm skin tones, and beautiful Indian features. I glance down at my filthy hands, feeling somewhat mediocre next to her beauty. Doc helps her from the step.

"A proper gentleman, I see. Why, thank you!" she says. She gives Doc a quick peck on the cheek before taking the lamp from Pickpocket's outstretched hand. A grin grows on Doc's flushed face as he touches his cheek, seeming stunned by her affection. I turn to catch Pete's eye, but his stare is locked on Doc, fury glazing his expression. I touch his arm and coax him to follow me. Seeming reluctant, he strips his gaze from them.

Fiery torches light the hallway, the flames' light twinkling off polished white marble tiles lining the floors. Old sconces and dusty portraits of England's leaders adorn the walls. The musty-smelling passageway is more sophisticated but narrower than those that led to the Lost City.

"Where are we?" I ask.

"In the secret royal tunnels," Lily says. "These are the passages that the royalty, top military generals, and other government officials once used to safely travel throughout the city."

I glance at Pete. He appears as surprised as I am and shrugs, still darting angry eyes at Doc as he stands shoulder to shoulder with Lily.

"I had no idea they existed," he says.

"Indeed," Lily says. "And you were not supposed to. No one was. There are numerous military bunkers, safe houses, and tunnels that led to important buildings built prior to it becoming the official palace of the monarch. Her Majesty even has a secret steam engine in one of the northern underground tunnels that leads to the surrounding counties."

Doc rubs his chin and he stares at the girl's black-and-gold-gloved hands. I wonder if the same questions running through my mind are running through his: Is Lily immune? And how has she survived?

I hold a hand out toward Lily. "Thanks for getting us out of there. Without your help, who knows where we'd be right now."

"Probably in Hook's laboratory," Mole says, shuddering.

Lily shakes my hand. "It's no bother. You're not the first I've rescued, and I hardly believe you'll be the last." Her gaze falls on Doc. "Although you are the most handsome bunch I've saved."

Doc's cheeks grow pink as he returns her smile with a crooked grin. Pickpocket rolls his eyes and Mole gives a hushed giggle. Pete gives an audible inhalation.

"I'm Gwen," I say, breaking the hushed tension. "These are the Lost Boys: Doc, Mole, Pickpocket, and their leader, Pete."

"It's a pleasure to meet you all," she says with a courteous nod of her head. She spins, lifting the skirt of her sari, revealing heavy combat boots adorned with several copper buckles. "We should be on our way. The Professor will be expecting me soon."

"Professor?" Doc asks, worry creasing his forehead. "Wait, who is the Professor?"

"She is the palace physician," Lily replies, ducking under a loose ceiling tile, waving us along. "She'll want to take a look at that injury on your arm." Lily nods at Pete.

"You're taking us to the palace?" I ask, halting and unsure if this is a good thing or bad. Even though the palace is where Joanna is and I was already headed there, an uneasy feeling crawls up my spine.

"Not exactly. The Professor will meet us in the infirmary beneath the palace. It is a secret room hidden behind the crematorium. Secret from the Captain," Lily says.

"As in Captain Hook?" Pete asks. He grips the hilt of his dagger.

Lily turns and tilts her head. "Of course. What other captain would I be speaking of?"

"Oh, now I know this is a bad idea," Mole says, fidgeting with the cuff of his sleeve.

Lily huffs an exaggerated breath. "Well, you're welcome to go back to the gallery, but I assure you with all that smoke billowing, that is not a simple bonfire." She whirls around and continues up the hallway.

The Lost Boys exchange worried glances.

"Come on," I say, tugging Pete's hand. "I don't think she means us any harm. And entering the palace this way is a whole lot better than having to fight our way through the soldiers."

"I agree," Mole interjects.

Pete casts a frustrated glance at Pickpocket. "What about you? Do you think we should trust her?"

Pickpocket shrugs. "Where else are we going to go? We can't exactly go back. Gwen's right; at least this way we can get closer to the palace without losing anyone else."

Pete is quiet for a moment, and the fact that he hasn't asked Doc for his input doesn't escape me.

"I concur," Doc finally says. His gaze darts after Lily. "Besides, if the Professor is indeed a physician helping children in Everland, she is probably seeking an antidote or has already acquired one. It would be good for us to find out what she knows."

Pete gives a suspicious stare in Lily's direction before conceding. "Let's go," he says reluctantly.

· HOOK ·

The shrill cry of panicked children is music to my ears as it reverberates through the tunnels below Everland. Their voices are drowned out beneath the shouts of the masked Marauders. I clench and unclench my fists as I scan the vast chamber of the Lost City. Copper, chrome, and brass fixtures glitter beneath oil and gas lamps. Gears squeal from machines, each seeming to have a specific purpose. Pulleys, levers, and wheels attach to the stone walls and ceiling. Buildings stand lopsided along the circumference of the makeshift city. It's rather magnificent, but I can't shake the itch of annoyance. All this time, they've been right under my feet, literally.

"How clever of them," I say, taking in the intricate details of the underground town. "And here I thought the tunnels were caved in. Nothing but rubble."

"They were, Captain," Smeeth says, scratching his head. "We made sure of it. The ones that hadn't collapsed after the bombing, we blew the entrances ourselves."

I glower at him, my hands aching to wring his thick neck. "Apparently they weren't, Mr. Smeeth."

The children protest as the Marauders gather the boys, chaining them in groups. "Fascinating. I had no idea there were so many of you still running the streets."

The younger children sniff back tears while the older boys scowl at me, boys who are near my age or a few years younger. I recognize the fire within them, the stain of lost innocence. It's the same fury that rages in my heart and soul, a fire that has burned within me since the day of my thirteenth birthday. I have the advantage this time.

A tall, skinny boy lunges forward. "What do you want with us?" he demands.

I look him over, an amused grin tugging at the corners of my mouth. I flick the boy's thick goggles, making the teenager jerk. "And who might you be?"

"Justice is our interim leader," another teenager says.

I burst into laughter. I can't help it. The boy cowering before me is hardly intimidating, much less the head of an entire city of orphans. "Leader, eh? I don't have time for games, so I'll make this easy on you."

Justice takes a big breath and the muscles in his jaw tighten. He still trembles, but I can see he's steeling himself for a battle. "What do you want?" he asks.

"There are a lot of things I want." I pace in front of the rows of shackled boys. "World domination, the German crown, the cure to the Horologia virus, which I'm fairly certain lies within a girl of Everland. Now, where are Bella and the other girl?"

A small boy bursts from behind a pile of machine parts and stands toe-to-toe with me. His brown eyes glaze with rage. He's captivating in a chubby-cheeked kind of way and his determination is bigger than his stature. Something stirs within me, a piece of my former self longing for the days Jack and I adventured into the forest until dusk, playing in tree forts. I don't know who changed first, him or me. With the death of his father and my . . .

my disfiguration, we both became different people. The jubilant boy he once was died the day he buried his father, and my joy was lost the day my mother struck me, taking my innocence along with my eye. I stare at the young boy, recognizing the fierce expression. It's the countenance I saw in my own reflection, the same expression when Jack said we weren't brothers anymore before he bolted from his father's funeral. He blamed me, but I had done nothing other than offer Jack's father the spiced cider from my mother. It was the only kind thing I'd ever seen her do for anyone, and I wanted to be a part of that occasion. He was dead by morning.

"They're gone and it's your fault," the boy shouts. He throws a dirty teddy bear at me and pummels me with his fists. It doesn't hurt. Each time his little hand connects I feel nothing, empty.

"Mikey! I told you to hide," a teenager covered in dirt admonishes. His chains rattle as he lurches toward the boy.

I kneel in front of the boy and regard him, scrutinizing him from head to toe. "Perhaps you Lost Boys could be useful."

I try to snatch Mikey's wrist, but he bolts and hides behind the bigger boys.

"You leave him alone," the boy with the dirt-stained face shouts, tugging against his shackles.

Chains clattering, three urchins step in front of Mikey, attempting to intimidate me as they tower over me.

"If you want Mikey," Justice says, "you'll have to get through us."

"It's just as well. He isn't vital to my plan," I say.

"You won't ever find Bella or Gwen. They're too smart to get caught by you. Gwen and Pete are probably storming your stinky palace as we speak, and when you get back she's going to have rescued her sister and Bella and you'll have no one. Then she'll come back here for her brother, Mikey, and the rest of us," one says before sticking out his tongue.

"Gabs!" Justice growls, yanking the boy back. "Dozer, look after him."

The teenager with the dirty face waves Gabs behind him.

I pick up the stuffed bear and study it, piecing together the bits of information tossing about in my mind. Her sister? Is it possible that the girl the soldiers caught earlier is another sibling of these two? But that can't be. With the girls dropping dead so quickly, how is it possible two sisters and a brother have survived? Regardless, I need to get my hands on her, and the only way to her is through Pete.

"So my brother was telling the truth. She *is* headed for the palace," I murmur, standing and ignoring the three teenage boys still attempting to appear daunting as they hover near. "Well, we should be sure we're there to welcome her."

"Captain, what should we do with the Lost Boys?" Smeeth asks.

"Gather them up and bring them along. They may be useful. Especially that boy." I point my gloved hand toward Mikey, who cowers behind Dozer. What better way to convince Gwen to come out of hiding than to entice her with her little brother.

"No!" Dozer shouts, struggling to keep my men from reaching Mikey.

Turning toward the tunnel to leave the cavernous Lost City, I mull over the details I've just learned when a rock whirs past me, striking the stone wall. The low rumble of thunder churns within me, ready to explode. No one attacks me. Not without paying harsh consequences. I storm over to the teenage boy with a stone gripped in his clenched fist, the interim leader, Justice. What a conveniently appropriate name. I grip him by his shirt, my other hand reaching for my pistol, ready to remind him who he's dealing with, when Mikey wails loudly. An iron fist grips at my chest. He's just a boy, a child. He's already seen enough violence in his short life. I turn my gaze back at Justice. He scowls at me, unafraid. I shove him to the ground and leave my pistol holstered.

"You ought to know by now that boys are not immune," Justice says, bolting to his feet, ripping a glove from his hand with his teeth, and throwing it to the ground. He holds his hand up. Boils cover his fingers from the tips of the pads down to his palms. "You yourself said that you believe immunity lies in the girls. We have nothing to offer you!" Justice shouts.

I'm aware of this truth already, that the boys are not immune, and not just because the Professor has told me. My knuckles pop as I squeeze my fists. Face-to-face, I peer at the boy.

"On the contrary, you may be much more useful than I originally thought," I say, spittle spraying Justice's face.

Justice doesn't budge but stares back, unblinking.

"What do you mean?" Gabs squeaks.

My gaze, fixated on Justice, narrows. "I need Gwen. The entire Lost Boy tribe will surely be enough to entice Pete to make an appearance. Especially if I offer a few of you as snacks to my pets. Tick and Tock aren't picky. A crocodile's got to eat."

"No!" Jack says, his voice echoing from a darkened tunnel. He thrusts forward into the dim light of the Lost City, cuffed and standing between two Marauders. "You promised, Hook! You said you wouldn't hurt the Lost Boys!"

"Ah, yes, I forgot to introduce my stepbrother. I'm sure you boys know Jack. He's the one who led me to your hideout."

Justice's eyes widen. "Jack? All this time you were one of them?" he says incredulously.

"It's not what you think," Jack pleads. "Gwen was all he wanted. He doesn't want any of us. Just Gwen. Once he has her he'll let all of you go."

Gabs's lower lip quivers. "She's a Lost Girl. She's one of us. How could you give her up?"

"Jack is a Marauder now, not a measly Lost Boy," I spit. I grip Jack's chin and jerk his head, revealing the Marauder's mark blistering behind his ear. The Lost Boys gasp collectively and erupt in accusatory shouts and curses.

Jack wrenches his chin from my grasp and looks away. A deep line forms in his brow.

"You're nothing but a traitorous pirate!" another one of them yells.

The Lost Boys watch Jack in wonder, whispering between themselves. I consider my brother, his rage boiling behind his dark eyes. I could release Jack to the Lost Kids and, with a little encouragement, his punishment would be crueler, more brutal than anything he experienced at Lohr Castle. Perhaps, though, Jack could still be useful.

"*Pirate* has such a nasty connotation," I interject between the accusations. "We are Marauders, not pirates. We pillage, steal, kidnap, and murder at the pleasure of the Bloodred Queen." I nod to a group of Marauders, their rifles trained on the boys. "Take them to the palace, but keep Mikey close. I think we'll need him to coax his sister from hiding."

Justice kicks another stone at me. This time, I don't duck quite fast enough and it connects with my forehead. I reach to touch the lump I can already feel growing on my head and pull my hand away. Blood shimmers on the fingertips of my black gloves beneath the lamplight.

"Nice shot, but you will regret that, Lost Boy." I snatch my pistol from its holster. The sound of a single gunshot drowns out the collective gasps of the boys. Justice's eyes grow wide as he reaches for his chest. A crimson stain blooms on his waistcoat. He stumbles back, falling against a rock wall before slumping to the floor. His lifeless eyes stare coldly at me.

"Bloody pirate, I'll kill you!" Gabs says, throwing weak punches at me.

I flip the pistol in my hand, gripping the barrel, and smack him across the head with the butt of the gun. He flies to the floor in a crumpled heap. Blood bursts from a gash on his cheek. I stoop over him and smile.

"Time to go to Everland, Lost Boys."

· GWEN ·

The tunnel curves to the left, and after traveling for a while, we reach a gilded door covered in mismatched metal gadgets. Lily spins gears, switches levers, and tugs on wheels in an elaborate sequence. The door clicks. She pushes the door and steps into a dimly lit space. A faint antiseptic scent of alcohol tingles my nose. Sheets partition the space, creating three makeshift rooms. Cotton balls, bottles of alcohol and hydrogen peroxide, bandages, and other first aid supplies fill an open cabinet over a stainless steel sink. When we enter the room, Lily shuts the door behind us. A series of metallic grinding and clicks emanates from the other side of the door, securing us into the small room.

"Come on," Lily says, reaching a delicate hand out to Pete, "let's fix you up."

Pete takes her hand and gives her a lopsided smile as she guides him to a partition and pulls the sheet aside. Something new stirs within me, and I suddenly feel protective of Pete as I glance at her gloved hand in his.

"It's only a scratch. I'm fine," he says.

"Sit," she says, nodding to Pete. He settles on the bed, the bandage on his arm soaked through with blood. "I'll at least clean it and apply a fresh bandage before the Professor arrives."

Pete removes his dark green coat. He winces as he pulls off his shirt. I catch myself staring at his shirtless torso, noticing that the canvas of tattoos continues over his defined chest muscles and cut abs. The black and brown inks scrawl across his body in a network of pictures that look as if his flesh has been peeled back and his insides are made of the inner parts of a clock. Wheels and gears ink across his chest in place of a heart, lungs, and stomach. In the faint glow of candlelight, his body appears to be more machine than human.

Noticing my stare, Pete looks at his chest. "I always thought the world couldn't hurt me if I was machine, not flesh," he says, covering the tattoos with his arms. "I know. It's a silly boy's dream."

I force my attention away from the inked wheels, cogs, and bolts on his chest and to his eyes, which sparkle like green sea glass. My cheeks grow warm. "It's beautiful," I say, hearing the surprise in my own voice. He gives me a tired smile.

Pickpocket clears his throat, reminding me of the audience around me, and I feel heat crawl up my neck, face, and ears. Mortified, I berate myself. I've been brave in the face of danger, dodged bombs and bullets, eluded soldiers, fought others for supplies, but a shirtless boy makes my legs feel weak.

"How do you know the Professor will come?" Mole asks.

Lily pulls supplies from the cabinet and places them on a metal cart. "She comes nightly after the soldiers make their final rounds of the palace. Once they know she's secured in the lab, she tends to her patients here."

"And who are her patients?" I ask, settling down on the end of Pete's cot.

"Other orphans. I search the streets for abandoned children and bring them here for treatment before they are sent from Everland to safer territory," Lily says.

Pete's mouth turns up in a crooked smile. "Sounds like a familiar story," he says.

Lily's brows rise in a curious expression, but then she returns his smile. "As I'm sure you know by now, everyone is infected by the virus even if they aren't showing symptoms. Inevitably we all will be sickened by the Horologia virus. Without her treatment, we will all die. Especially the girls."

"What about you?" I ask, finally addressing the unspoken question I'm certain we all are thinking.

Lily pulls off her gloves. Scabs cover the tips of her fingers. My hope plummets.

"You're infected with the virus, too?" Doc asks, appearing equally disappointed.

Lily gives him a puzzled look. "Isn't everyone?" she says, pulling on latex gloves.

"Gwen's a real Immune," Mole says. "Or at least that's what Doc thinks."

Lily glances down at my hands. Something flicks in her gaze. She turns her eyes to Doc and he nods in affirmation. Lily grips my hands, inspecting each of my fingers. "Fascinating!" she exclaims. Her eyes grow wide. "You must be the one the Professor has been searching for."

"Searching for me?" I ask with some apprehension as I slip my gloves back on. "How did she know I existed? I've just found out myself that I'm immune."

Lily brings her supplies over to Pete's bedside. "The Marauders were bringing children to her lab daily. Even though she could escape at any time, the Professor has remained here as a prisoner, believing that there was only one child who was truly invulnerable to the virus. One person who she swore would be resistant. She refused to leave until she found the Immune whose blood contained the antidote to the Horologia virus. I think it was you she must have been speaking of," Lily says. She peers at me, excitement in her dark eyes. "For nearly six months now I've been sneaking around Everland rescuing kids, bringing them here for treatment, and then sending them away to safer lands, along with medication." She spins on the heels of her boots, rushes to me, and grips my arms. "With you here, we could all leave Everland *for good*. If you really are the Immune she is looking for, we can have a true antidote. Not just medicine to treat the symptoms. A real cure!"

The weight of her words settles on my already tight shoulders. Inching backward, I move closer to Pete. Detecting my uneasiness, he grips my hand. The warmth of his fingers intertwined with mine brings a wave of calm over me.

"How has the Professor been able to save the kids without getting caught?" Doc asks. "Hook has been taking children off the street for the last year. What does he think she does with them? Certainly he must suspect her?"

"Hook insisted that once it was decided that the captured children were not immune, they were to be euthanized. Their bodies were to be incinerated so that the virus would not spread," Lily says. "The Professor led Hook to believe that they had been cremated; meanwhile, she treated them until they could safely travel. My job was to take the children away. I was one of the Professor's first patients. When Hook brought me to the palace, I was sure I was going to die, but the Professor saved me." Lily shrugs. "Since then we've been a team."

"How many others have you saved?" Pickpocket asks.

"You mean how many others has the *Professor* saved," Lily says. "She is the one who treats them. There are many. Granted, none of us are cured of the Horologia virus, but she has kept us alive, treating the symptoms and supplying medicines to other survivors."

"Where are the other survivors?" Pete asks.

"Northumberland," Lily says. "The Queen of England escaped through the royal tunnels when the bombs dropped. One of the steam railway tunnels leads to Alnwick Castle. The Duchess of Northumberland has taken Her Majesty in, along with survivors who escaped with her. Together they are treating the survivors of not only England, but all citizens of the United Kingdom, and are preparing to strike back to reclaim Everland as their own."

"The Queen is alive?" I breathe. "How many survivors are there? Can they help us now?" I ask with urgency.

"As far as those who escaped with the Queen: a few workers, family, the Royal Guard, some military. I'm unsure how many have gathered there from the rest of the United Kingdom," Lily says.

"Military? Guard?" Pete asks, rage spitting from his lips. "Why haven't they come to fight the Marauders?"

Lily frowns and slowly shakes her head. "Only a handful of the Queen's military and guard escaped, a few dozen at the most, not nearly enough to stage a counterattack. Even if they had the numbers to attack, the priority is to treat the sick and dying. They are not prepared to strike yet."

I reach for the metal tags and my fingers graze across cloth and skin where the necklace once rested. I jerk my hand away, sickened by the empty space that held the only item I had left of my father's.

I blink, trying to hide the tears burning my eyes.

Lily ties off the bandage on Pete's arm. "There you go," she says. She presses two fingers to her pink lips, kisses them, and places them on the bandage. "Healed with a kiss. You should feel much better soon. The bullet merely grazed you."

"Lucky for me," Pete replies with a quirky grin.

Annoyed, I drop my gaze to the floor. Something glitters beneath the lamplight, catching my eye. Bending, I run a finger across the hint of gold dust sprinkled on the floor.

A small cough breaks the silence from behind one of the curtains. Pete's surprised eyes shift from the noise to Lily.

"Who is that?" Pete asks sternly.

"Another rescue," Lily says, removing her gloves and dropping them in a rubbish bin.

The patient says something so weakly that I barely hear her voice. I dart across the room and rip open the sheet dividing the two cots. With a glassy gaze she peers up, dark circles puffy beneath her eyes. Her face is pale and her breathing is quick and shallow.

"Bella!" I shout, tears threatening to fall.

The young girl's eyelids flutter before her eyes roll back and she plunges into unconsciousness.

· H O O K ·

The hallway rumbles with the chatter of soldiers discussing the arrival of the newest female as they peer beyond the bulletproof window. Inside the Professor's lab, I inspect the unconscious girl, awed by the condition she is in. Although her fingers show signs of infection, for the most part she appears to be extraordinarily healthy. Compared with the other children that have been found, she is nearly perfect.

"Has the Professor seen the girl?" I ask Smeeth.

"She's just finishing up in the crematorium down in the basement. She should be up shortly."

I nod curtly.

"I've seen worse," Smeeth continues. "She doesn't appear to be too far along. In fact, I'd say she's the healthiest specimen I've seen. She is in remarkable condition. I'm not sure how she's managed to survive this long, but I hope she's a good candidate for further testing."

Seizing the patient's chart from the bed, I flip through the pages. "Do we have any identification on who she is?"

Smeeth stares at me with a puzzled expression. "Not that I'm aware of. Why?"

The chart offers nothing out of the ordinary: height, weight, and description. I watch the girl with a newfound appreciation, and I sort through jumbling thoughts as if piecing a puzzle together. "If she's been able to stave off the virus for this long, she must have had some help, something to assist her in building enough immunity to keep the virus from affecting her like the others. Maybe the Professor is wrong. Perhaps it may be possible to concoct an antidote from her cells. You do know what that would mean, Mr. Smeeth?"

"What, Captain?"

"She could be our ticket out of Everland. We might not need the other girl," I say, observing this girl with interest. "When can we wake her?"

"If you're right, I'm sure the Professor will be interested in speaking to her to find out if there's an environmental factor or something else keeping her alive."

I place the patient's chart on the foot of the bed. Footsteps echo in the staircase that leads from the basement cremation chamber to the lab. The Professor steps into the room, pulling on a pair of gloves.

"So let's see who our . . ." She stops midsentence. Her eyes stare in shock at the young girl. Suddenly, it clicks.

Upon seeing the Professor's expression, rage strikes me in the gut like lightning, confirming what I'd just deduced. I ball my fists, holding back the anger, reminding myself that she, like my own mother, will lie through her pretty white teeth as long as it is to her own benefit.

"Professor?" Smeeth says, furrowing his brow. "Is something wrong?"

The woman draws near to the patient and gently touches the girl's cheek.

"You know her, don't you?" I snarl, more as a statement than a question.

The Professor regards me, shaking her head, seeming to search for lost words. Finally, she drops her gaze back to the patient.

She brushes a ringlet of hair from the girl's face. "This is my daughter."

"You said you had no children," I say, my voice trembling behind clenched teeth.

The Professor nods, her worried eyes flicking from me to the young girl. She glances at her watch as she rests her fingertips on the girl's wrist. "I thought she was dead. I've watched hundreds, thousands, of kids come through here, hoping any of them were Joanna. When she never showed up, I assumed the worst." The Professor strokes Joanna's hair. "I can't believe it's her. She's grown so much."

"She obviously is not the one you said was immune," I declare, tossing Joanna's file onto the counter. "This virus has annihilated the adult population and almost every female we've come across. Yet somehow both you and your daughter managed to survive it, and you claim that there is only one child that is immune. How is that possible?"

The Professor says nothing. Fury boils over within me. I swipe the counter, sending the file and medical tools clattering to the floor. I growl and grab the Professor's frail arms with viselike hands. She yelps in pain.

"What are you hiding?" I demand.

With a frightened but defiant stare, she glares back at me.

Her insubordination rattles me. I press my lips together, fighting the urge to slap her.

"Perhaps this will convince you," I say. Pulling my revolver from its holster, I raise it to the Professor's chest. She shudders but stands tall.

"Captain, wait!" Smeeth says, stepping between the gun and the Professor.

He is like kerosene, fueling my anger.

"Soldier, stand down!" I snarl.

The Professor guffaws and stares at me with unintimidated, unyielding eyes. "You'll never pull that trigger. You need me."

I cock the hammer of my gun back.

"Think this through," Smeeth says, holding his palms up. "She is the only one left who knows how to develop the cure for the Horologia virus. You kill her, you kill any chance we have to find the antidote."

I study the Professor, searching for any sign of fear. There is nothing. Smeeth is right and she knows it. "You have a valid point. Your daughter, however"—I turn my revolver toward the unconscious girl—"is not vital to my plan. She is not the Immune."

Just as I expected, the Professor's resolve dissipates. She throws herself over the girl's body, shielding her from my aim. "No!" the Professor pleads, the blood draining from her face.

Smiling widely, I lower my weapon. "Ah, just as I thought. I want answers and I want them now. There's something keeping her alive. Start talking."

The Professor's eyes glisten as she sits up and laces her fingers into her daughter's hand. "Sixteen years ago, I had just begun working for the biological weapons laboratory. Three other researchers and I were assigned to study the Horologia virus. It was sent to us by an anonymous rebel of . . ." The Professor hesitates, as if struggling to continue. She sighs. "It was sent from Germany."

Disbelief and rage flood through me. My knees grow weak. I lean against the counter to steady myself. It was one of my own who sent this virus here. But why? And who? As if reading my mind, the Professor continues.

"We don't know who sent it, only that it came from Germany with a dire warning that it would potentially be used against England. I was commissioned to create an antidote in the event Germany attacked England." The Professor lets out an audible breath, appearing reluctant to share more.

I swing my pistol, its barrel aimed at the Professor. "What else do you know?"

The Professor gathers herself and stands, straightening her lab coat. "Immediately, it was apparent the virus was meant to destroy whole populations. Not only cities, but entire countries. After months of research, we were able to isolate and create not only an antidote, but also a vaccine. But the base of the virus was developed with an ingredient so rare that we couldn't re-create enough. It was impossible to generate enough of the vaccine to protect England with the small sample we had. Just enough to vaccinate a few individuals. Once I knew the vaccine was safe, I began to vaccinate her." The Professor nods toward the unconscious child. "I knew that it was only a matter of time before the treaty was as worthless as the signatures on it. Peace can only last so long."

I watch the young girl as her chest rises with each inhalation. "But if she's vaccinated, why is she showing symptoms?"

The Professor frowns. "Immunity required a series of three doses over fifteen years. Joanna has received only two. She wasn't scheduled for her next for another three years. Considering how rapidly the population succumbed to the disease, it's no surprise that she's showing signs. Without the third shot, she wouldn't have developed the immunity to entirely resist the virus." The Professor drops her gaze, a crease deepening between her eyebrows.

I regard the Professor, looking at her from head to toe. "If you had access to the vaccine, then you must have vaccinated yourself, too."

The Professor shakes her head. "The program was shut down. With England at odds with Germany and the funding for the project dwindling, Parliament was more concerned about defending the country, not some obscure virus that no one had seen before. I was reassigned to study more prevalent biological weapons. Only a small portion of vaccine was developed, but with tensions between England and Germany rising, I wasn't going to take the chance. I stole the vaccine and used it on her. I didn't make enough to vaccinate myself before the program closed. The only way I survived the initial outbreak was because lab protocol required we dress in hazmat suits while working with the specimens. Luckily for me, I happened to be in the lab when you bombed London." Sarcasm laces her voice.

"But there's a third shot out there that you intended to give her. Where's the vaccine now? Is it with the antidote?" I ask, the hope in my voice betraying me.

"*Everything* was destroyed." The Professor's voice hardens.

"When you bombed London, you not only released the virus, but you destroyed the vaccine along with the cure."

I holster my gun and step to Joanna's bedside, scanning the length of the child. "What about the girl? Can you harvest the antibodies from her to develop an antidote?"

The Professor cringes, but joins me at the girl's bedside. She lifts her daughter's hand and inspects her fingers. "Her body is starting to succumb to the virus. The antibodies aren't working. They may have kept the virus at bay, but her immune system is weakening. I could try, but I can't promise anything."

"And what about your other children?" I ask, holding back the grin I feel creeping at the corners of my lips.

Her glassy gaze flicks toward me, wide with surprise. "Other . . . children?" she repeats, her voice trailing off.

I pull the military tags from my pocket and hold them up so that she can read the etching engraved into the metal. The name G. DARLING dangles from the chain before her beautiful eyes.

The Professor gasps. She takes the chain, wraps her fingers around the tags, and holds them close to her chest. "Where did you find these?"

"Let's just say it appears Joanna is not your only child," I say.

Tears spill from her eyes, streaking her pink cheeks. "Gwen's alive?" she asks, searching my face for answers.

Gwen. The last time I saw her she was chasing Pete's shadow just outside of Everland.

The Professor turns, clutching the tags close. "Only Gwen was old enough to receive all three doses. She is the true Immune, *if* she survived the bombs."

Again she appears to search for affirmation of her daughter's survival in my expression. I give her nothing. My thumb grazes her cheek and she pulls away, clearly disgusted. She is truly beautiful, exquisite, with her soft locks and bright eyes. Perhaps I've been looking at her all wrong. Although she embodies everything a mother is, there is something lovely about her. I've never received the love of a mother; I never will. However, with humanity on the brink of extinction, perhaps she is more than that.

"What would you say if I offered you a partnership? You and I, together, ruling more than just that measly country my mother controls. No more running from Germany or living in what is left of England. We could be royalty. We could rule the world," I say.

"Why would I ever align with you?" the Professor asks, her bottom lip trembling.

I tuck a loose curl behind her ear. "Professor, do you believe in ghost stories?"

"I don't understand," she says, fumbling over her words.

I pull the Professor into me, my lips nearly touch hers. Her heart beats rapidly against my chest. "I believe my pal Pete has rescued another child. Little does he know she is not at all the orphan she claims she is," I whisper so close to her ear I can smell the hint of lavender.

Gently, I escort her through the door, letting it slam shut behind us. I take her hand in mine. She tries to pull away, but I grip it tightly. "It's a lovely night for a family reunion, isn't it?"

· GWEN ·

Bella! Bella, talk to me!" Pete says, jostling Bella awake.

"Pete, it hurts," Bella whispers, squeezing her eyes shut tight as she holds her hand up, revealing blood-soaked bandages around her fingers.

He spins toward Lily. "What have you done to her?"

With shock masking her face, Lily takes a step back. "I found her like this. She almost plunged to her death off Big Ben. I saved her."

Pete whips his gaze back to Bella.

Lily joins him hesitantly. "She is the worst I have seen in a long time and the Professor has not been in tonight. I've been waiting for her to bring in the medicines."

Pete snatches up his rucksack and pulls out the needle Doc gave him earlier from the side pocket. He uncaps it with his teeth and sits on Bella's cot.

"Wait! We should consult with the Professor," Lily protests, but she is too late.

Pete pauses for a split second and then he plunges the needle into Bella's shoulder. She grimaces in pain. Pete throws the needle in the sink. "Bella? Bella, please talk to me." She rolls over instead of answering. Her body trembles as she quietly sobs.

"What was that you gave her?" Lily says, pushing Pete away from Bella.

Pete's shoulders stiffen and his green eyes grow hard. "Let's hope it's the antidote."

I sit on Bella's bed. "Bella?" I say. She looks at me, her black eye makeup streaking her cheeks with dark-tinted tears. I place my hand on the inside of her wrist. Blood pulses through her veins against my fingertips, as steady as a summer rainfall, a heartbeat that now contains my white blood cells. "You're going to be okay," I say, smiling at her.

Bella nods, and the tightness in her shoulders melts into the mattress. She takes a breath and I feel her pulse slow, see her breathing return to regular, deep breaths. "Gwen," she says in a small voice. "I almost had him. I had Hook in my sight, but . . ."

"Bella, what were you thinking?" Pete says in a voice so loud it reverberates in the small room. "No one goes into Everland alone. No one! Especially not you! You could've been captured, or worse yet, killed."

I glower at Pete, a silent warning for him to back off. Pickpocket taps him on the shoulder and nods toward the far end of the room. Pete steps back, tripping over Bella's metal wings, and leans against a far wall, not saying anything more. It is then I notice the mangled copper and jagged film of her left wing. I suck in a breath, trying to swallow the lump in my throat. Her beautiful wings . . . broken. Tears well up in my eyes, but I blink them back as Bella's fingers graze my arm.

"I thought if I could take him down, then maybe I could get Joanna, and no one else would have to risk their life," she says, blinking with tired eyes. "I wanted to prove that I'm just as good as any Lost Boy."

"Shh," I say, taking a cool, wet cloth from Lily and brushing Bella's forehead with it. "That was very brave, the bravest thing I've seen anyone do, but you don't have to prove yourself. I knew you were extraordinary the first time I saw you." Bella forces a small smile. "You need your rest," I say.

"I'm glad you're here," she whispers. "I'm sorry about what I said. I don't really hate you." Bella closes her eyes.

"I know. Try to sleep now." I lean down and embrace her, grateful for the opportunity to provide her comfort. Comfort I wish I had given Joanna the last time I saw her. I wish I could give it to her now. As my pulse slows, fatigue sets in, and I want to lie next to her to rest for just a while, but there's no time for sleep. Not until Joanna is safe.

Mole looks worried. "Is she going to be all right?"

"I don't know," Doc says, starting to remove the bloody bandages from her hands. "When will the Professor be here?"

"She should have been here already," Lily says, glancing at the delicate gold pocket watch hooked to a broken chain-linked belt. "It is not like her to be delayed like this. Something is wrong."

"Then we should go find her," I say, standing. "Bella needs help now. And Joanna is somewhere inside the palace."

"We can't do that," Lily says, stripping her latex gloves from her hands and replacing them with black warrior gloves embellished in gold. "The door is locked from the inside of the lab and is covered by a cabinet. There is no way to get in there from this side without a key. Only the Professor can open the door."

Standing, I turn to Pickpocket. "Can you get us inside?"

Pickpocket grins and pulls his lock-picking multitool from his pocket.

A wrinkle of curiosity forms on Lily's brow.

"Show me the door," Pickpocket says, extending a hand for her to lead the way.

"Mole, you stay here with Bella," Pete says.

Doc continues to remove Bella's bandages. "I'm staying here as well. I want to take a look at Bella's hands."

Mole bites his lip, suddenly appearing younger than his twelve years. I wrap my arms around him and lean my cheek on his tousled brown hair. "We won't be long," I reassure him. He squeezes his arms around my waist.

"Promise?" he whispers.

"I promise," I say, kissing the top of his head. Again I feel the sudden pang of loss. I miss Mikey. I miss Joanna.

Lily motions for us to follow her and, with a gas lamp in her hand, she leads us to a walk-in closet on the far side of the room. Inside are metal shelves stacked with sheets, pillows, and other bedding. On the back side of the closet is a steel door much like the one at the entrance of the infirmary. Only this time there is a single slot for a key.

Pickpocket manipulates the tool into the lock, and within seconds the latch releases. "You'd think for a secret door in the palace, they'd have a harder lock to pick," he says.

"Impressive," Lily says. "Where did you learn to do that?"

Pickpocket places the tool in his breast pocket. "Let's just say I've seen more than my share in the clink. You learn a thing or two during your stay," he says, winking.

"Ah, I see. You're one of those bad boys," Lily says, winking back at him.

Pickpocket smirks, watching her with a dreamy countenance. I roll my eyes. Her smooth, exotic accent grates on my nerves as I watch Pickpocket practically melt in front of her.

Pete turns the knob. The door swings inward. A wooden wall blocks the entry into the room. Pete gives us an apprehensive glance before he places his hands on the wooden panel.

"Wait!" Lily whispers, stepping between Pete and the back of the cabinet. Her hand rests on his chest. Their faces are close enough that it would take only the slightest of movements for them to kiss. A stupid grin flashes across Pete's face. I look away, frustrated with Lily's flirtations, first with Doc, then Pickpocket, and now Pete. Next to Lily, who is flawlessly beautiful, clever, and exuberantly confident, I feel plain. She is everything I admire in Pete: selfless and willing to put her own needs aside to rescue strangers. I, on the other hand, have turned others away, even fought them over supplies. I wouldn't blame Pete for choosing Lily over me. Worse yet, I ought to be worried about rescuing my sister instead of fussing over a boy.

"We need to be careful," Lily continues. "The soldiers could walk in at any moment."

I shove myself between Lily and Pete, slide the cabinet open just a crack, and peek through the opening. "I don't see anyone in there, and we're not going to get anywhere standing out here."

Lily starts to protest, but I ignore her, heave the door open, and step through.

"You do know what the Captain will do to you if he discovers you in the palace?" Lily says from the doorway. She folds her arms across her chest, defiance radiating from her stern expression.

I mimic her stance, holding my ground. "No, but I don't intend to find out," I say a little too abrasively. "Pete, are you coming?"

Lily places her hand on the bronze hilt of her sword and hesitates. "If the Professor returns to the lab, more than likely she will be escorted by the Captain's guards. I'm coming with you." She pulls the blade from her belt.

Pete glances at the sword, its blade etched with intricate carvings. He whistles. "Now *that* is not a butter knife," he says, pointing at Lily's weapon.

Lily smiles brightly.

Another twinge of resentment prickles at me and my cheeks grow hot with jealousy.

"It's almost as fine as those daggers Blade gave to you," he says, smirking at me.

Reaching my hand out, I pull Pete into the room, feeling vindicated.

"Do I detect a hint of jealousy?" Pete asks in a quiet, mocking tone.

"Don't flatter yourself," I retort.

I hesitate, stealing a glance at Lily. Her eyes dart from Pete to me, and she gives me a slight knowing look. Pete chuckles but lets me lead him into the lab. Pickpocket and Lily follow behind us.

The dimly lit room is empty other than a metal gurney and huge incinerator.

"This is the crematorium," Lily says, nodding to the oven. "Follow me."

She takes the lead, climbing two stairs at a time up a narrow concrete stairway. When we reach the top, we step into what looks like a doctor's laboratory. It smells of disinfectant and something else, something floral and familiar. The white walls, tile, and counters give it a sterile appearance. Gadgets fill the room, each piece rigged with wheels, levers, gears, and pedals. Cabinets line the walls, revealing bottles, containers, bandages, and other medical supplies behind their glass doors. A gurney stands in the middle of the room, its sheets disheveled. Lying on the white pillow is a brass bracelet: buttons from a military uniform. My father's uniform. Joanna's bracelet.

The metal buttons clink as I pick up the band. I rub my thumb over the military insignia, remembering how brightly they shone on my father's jacket, carefully cleaned and polished. My heart leaps at the sight of the tarnished buttons.

"Joanna's been here," I say, glancing around the room.

Pete rests a hand on my shoulder. "At least we know for sure she's in the palace."

"Or she *was* here," Pickpocket says, peering into a glass cabinet.

I smell the faint hint of the lavender wafting from the sheets. Its scent reminds me of the lotion Joanna took from my mother's room the night we left our home. "It was recent," I say, scanning the room.

"Look at these supplies," Pickpocket says. He pulls out his multitool and picks the cabinet lock with ease. Pete joins him, and together, they stash supplies in their rucksacks.

"What do you think you are doing?" Lily says indignantly. "Those are the Professor's supplies."

"Look," Pete says, whirling around to her. "I have an entire city of kids I'm responsible for. We don't have access to supplies like these."

I step away from the cot, noticing the floral scent isn't just on the bedding. Feeling like Mole, I follow the smell. I open the cabinets near the bed. They are full of linens and bandages.

"An entire city of children?" Lily says with surprise. "Why haven't you mentioned this? We must bring them here."

The smell grows stronger as I search a metal rolling cabinet next to the sink. More gadgets and levered devices line the shelves.

"I am not bringing them into Everland," Pete says heatedly. "They're better off in the Lost City."

"But you have to," Lily argues. "I promise you, they will be safe with the other survivors. The Duchess will provide them with everything that Everland can't: shelter, food, and medical care. You can't stay here. It's not safe."

Beneath one of the two steel sinks, something rumbles. Pete grabs his dagger from its sheath and places an arm up as if to protect the rest of us.

"Who's there?" he demands.

Stepping in front of him, I stoop by the doors. The scent of lavender permeates the air. A tiny whimper escapes from below the sink. Slowly, I open the doors.

A small girl hides her face as she wraps her arms tighter around her knees drawn up to her chest. Blisters dot her quivering fingertips.

"Joanna!" I exclaim, pulling my sister from the cupboard and into my arms. My pulse beats against my collarbone, where

Joanna's face rests. Relief washes over me and I swallow the lump in my throat. I bury my nose in her hair and breathe in her floral scent.

My sister's surprised gaze meets mine. She wraps her arms around my neck. Fresh tears stream down her cheeks. She squeezes so tight I can barely breathe, but I don't care. "I knew you'd come for me," she whispers.

With the back of my hand, I brush a tear from my own cheek. "I'm your sister. I'll *always* come for you."

· H O O K ·

ightning paints the black sky in streaks of gold, filling the air with the faint smell of electricity. The flames from the burning buildings cast eerie shadows on the palace walls. Chains rattle as the line of Lost Boys cough on the thick smoke, grumbling among themselves. The Marauders cackle through their masks, prodding them with the barrels of their guns through the palace's gilded doors. The Professor whispers words to the children, squeezing the littlest ones to reassure them.

Smeeth tips his face toward the sky. "A storm is coming, Captain. It could make traveling a bit dicey. Perhaps we should consider postponing until it passes?"

"Storm or not, we leave tonight. I'm not staying one more day in this roach-infested country."

"Beg your pardon, sir," Smeeth says, "but I don't believe the zeppelins will be able to navigate through this weather as it is. Add all these Lost Kids, and our fleet is sure to be doomed."

I slap Smeeth on the shoulder. "Who says we're bringing them?"

His forehead wrinkles. "But, Captain, you promised Jack that you wouldn't harm the children. If we leave them here, they will surely die. There is nothing left of Everland. We've burned it to the ground."

"I am a man of my word. I'll keep my promise to my brother. I won't lay a single finger on them," I say, admiring the Professor's stunned expression as she takes in the swarm of sniveling Lost

Boys. It baffles me, this *feeling* for children that she seems to possess.

Frown lines form on Smeeth's brow, but he says nothing more.

"Hook!" the Professor shouts, storming toward me. She wears a clear hazmat face mask. Behind the transparent shield I see her perfect ruby lips frown. Her eyes shimmer above her tear-streaked cheeks. "Where did you find these children? There are over a hundred of them."

"Let's just say a little birdie let me know of a vast underground Lost City, brimming with boys who needed a mommy." I jut out my lip in a sarcastic pout.

"You know they don't have the antibodies. They won't give you the cure. Why are you taking them as your prisoners?" the Professor says.

"You're right, Professor. They, too, will succumb to the Horologia virus. However, that doesn't mean they can't be useful. Among these boys may just be the one who will get me what I need."

"What more do you need? You have my daughter," the Professor shouts.

"Incentive," I say, waving a soldier over. "The final piece to entice Gwen to turn herself over to me: her entire family."

"Mum!" the little boy yells as he breaks free from the guard's hold.

The Professor's eyes grow wide and I'm certain she recognizes that young voice. She spins, drops to her knees, and clutches the boy in her arms as he nearly bowls her over, running into her embrace. "Mikey, you're alive!" She holds him at arm's length and brushes his hair from his eyes. "Are you hurt?"

His bottom lip quivers as he shakes his head.

The Professor pulls him into her arms again. "Oh, Mikey, I missed you so much."

I nod to the guard, and before she has a chance to notice, Mikey is snatched from her.

"No! No! Let him go!" she screams, racing after the guard as he pushes the boy through the palace doors. Guards block the way and the Professor attempts to chase after the Marauder. Mikey's wails become faint as the door slams shut.

The Professor whirls around and her eyes drill through me with fury. She marches up to me and shoves me, but she is smaller than I am, and I hardly budge. "Give me my son back now!" she screams.

I half expect her anger to rekindle the fear I felt as a child, but I feel oddly numb. "Once Gwen surrenders and you give me the cure, I will release both your daughter and your son," I assure her.

"It could take years to find a cure!" she yells.

"Perhaps," I say smugly. "But I suspect you'll hurry the process along. We're leaving tonight, and the Darlings are coming with me."

She presses her lips together and steals a glance toward the other Lost Boys. "And what about them? What are your intentions with the other boys? They can't help you."

"That is not your concern," I say, smiling as widely as I can. I nod to Smeeth. "Take her back to the lab to get her supplies. I want it packed and ready to go within the hour. We'll meet in the palace courtyard before our departure."

"Come along, Professor," Smeeth says, gently taking her arm.

"I'll never come with you!" She glares at me but allows Smeeth to guide her back inside Buckingham Palace.

"Captain, what do we do with the boys?" another Marauder asks.

I can't wipe the grin off of my face as I watch the kids peer at me with frightened eyes. "Lock them up in the ballroom! And make sure they're comfortable—they'll be staying in Everland for a while."

· G W E N ·

Joanna brushes away a stray tear from her face. "Gwen, I'm so sorry."

I look at her, puzzled. This has nothing to do with anything she's done. I'm to blame. "Joanna, you did nothing wrong. This isn't your fault."

"I didn't mean what I said," she says.

My chest aches to see her like this.

"You're a great sister. The closest thing I have to a mother since, well, since Mum disappeared. I shouldn't have been so cruel to you." She wipes her eyes with the back of her hand.

Hugging her as tight as my arms possibly can, I hold back the flood of tears that threaten to spill over. "You are the best sister, too," I say. I wipe a tear from her cheek.

"Where's Mikey?" she asks.

I rub my thumb over her cheek, wishing I could wipe away all evidence of the toll Everland and the war have taken on her. "He's safe," I say brightly, trying to hide the doubt brewing in my gut. I shouldn't have left him. He should be here with Joanna and me. "Mikey's fine!" I say again, more for myself than for my sister.

She sighs and the tension in her shoulders slips. "I was sure the Marauders were going to find him. I should have blown the candle out after you left. It's my fault they came. I'm sorry, Gwen. I should've listened to you."

My heart clenches and I avert my gaze from her. I am the one who was supposed to protect my sister, and yet she was kidnapped on my watch. If it wasn't for Joanna's quick thinking, Mikey would've been taken, too. "No, it's my fault. You and Mikey were my responsibility, and I left you alone."

Joanna frowns and wraps her arms around my waist. "Don't blame yourself, Gwen. Without you, who knows where Mikey and I might have ended up? We could have been caught by Hook a long time ago."

Her words do little to soothe the sick feeling in my stomach.

"Your hands look better," I say, changing the subject. Taking Joanna's hand in mine, I inspect her fingers. Although her nails are still black with decay, the sores are not as angry-looking as they were when I last saw her. They have been carefully cleaned and a thick ointment has been applied to them. "Who did this?" I ask, slipping her button bracelet onto her wrist.

"I don't know," Joanna says, shaking her head. "When I woke up, my hands already looked like this."

Turning to Lily, I ask, "Did the Professor ever tell you her name?"

Fidgeting with the chain around her neck, Lily shakes her head. "I've always just called her Professor."

"Not to interrupt you, guys," Pickpocket says, leaning up against a counter with his arms folded, "but as noble as this Professor sounds, we are in Hook's lab. That codfish could walk in at any time now. We have Bella and Joanna. I don't care where these safer lands are, but I think we should gather the rest of the Lost Boys and head that way now before we get caught."

"What about the Professor?" I say, my voice shaking. "We can't just leave her here. She was waiting for me. We have to bring her with us!"

"Look, Gwen, we've done what we came here to do," Pickpocket says. "And Doc seems to believe that antidote he gave Bella is the cure. We don't need her."

"But look at the children she has helped. And what about Jack?" I ask. "He could be here, too."

Pete drops his gaze to the floor and bites his bottom lip. He hesitates before responding. "We don't know that Jack is here, and we can't risk our lives trying to find out," Pete says. "As for the Professor, Lily can let her know she's found you, and she can flee the first chance she has."

Lily's brows draw together as she looks at her watch again. Her gaze shoots back toward the lab door. "Something must be wrong. She's never this late. The Professor usually meets me by now to sneak the kids out of the lab."

Standing, I place my hands on the hilts of my daggers. "I'm staying. The Professor deserves the chance to be rescued after all she's done. The rest of you go, and take Joanna with you."

Shouts erupt beyond the lab door.

"Back to your cage," a harsh voice says, chortling. "Ahem, I mean lab. Captain's orders are to bring you and your supplies to the courtyard when you're done."

A woman protests loudly as keys jingle in the door lock.

"Get back to the basement!" I whisper, pushing Joanna toward the staircase. We hurry down the steps and through the sliding cabinet. Pete moves the cupboard in place, plunging us into darkness. Next to me, Joanna shakes in a fit of tremors. I wrap an arm around her. Muffled shouts rise from behind the wood panel and after a minute, the room goes quiet. Listening intently, I hear nothing at first, but then the cabinet shudders. I push Joanna behind me and grab both of my daggers. In the blackness, Pete's daggers let out a metallic scraping sound as he releases them from their sheaths. The click of a gun being cocked to my left assures me that Pickpocket is nearby.

The cabinet slides open. My heart beats rapidly as I get ready to throw my blade, but I don't get the chance. Both Pete and Pickpocket storm into the crematorium, knocking the intruder down to the floor. Lily bolts to Pete's side, trying to pry him off the newcomer.

"Wait!" Lily shouts.

"Who are you?" Pete growls, his daggers aimed at the figure.

"The Pro . . . Professor!" a familiar female voice says, fright evident in her tone.

I peek through the opening, brushing a loose curl from my face. My breath catches when I see her eyes, eyes that are a mirror image of my little sister's. For a fraction of a second, I wonder if I'm dreaming.

"Mum?" I ask in disbelief.

My mother stares at me and covers her mouth with a hand as she gasps. "Gwen?"

I drop my blades, sending them clattering onto the floor, and push my way through Pete and Pickpocket and into my mother's arms. Joanna·follows behind me. Hot tears rain down my face. I inhale, and her sweet lavender scent consumes me, lifting from me a heavy cloak of despair.

My mother kisses my cheek, and then Joanna's. "My girls! Look at you!"

I brush a tear away with the back of my hand.

"Gwen, is it really you?" she asks, lifting my chin. My mother breathes a sigh of relief, brushing the loose strands of hair out of my face with her hand. "How did you get here?" The rough fabric of her lab-coat sleeve brushes against my cheek. I notice the emblem of the Marauders on the lapel. My relief gives way to anger as my heart pounds.

"I came to save Joanna." My words spill sharply, a hundred questions piercing my thoughts. "You're the Professor?" I ask.

"Why didn't you come get us?" Joanna demands, her voice laced with venom.

I place my hand on Joanna's shoulder and she stiffens.

Pain etches my mother's face as she draws her hands back. "Ever since the war, I've been a prisoner. When the bombs destroyed the lab, everyone evacuated except my team and me. I was moving the refrigerated locker that held the Horologia virus to the fallout bunker when the ceiling collapsed. The Marauders found me pinned beneath a concrete slab. I was imprisoned with other survivors the soldiers captured. When the adults started dying off because of exposure to the virus, the Captain brought me from the holding cells, knowing my background in researching biological weapons. It became my job to try to find a cure for the virus. I couldn't leave, not without knowing you kids were okay. I thought about you every single day," my mother says.

"You knew about the virus," I say, accusation thick in my voice. "All this time you knew it existed, and you never mentioned it? You were working with the government this whole time?"

My mother's brows lift in surprise. "You were children. There was no reason to worry you with what my job entailed or who I worked for. I did it to protect you."

She reaches for Joanna and me. Joanna jerks away and wraps her arms around my waist, burying her face in my chest. I hold her close, listening to her sniffle through tears. My heart cracks with each of Joanna's sobs, hairline fissures growing into fractured hunks of tissue and sorrow. "We mourned your death every single day," I say, fixing my gaze on my mother.

"It doesn't explain why you stayed here," my sister says angrily. "You abandoned us! Why didn't you come for us?"

My mother closes her eyes and covers her mouth, holding back a sob. "At first, I tried everything I could do to escape," she says. Another flash of pain erupts across her pale face. She shakes her head, taking in a breath, and her eyes meet mine. She is calm and composed now, setting aside her own emotions. Just like in the days before the war, she is the image of stability, strength, and fortitude. Everything I have tried to be.

"I only discovered the secret room and tunnels six months ago. By then I knew my best chance of finding you was to stay here. Hook was bringing a dozen children in every few days. I hoped it was only a matter of time before you would show up. If

I had left to find you and Hook captured you, I would never have known."

Unable to take my stare off the emblem on my mother's lapel, a profound ache ensnares me. "What about Dad? He never came for us either," I say in a soft voice.

My mother refuses to meet my gaze. "I haven't heard from him since the day he was deployed. I can only assume that he's . . . that he didn't make it."

My heart splinters into tiny, searing shards. Although I knew the truth, something, a fragment of hope inside me, willed for him to be alive. But if my mother believes he's gone, what hope is there that he made it at all? Joanna turns her head into my shoulder and weeps.

"I think we should go now," Pickpocket says, gently patting my sister on the back. "We've got the girls back and the Professor. Let's get out of this hole."

"Agreed," Pete says. "We need to start back to the Lost City."

Pete starts to turn toward the infirmary and we follow him, but my mother does not move.

"Mum?" I ask.

The blood drains from her face.

She covers her mouth. "Did you say the Lost City?"

"Yes, that's where we're from," Pete says, gesturing to Pickpocket. Pete's brow furrows as the alarm in her expression seems to register. "What do you know?" he asks urgently.

My mother closes her eyes tightly and shakes her head. "The Marauders have captured the Lost City."

"No, that's impossible," Pete argues.

My mother's hands tremble. "Hook has apprehended someone who knew the Lost City's location. They took everyone they could find and now they're burning down what's left of Everland so that there is nowhere for anyone to hide. The Lost Boys are locked in the ballroom, and he's gathering all of us in the courtyard to leave Everland tonight."

The muscles in Pickpocket's face harden, his cheeks flushing bright red. "No one knows where the Lost City is. Who could have told him?" he asks through clenched teeth.

"I don't know," my mother says. "They didn't tell me anything else."

"It doesn't matter who told him," Pete says. "We're getting those kids back."

An icy chill races up my spine. I feel like I've fallen into the Thames during the dead of winter. I place a hand on Pete's arm. He turns to me, his gaze sizzling with anger.

"Mikey," I say, his name catching in my throat. *You look after my brother and I'll keep my eye on yours.* Dozer's words come flooding back to me. I briefly hope that Dozer and Mikey escaped, but then where would I begin to search for him?

"Mikey's here with the others," my mother says.

"What are we going to do? How are we going to get him back?" Joanna asks, worry lining her doll-like face.

Pete sheathes his dagger. "We are not abandoning any of the Lost Boys. Pickpocket and Mole will come with me. Lily, you take everyone else north." He faces me, his jaw rigid. "I'm rescuing all of the Lost Boys, Mikey included."

"I'm coming with you," I insist.

"As are we," says Doc from behind us. He watches us, weariness mixed with steadfast determination masking his face. Behind him, Mole smiles next to an ashen but alert Bella. I feel my jaw drop, and I'm astonished by her sudden burst of energy. I wrap my arms around her, burying my nose in her hair.

"Bella?" I ask. "You're okay!"

"I'm much better than a half hour ago," she says, snaking her arms around my waist.

Lily steps toward Doc. She glances at Bella's hands. Each finger is neatly wrapped in thin bandages, allowing Bella to slip her medicated gloves back onto her hands.

"Nice job, Doc," Lily says, smiling shyly at him.

Another grin grows on Doc's face. "Fortunately, Bella's received great medical care. I merely followed up, although I haven't ever seen her bounce back so quickly. I think this new formula with Gwen's antibodies is the real deal, but we never would have been able to help her if you hadn't kept her alive."

Lily drops her stare to the floor and she blushes. "It was my pleasure."

I see a flash of admiration in Doc's eyes as he smiles timidly at Lily. My heart swells with hope for the brokenhearted Lost Boy. Since he has loved and lost once before, I wonder if another could mend his heart. Another like his first love, Gabrielle.

Pete, noticing the flirtatious exchange, glowers at Doc as he helps my mother to her feet. She looks resolved.

"With all those children here, I should stay," my mother says. "Some of them may need medical attention."

"No, Mum!" I say. My stomach grows sick at the thought of leaving her behind. "We've just found you. I am not losing you again. Besides, if they've captured Mikey, I should be here for him. He's my responsibility!"

My words echo in the concrete room. *My responsibility!* My mother shakes her head. I realize that the obligation to care for him is no longer mine. Guilt tugs at my heart, and I look away. My mother tilts my chin up so that my eyes meet her.

"It's not your fault, Gwen," she says, as if reading my mind. She places a hand on either side of my face. "Joanna and Mikey are lucky to have you. You've gone beyond what any fifteen-year-old girl should have to do. You kept them safe in circumstances when I couldn't."

My eyes burn with unshed tears. I can't bring myself to look at her. "I lost Joanna, and now Mikey. I've failed them both."

"I failed *you*," my mother says. "I should have found a way to come home. This is my fault, and I intend to make it right. We *will* get Mikey back, and we'll be a complete family again."

The image of my father's military tags lying scattered among the debris in the café comes back to me. I finally meet my mother's eyes. "We'll never be complete." A stray tear rolls down my cheek.

Joanna twirls her bracelet around her wrist, drawing my mother's attention. She frowns, her stare set on the copper buttons. Tears pool in my mother's eyes. "I miss him, too," she says.

My mother reaches into the pocket of her lab coat and pulls out my father's military tags. She slips them over my head and I feel the cold metal tickle my neck. "Where did you find these?" I ask, holding the tags between my fingers and half expecting them to disappear.

"He'll always be with us. Always," my mother says. She doesn't answer my question, but it's all I need to feel whole again.

Pete breaks the grief-stricken moment. "I am the leader of the Lost Boys. I can't abandon them," he says matter-of-factly.

My mother gives him a weary smile. "These boys have been under your care long enough. Lily will lead you to where the other children have taken refuge. I'll get the Lost Boys and send them as soon as I can."

"How are you going to get them out?" Pete asks, urgency lacing his voice.

"I'll incapacitate the soldier who comes to retrieve me, and get into the ballroom." She pulls a vial from her pocket and holds it up. "A liquid sedative should take care of him."

"No," I protest again, glancing around. No one speaks. "Pete, we can't leave her to rescue all those kids alone."

Pete stares at the ground, kicking a loose rock with his boot.

"Bella? Doc?" I say. Bella joins Pete and takes his hand. Doc frowns, shaking his head.

"Pickpocket? You can't believe this is the right thing to do," I say.

He shrugs. Next to him, Mole drops his chin to his chest.

"Gwen," my mother says. "Go. I will be all right." She kisses Joanna's cheek and then mine. She turns to Lily. "Be sure they get to Northumberland safely."

"I will, Professor," Lily says with a nod.

My mother starts to shut the steel door, but hesitates. "I love you girls. I never stopped waiting for you."

A noise outside the lab startles my mother.

"Go! Get out of here now!" she says, pushing us toward the opening.

Joanna shakes her head, her eyes wide with fear. "No, I'm not leaving without you!"

Bella, Lily, and the Lost Boys bolt through the opening, but I'm frozen as I watch Joanna back toward the staircase to the lab.

"I won't lose you again!" she says.

The door to the lab swings open with a metallic clang and deep male voices call for the Professor.

"There's no time! Get out of here!" My mother tries to push Joanna toward the opening, but she throws herself to the floor, reminding me of a tantruming child. Taking her by the hand, my mother tries to drag her to the door, but to no avail.

"I won't go without you!" Joanna shouts.

My mother peers up at me with terror in her eyes. She nods. "Go, Gwen."

I shake my head. "No!"

My mother leaves Joanna's side and starts to push me toward the opening. My eyes lock on Joanna's, imploring her to come with me, but her stare is resolute; she's determined to stand her ground.

My mother shoves me through the opening. "I love you, Gwen." With those final words, she hurriedly closes the door, and the only sound I hear, other than my rapid breath, is the cabinet rolling back into place.

· HOOK ·

The lab is empty. Professor Darling and the girl are nowhere to be found. There's only one other place they could be. I storm down the flight of stairs to the crematorium. When I reach the bottom level, I find the Professor sitting against a cabinet. Her daughter sits in her lap while she reads from a book. Joanna's face erupts in a bright smile as her mother tells the story with exaggerated hand motions. The dark leather spine reads *The Clockmaker and the Midnight Elves* in elegant script.

My knees nearly buckle beneath me as a long-forgotten memory consumes me, striking me speechless. Jack's father, my stepfather, who once cared for me as if I were his own, read to us from his favorite collection of stories in the castle library. It has been boarded up and locked away since his death, and I hadn't thought about it until just now.

The Professor, still unaware of my presence, reads about tiny elves that sneak into an old clockmaker's workshop to restore a magical grandfather clock. I feel a flare of jealousy for all the times my mother didn't read to me as a child.

I storm over to her, ready to wrench her from the floor. Just as I place my hand on her arm, her daughter dashes from her lap. I see the Professor reach for her pocket, and something silver glints in the lamplight. Swiftly I grip her other wrist with my free hand, just as she's about to plunge a needle into my chest. My fingers squeeze, digging into her soft flesh. She cries in pain, sending the needle smashing to the floor.

"Story time is over!" I shout.

· GWEN ·

No! No! No!" I scream as Pete drags me from the closet and into the infirmary.

Lily carefully shuts the steel door and follows us into the room along with everyone else.

I rip myself from Pete's grasp. "I'm not leaving them!"

"Stop it!" he yells, a finger pointed into my face. "You're going to get us all killed carrying on like that."

"Pete, you can't possibly believe my mother can save all of those kids on her own," I protest. "My entire family is locked in that palace. We have to save them."

Pete returns to the closet and leans against the door, his ear pressed up against the steel. "You're absolutely right, and no offense, but I trust your mother about as much as I trust Hook. Anyone who aligns themselves with a Marauder is a traitor."

The hair on the back of my neck bristles. "My mother is not a traitor! You heard what she said. She's willing to risk her life and stay here to rescue the entire group of Lost Boys."

Pete says nothing.

"Are you listening to me?" I ask, tugging his arm and pulling him around to face me.

"Not really," he says, annoyed. "I'm trying to figure out if the soldiers have left yet."

I lean my cheek against the cold metal. Holding my breath, I listen for the deep, husky voices belonging to the Marauders. Their words are nothing but murmurs behind the steel door. I strain to make sense of their muted voices. My mother responds in loud protest. Finally, a heavy door slams shut and the adjacent room is silent.

"They must have taken them from the lab," Pete says.

"Pete, what are we going to do?" I ask.

"*We* are not doing anything," he says, waving a hand in a gesture that appears to indicate he is speaking of the entire group. "Doc, Pickpocket, Mole, and I will rescue the boys. You and Bella are going with Lily."

"What about my mother? Joanna and Mikey?" I protest.

"I'll do my best to get them out, along with the rest of the Lost Boys, but she's been sending kids north for months. She'll find a way to get herself and your siblings to the safe lands," Pete says. "But there's no way she can get all of those Lost Kids out on her own, even if she isn't conspiring with Hook. I'm not leaving without those boys."

"And I'm not leaving my family behind," I say, clenching my teeth. "Besides, even if you manage to rescue the Lost Boys, who knows what Hook will do to my family?"

"Look, if I can, I will try to get your family out, too. But I'm not going to risk *you* being captured. You are the key to curing the virus. We need you!" Pete shouts, startling me. His expression softens as he takes in my surprise. He reaches for both of my hands. "*I need you,*" he says, stumbling through those three words in a quiet voice. His eyes meet mine. "I've lost almost everything important to me. My parents, my sister—and I nearly lost Bella." He glances at Bella, and she gives him a shy smile. His eyes turn back to me. They are marked with worry. "I can't lose you, too."

I ignore the tingle in my chest at the words *I need you* echoing in my mind. "You're not leaving me behind. Pickpocket, you have to be the voice of reason here," I object.

"Better get this door unlocked again," Pickpocket says without looking at me. He struggles with the lock before it gives a distinct click. Opening the door, he peeks through the gap. He clears his throat. "The coast is clear," he says, sliding the cabinet open.

Lily glances at me, grimaces, marches up to us, and paces. The bent metal chain on the pocket watch clinks with every stride. "Gwen is right. You would be outnumbered at least twofold even if the Lost Boys were capable of fighting for themselves. You're going to need our help. It is unreasonable to believe that the Professor and a few Lost Boys can take on an entire army of Marauders and lead the escape of . . . how many Lost Boys did you say?" she asks, halting in place.

"A little more than a hundred," Pete says.

Lily shakes her head. "Her Majesty's train was meant only for her, her family, and her personal guards. Two dozen at most. The train will not hold all of the Lost Boys. It was constructed with a single car intended for a quick escape. They'd have to hunker down here too long. They'll surely be caught. We will have to find another way to get everyone out of Everland," she says, pacing again.

"Blast!" Pete says, kicking the steel door.

"Wait! What if . . . ?" I waver, thinking of the numerous things that could go wrong. Biting down on my lip, I weigh the pros and cons. It'll be risky, but it'll ensure that everyone escapes. Everyone . . . but me.

"You have an idea, Gwen?" Doc presses.

"It might be a crazy suggestion, but what about Hook's zeppelins?" I ask.

"Yes!" Lily says excitedly. "The *Jolly Roger* is sitting at the far end of the royal gardens along with the rest of his fleet. His ship is certainly large enough to accommodate your group."

"Won't there be soldiers protecting it?" Mole asks, wringing his hands.

Pickpocket pulls his revolver from its holster and spins the chamber, checking to see if it is full. "Oh, we'll take care of them."

Pete places both of his palms on my cheeks and plants a wet kiss on my forehead. "You're brilliant, Gwen Darling!" Pete exclaims. My face grows warm, but no one else seems uncomfortable about his public display of affection.

"If Hook's intentions are to leave tonight, more than likely his men will be preparing the zeppelins for departure. That would be the optimal time to rescue the Lost Boys. They will be in the holding cells constructed within the ballroom. That's where they took me when I was captured," Lily says.

"We'll head there straightaway," Pete says.

"I'm going after my mother," I say, placing my hands on the hilts of my daggers. "Can you get me into the courtyard?" I ask Lily.

Lily's gaze flits from me to Pete and back. "Yes, but it could be dangerous. I have no idea how many soldiers will be accompanying Hook."

"I don't care," I say. "I'm the one Hook wants. He won't hurt me—he needs me alive."

Doc regards me for a moment. "You're up to something, aren't you. What's your plan?"

I shake my head. If they knew, they'd never agree to let me go. I turn to Lily. "When can we leave?"

"No, Gwen, it's too risky," Pete says, worry creasing his forehead.

I face him, unblinking. "I am not leaving Everland without my family."

Pete steps toward me, his stare holding mine. "I promised to get your family back to you unharmed. You've held up your end of the bargain and helped Bella; now it's my turn to hold up mine."

I fold my arms, indignant and attempting to be unmoved by his show of regard.

"Technically, you already held up your end of the bargain. You helped get Joanna back," I say, raising my brows. "It wasn't your fault she refused to come with us. My mother and brother were never part of the deal."

"I'll go with her," Bella says, joining me on my right and wrapping her gloved fingers in mine. I wait for her to wince, expecting the sores on her hand to send shooting pain through her, but she only smiles.

Bella has already risked her life for me once. This time, I cannot guarantee her safety. I start to object, shaking my head in protest, but Bella's warning expression forces me to reconsider. If I deny her, she'll follow me anyway. As stubborn as she is, I make a silent vow to get her to safety the first chance I get, or die trying.

"There's a tunnel entrance not far from the *Jolly Roger*. It won't be easy, but it will give us access to the palace courtyard," Lily says. She glances down at Bella. "I think with Bella's help we can get you in there. Once you have your family, we'll leave Everland . . . for good."

Suddenly, the weight of jealousy slips as I am filled with gratitude.

"Perfect!" I say with feigned enthusiasm, knowing my feet will never board the zeppelin. "You boys search for the holding cells. When you find the Lost Boys, meet Lily at the *Jolly Roger*. She may need Pickpocket's help to jimmy the lock."

Pickpocket replaces the revolver in his holster and laces his fingers, cracking every knuckle. "Piece of cake."

Pete shakes his head. "I don't like it. I won't let you face Hook without me."

"Pete's right," Doc says. "One of us should go with you."

"I'll be fine," I say. I turn to Pete. "You be careful. And don't get caught."

Pete takes both of my hands in his. He hesitates, gazing into my eyes, and for a moment I'm certain he's going to kiss me. My pulse beats wildly and my breath quickens. I don't know if my racing heartbeat is because of anticipation or fright. The pause seems to last forever, and just when I'm sure his lips are going to touch mine, he gives me a playful nudge.

"You and I, we're Lost Kids. Neither of us will be caught," he says, staring at his boots.

My heart shrinks and I feel my smile slip.

A hand rests on my shoulder. I turn to see Doc's resigned expression. "Be careful," he says, patting me on the shoulder.

Trying to shake my disappointment, I wrap my arms around Doc's neck. "Thank you for helping me save Joanna," I whisper into his ear. I feel the muscles in his face pull up into a smile against my cheek before he releases me.

"It's my pleasure," Doc says. "Saving people, it's what I do, and I will always be there when you need me."

I release him, grateful for his offer. I've grown fond of Doc and feel indebted to him for his help. I know I'll never be able to repay him or any of the Lost Boys.

"We should get going," I say.

Bella follows Lily as Pickpocket, Doc, and Mole step through the opening and into the lab. I start to turn, but Pete grabs my elbow and pulls me into a bear hug.

"Please, Gwen. I need to know you will be safe. Promise me you're not going to do anything dangerous," he says quietly into my ear.

Safe is a word I have not known in a very long time. The weight of responsibility, the burden of being the one in charge, threatens to drop from my shoulders, and the little girl within me fights to break free of the bonds I've placed upon her. My eyes well up with tears as I rest my cheek against his chest, hearing his steady heartbeat. Silently, I admonish myself for being so childish, so easily moved to tears, when Pete pulls back from me to look me in the eye.

"Gwen, I—" He stops himself abruptly.

"Yes, Pete?" I ask, trying to steady my own pulse.

He purses his lips, as if struggling with what to say next. "You're the bravest girl . . . no, you're the bravest woman I know."

The word *woman* settles over me like a brand-new coat: unfamiliar but comfortable, soft, and warm.

With my sixteenth birthday coming, I consider the implied sophistication that comes with being referred to as a woman. Suddenly, I feel self-conscious. I consider that it's still been too long since I've last bathed. And that my hair is one tangled knot these days. My dirt-stained hand rests on Pete's chest with fingernails that are broken, cracked, and filthy. Briefly, I wonder if Pete is right, if a woman does lie beneath the mask of grime that covers me; grime that belongs to Everland.

"Pete, any day now," Pickpocket says from inside the lab.

I drop my hand from Pete's chest, but before it falls, he places his on mine. "Be happy, Gwen. Only think happy thoughts. If things don't go right, if something happens to me, get out of Everland. Forget about today, forget about me. Just . . . just be happy."

Wiping away a tear from my cheek, I give him a disingenuous nod. I struggle with Pete's words. *Be happy.* Finding Joanna and my mother made me happy, but now . . . now the prospect of having my family together does not seem to be enough. Without Pete and the other Lost Boys, it'll never be enough.

Pete briskly turns and steps inside the lab, pulling the steel door shut behind him. My pulse races and the world seems to slow down. My heart feels as if it is spiraling, a bomb plummeting to earth, uncertainty eating a hole in my gut.

"Wait!" I call, forcing the words out as a heavy sensation chokes me. Pete stares through the cracked door with piercing green eyes. Eyes I know I will never see again if I go through with my plan.

"Pete?" I say, my voice cracking. "Please don't die."

Pete gives me a dazzling smile and bows. "To die will be an awfully big adventure." He blows me a kiss and pulls the heavy door shut with a metallic clank, leaving me alone in the dark.

· GWEN ·

The dimly lit walls close in on me and the air feels thin. I gasp as a swell of energy surges through me. I race into the infirmary. Bella and Lily are gathered together, excitedly exchanging conversation, sometimes talking over each other.

Gripping Lily's elbow, I pull her to attention. "I don't feel right about this. We can't let them go alone," I say, breathing rapidly. "What if they get caught?"

"You can't worry about him," she says in a stern voice.

"Him?" I ask.

Lily folds her arms. "You're concerned about Pete."

My breath catches, caught between denial and truth. I drop my gaze. She's right, but it's more than just that. I'll never know if he makes it out alive.

As if reading my mind, she places a soft hand on my arm. "They'll be okay. Those boys are the bravest I have met. Smart, too."

The simple gesture and the confident tone in her voice curbs the edge of my anxiety. Taking a final glance up at the steel door, I nod. "You're right. We stick to the plan."

Lily takes my hand into hers, intertwining her gloved fingers with mine. She gives my hand a reassuring squeeze. "Come on. Let's rescue your family."

"So how are we getting into the palace courtyard?" I ask.

"You're probably not going to like this plan." Bella smiles, her complexion glowing with a new healthy radiance she did not have earlier. She links her arm in mine. "It's time for the Lost Girl to learn how to fly."

Lily looks at me with unblinking, wide eyes. "Are you sure about this? If Hook captures you, we can't come back to rescue you. There are too many children's lives at risk to stall our departure."

"Don't worry about that. I'm going to give him *exactly* what he wants," I say, articulating each word.

Bella shakes her head. "I hope you know what you're doing."

Soon enough, we are trudging through murky water in a dark tunnel. The smell of damp dirt fills the narrow passage as I duck beneath a low ceiling. The intertwined tree roots give the illusion of lace. Lily takes the lead while I follow, Bella close behind me. Water seeps into my leather boots. Unlike the carefully engineered royal tunnels, the muddy channel feels more like an underground animal burrow than a passageway. I lumber on, trying to keep myself upright while my shoes sink into the muck.

Lily, on the other hand, travels with ease, her long, dark hair swinging behind her. She marches forward, each step sure and steady. Her slender hands grip the skirt of her sari, holding it above the waterline. The metal chain around her waist tinkles in the cavern like the ringing of miniature bells.

Thunder rumbles ahead. A rusty old ladder leaning against a rocky alcove appears from the shadowed darkness; a small hole above it opens to a stormy sky. The flash of lightning illuminates the passage for a moment before plunging us into the dim light of Lily's lantern.

"This leads into the gardens behind the palace. Follow the tree line toward the building," Lily shouts over the crash of thunder. "It will take you to the northwest corner."

"What about you?" I ask, my eyes fixed on hers.

Frowning, Lily nods. "I'll be taking a nearby passageway just to the west. It ends several meters from the *Jolly Roger*. I'll sneak aboard and prepare it for departure. When Pete, the Lost Boys, Bella, and your family arrive, we'll leave for Northumberland."

Pete, Lost Boys, Bella, and my family. No mention of me. She knows my plan, my secret. I'm sure of it. My chest wells with gratitude as she smiles weakly at me, acknowledging the unspoken words between us.

I nod. "So how are we getting inside to the courtyard?"

Another bolt streaks the sky, lighting Bella's face. "That's where I come in. We're scaling the walls."

My eyes dart toward Lily. "Scaling the walls? Of the palace?" I ask in disbelief.

"It's the only way in without drawing the attention of the guards," Lily says. "There are soldiers guarding every entrance."

I peer up at the darkness beyond the opening. Lightning rakes across the midnight sky.

"The only trouble will be traveling in the darkness," Lily says. "They'll spot you right away with a lamp. With the cloud cover it'll be hard to scale the wall without the moonlight."

The corners of Bella's mouth turn up and her blue eyes sparkle in the lamplight. "And that's why you need me here. How do you think I travel by the rooftops at night? Lily, can you dim the lantern?"

Lily turns the brass knob, and the hiss of gas quiets until only a small flame remains. Bella's face is shadowed in the dark, but even in the minimal light, I can see her chin tilted up toward the opening in the ceiling. Another roll of thunder rumbles the earth.

"Watch this," Bella says. She pulls something from her pocket and blows a breath across the palm of her hand. Lightning brightens the cavern again. This time the air is filled with a metallic glitter, sparkling like the brilliant gold rays of a sunrise on a clear morning. The fine powder shimmers and floats to the ground.

"Gold dust," Lily says, surprised.

"Pixie dust," I correct.

Lily turns the lanterns back up and the floor sparkles in the dust's luminescence.

Bella's expression is bright with excitement. "That storm is close enough that we'll have plenty of lightning to reflect off of the dust. I'll go first and leave a trail for Gwen to follow."

Lily whistles. "That's bloody brilliant!"

Bella grins and starts up the ladder. "Come on, Gwen. It's time for your first lesson."

"Lesson?" I ask.

She winks, her long lashes fluttering like the wings of a butterfly. "I wasn't kidding when I said I was going to teach you how to fly."

"But you don't have your wings," I say.

Bella shrugs. "I don't need wings for this adventure."

Hesitantly, I follow her. I prop my elbows on the muddy ground and pull myself out of the narrow opening. We find ourselves near a small grove of trees. Two soldiers guard the garden entrance into the palace. Across the vast overgrown lawn in the far distance, torchlight surrounds a large silver zeppelin that hovers above a wooden ship fitted with propellers. A long ramp leads to the door, and dozens of soldiers are carrying crates and boxes into the vehicle. Other smaller zeppelins surround it.

"That must be the *Jolly Roger*," Bella says, pointing to the largest ship, which is adorned with a skull-and-crossbones figurehead.

The faint smell of smoke and burnt wood carries on a cool breeze. A crack of thunder bursts through the air, followed by another bolt of lightning, casting the smoke-and-cloud-filled sky in an orange haze. Bella must smell it, too. She turns, facing the palace.

Beyond the palace walls, the city is ablaze.

Everland is on fire.

Bella watches the burning city and her bottom lip turns up in a pout, but she says nothing. A heavy sense of sorrow hangs in the air, mixing with ash as the city burns. The last thread of hope inside of me that believed England would one day be restored snaps. There is nothing left of London. All that remains is Everland, a city of sorrow, destruction, and embers. Although my heart severs in two, I remind myself of Northumberland, a light in the midst of despair.

"Ready?" I ask.

Bella nods and leads the way. We follow the line of trees to the northwest corner of the palace, keeping within the shadows. The palace roof towers above us, nearly three stories high.

"Are you sure about this, Bella?" I ask. "It seems so high. You could fall."

"We will both be fine. Trust me," she says with a sly smile.

Another crack of thunder startles me. Bella looks up at me, the light in the sky making her bright eyes appear almost green in its glow. She touches my trembling hands. "We have to hurry before the rain comes. I'll go first and you follow behind."

She crouches down and darts from the trees, paying no attention to the soldiers in the distance. I follow her lead. Bella grabs onto a stone in the wall and climbs effortlessly. When she reaches the top ledge of the building, she grunts as she pulls herself up, but her expression shows no hint of discomfort. She is the healthiest she's been since I've met her.

Bella peers over the ledge. She waves a hand at me, coaxing me to join her. Stepping out of the protective cover of the trees, I sprint toward the wall. When I reach it, I close my eyes and take in a breath. The air smells faintly of rain and electricity. Another burst of lightning brushes the sky, but all I see is the fiery red glow behind my eyelids. A light dusting of flecks falls on my cheeks, reminding me of family trips and playing with my sister and brother in the powder of fresh-falling snow, flakes catching on my lashes.

Slowly, I open my eyes and see specks of gold shimmer on my cheeks, barely within my vision. My jacket and boots glitter in an iridescent display. I blink, staring up the wall of the palace. Dust powders the broken and chipped bricks, revealing ledges large enough to stand or hold on to. Like a treasure map, a gold trail leads to the top of the building where Bella waves, beckoning me in whispered excitement.

"Come on, Gwen. You can do it!" she says.

At first, I hesitate, scanning the face of the wall. Bella's bright blue eyes peer down at me. She radiates with confidence and something else. *Faith*. Faith in *me*.

Trust me, she said. The same words Pete offered me at the start of my journey to Everland, to the palace, and to finding my family.

I follow the gold trail with my eyes. *Pixie dust*, I think. Feeling a smile grow on my face, I curl my fingers over the notches in the stone and climb.

· HOOK ·

Tilting my face to the sky, I blink as a small drop of warm rain splashes my cheek.

"Are you sure you don't want to postpone our departure, Captain?" Smeeth says, watching the soldiers heft boxes into the zeppelins.

Closing my weary eyes, I keep my face turned toward the stormy night. "A year, Smeeth. One whole year, I've been stuck here in Everland. And all for what? Because my mother wanted to rule the world and now . . ." I pause and sigh. "And now it's my chance to be more . . ."

"More than what, Captain?" Smeeth asks.

I turn my gaze toward my ship, the *Jolly Roger*, the only gift from my mother, but so undeserved. She is right. She's always been right. I owe her, but my debt is too large to pay. I will forever be indebted to her unless I finally rid myself of her. "To be more than just a bandit, destroying and stealing, like a thief . . . like a ruthless *pirate*," I say, the word leaving a foul taste. "My mother's pirate!"

But Smeeth is staring past me with a curious expression on his face.

I spin, searching for whatever has drawn his attention. A bolt of lightning races through the night sky. Across the tall, grassy field, beneath the haze of smoke, the shadow of a person clings to the base of the palace, her long hair flapping in the wind. On the roof above her, another figure leans over the ledge. The slight glint of gold flickers on the face of the wall as the sky pulses with electricity. Something in my gut stirs, and I know that the figure on the wall can only be Gwen.

"Smeeth," I say, pulling my night-vision goggles over my eyes, "it appears we have ourselves a few more guests. Take as many men as you need to the rooftop to greet our new arrivals."

"Yes, Captain," Smeeth says before hurrying off.

I clench my fists. The cure is so close I can almost taste it.

Moments later, my soldiers and I head for the ballroom. Footfalls on the stone floor echo through the dark, dank room as I inspect each diminutive cage stuffed with Lost Boys. Small shadows whimper and sniffle behind the cold steel bars. Torches cast a dim light on a group of boys huddling together in the last cage. A guard opens the metal door, the hinges shrieking my arrival. The oldest of the boys lifts his chin, releasing a tearful child from his arms. He lunges toward me, but two large soldiers stop him.

"Let us go!" the boy named Dozer growls.

I ignore his words. A glint in his gaze sparkles when it falls on the smaller, crying boy. I grip the dirty teddy bear in my hand.

"Aw, now, now. There's no reason to cry," I say with sarcastic sympathy in my voice. I hold the bear with an outstretched hand. "Dry those tears, Mikey."

"Stay away from him!" Dozer wriggles in the soldiers' grasp until one guard slaps him across the face and flings him to the ground. Dozer howls as he lands on the floor. Holding his arm, his face etches with pain. "Bloody pirate," he says, spitting through a cut on his lip.

"You Lost Boys try my patience," I say, nodding to a soldier. "Bring the Professor's boy."

Picking Mikey up, the guards follow, slamming the door behind them.

"No!" Dozer says, racing to the door and gripping the steel bars. "Leave him alone!"

"Let me go!" Mikey whines.

The Lost Boys erupt, shouting for Mikey's release.

I address the boys in the cages. "Don't worry, Lost Boys. Once I have the girl, I will leave Everland and you can return to your happy hollow." Turning toward the exit, I take a few steps before pausing. "Or at least what's left of it."

The ballroom door slams shut like the lid of a coffin as I leave behind the noise of protests.

· GWEN ·

Pain shoots through my cramped and bloodied fingers as I grasp the ledge of the palace. My feet slip. A scream threatens to escape, but I grit my teeth as I dangle precariously from the wall. Two tiny hands wrap around my wrists. I turn my gaze toward Bella and blink away the light sprinkles of rain.

"Come on, Gwen," Bella grunts. "Get your feet underneath you."

The sky lights up in a brilliant white flash.

"Right there," Bella says, pointing to the wall. "Put your foot on that stone."

A pile of Bella's gold dust sparkles on a small crevice. I swing my leg, wedging the lip of my boot into the crack, and stand wobbling before catching my balance.

"There you go. You have it. Now pull yourself up," Bella whispers.

I prop my elbows on the ledge and heave myself onto the roof. Tired and breathing heavily, I roll over onto my back and stare at the sky, willing my heart rate to slow. Clouds and smoke span the night, except for one small break barely large enough to reveal two twinkling stars. The irony strikes me, and I decide there is only one thing to do. I wish on the dual stars: one wish for the safety of my family and the other for Pete and the Lost Boys.

"You did it, Gwen," Bella says in whispered enthusiasm. She helps me up; the glow of the rooftop gas lanterns cast dancing shadows on her face. "You really did it."

"I did, didn't I?" I say, still relishing the moment.

Bella nods, her expression bright with excitement. "Just like a true Lost Girl." She reaches in her pocket and holds her hand out to me. "Take this. You earned it, and you're probably going to need it."

Bella pours glittery powder into my open palm. Carefully, I put the dust in my pocket.

"Thanks, Bella."

A crack of thunder slices the air now. When the next flash lights her expression, it changes from excitement to horror. I turn to see what she is staring at.

The door opens. Smeeth and two soldiers step onto the roof. I push Bella behind me and pull out my dagger.

"Well, well, look what we've got here," Smeeth says, his night-vision goggles pulled onto his face. "If it isn't Miss Bella and the Professor's daughter, I presume."

I take Bella by the hand and spin around to run the other direction when another door opens behind us with two more soldiers.

"Don't be frightened," Smeeth says. "We want to have a little chat with you, that's all. No need to run out on us."

"You know I could jump off this building and be gone before you made it halfway here," Bella says with defiance.

Smeeth nods and laughs. "That is true, Miss Bella. But it isn't you we want." Smeeth clasps his hands behind his back. "I'm here for Miss Darling."

I take a step back, protecting Bella with my body. "What do you want, Smeeth?" I ask.

Smeeth turns his face to the sky. "In this bloody weather, a spot of tea would be nice, but alas we will not be attending any parties. It's more of a family get-together. However, don't feel left out, Miss Bella; I'm sure the Captain will find a suitable use for you."

"Run, Bella," I whisper.

Without hesitation, Bella sprints to the ledge. She opens her arms as if they were wings, ready to dive into the nearby tree. She is stopped by two soldiers climbing over the edge of the building. Bella shrinks back with a look of dread as one soldier towers over her. She hurries toward me and wraps her arms around my waist.

"Gold dust," the soldier mumbles, walking toward us with purposeful steps. He rubs his fingers and thumbs together as glittering specks fall to the ground. "Brilliant, really. Had no trouble climbing the wall with the trail you left behind." The soldier crouches and peers at Bella. "Once the Captain is done with you, you'll be showing us where the gold is, little girl. Ain't that right?"

Bella looks at me with a glassy stare.

"You want gold?" I ask, feeling adrenaline course through me. I give Bella a sideways glance and wink. "You can have it." I reach in my pocket and throw the dust into the soldier's face. Bella follows suit, sending her powder into the direction of the other Marauder. They paw at their goggles, attempting to wipe away the dust.

"Brats!" one of the soldiers screams, and stumbles to the ground.

I kick the soldier's shin with the toe of my boot and grab Bella's hand. We start for one of the doors when two more soldiers burst through it, blocking our escape.

Smeeth's dazed expression quickly turns to anger. He pulls his gun from its holster and aims it at Bella and me. "You cheeky scamps! I've had just about enough of your nonsense."

As Smeeth trains his weapon on us, the soldiers move past him, closing in on Bella and me. Bella grabs her slingshot from her belt and turns her back to mine, fending off the advancing men behind me. I hold my dagger, ready for Smeeth and his guards. The Marauders hesitate.

"Ladies, it doesn't have to be this difficult," Smeeth says, still directing his revolver at us.

I search for an escape, but we are surrounded, with nowhere to go except over the eastern wall and into the quad. A wave of nausea rolls over me. I breathe, smelling the scent of ash and smoke.

"This is ridiculous," one of the soldiers says. He snatches Bella and pulls her into him, clutching her arms as she struggles against his hold.

Smeeth steps toward me. His copper gun reflects a flash of lightning as he points the weapon at me.

I seize my second dagger, aiming one at Smeeth's head, the other at his heart.

"I wouldn't do that if I were you," Smeeth says, his stare stone cold.

Gripping my daggers tighter, I feel my blood pulse against the hilts. One flick of my wrist, that's all it would take to plunge the sharp blade in between his eyes, but my stomach churns at the thought. My attention darts from his forehead to his finger wrapped around the revolver trigger.

"You won't hurt me," I say, aiming my dagger at him. "Hook needs me."

Smeeth scowls and steps forward.

"You take one more step and I'll pin your skull to the wall," I say, hoping the slight tremor in my hand doesn't betray me.

Smile lines grow in the corners of Smeeth's mouth. "Now, now. Let's be reasonable. We wouldn't want anyone to get hurt." He pulls the hammer back on his gun and aims it at Bella.

"Drop your weapon," I say, my clenched jaw aching. The hilts of my daggers slip in my sweaty palms, but I keep my aim steady.

Smeeth chuckles, an amused expression on his face. He wipes a mocking tear from his eye. "Or what? Even if you manage to strike me down with your knives, the bullet is always faster than the sword." He places his gun on Bella's temple.

Bella purses her lips and stares at me with ferocity. Although she has put on a brave face, she shudders, and I'm not sure if it's from fear or rage.

"Don't worry about me," she says, gritting her teeth with every word. She nods toward the balcony. "The Lost Boys need you. Your family needs you. Just go!"

"I'm not leaving without you, Bella." I flip one dagger in my hand, its tip aimed at my neck. "Let Bella go, or I'll slit my own throat."

Bella struggles in the soldier's grasp. "Gwen, no!"

Smeeth falters, and the barrel of his gun slips.

Smiling slyly, I squeeze the dagger's hilt. "Ah! Just what I thought. What would your precious Captain do if I died within meters of you? Shoot you? Feed you to his precious crocodiles? Now, put your weapon down."

Smeeth's brows knit together and he drops his revolver, sending it clattering to the floor.

"That's a good boy," I say in a mocking tone. "Let. Bella. Go!"

The Marauder doesn't budge.

I sigh. "Fine. Have it your way," I say, pulling the knife closer in to my throat. Its razor-sharp point bites into my skin. Warm liquid drips down my neck and seeps into the collar of my shirt.

"All right!" Smeeth shouts, holding a hand out.

With the blade stinging my neck, I wait for him to release Bella. My grip slips, but I clench my fist tighter on the dagger's hilt.

Pulling his goggles off, the anxiety on Smeeth's face washes away as his chuckle crescendos into roaring laughter. "Take Bella to the Captain," he shouts.

The Marauder pulls Bella toward the door. She struggles against his grip as a string of profanity spills from her lips.

"No! I said to let her go!" I shout, but I'm too late. Smeeth rushes me. Distracted, I lose my grip on one of the daggers, and it clatters at my feet. Smeeth lunges for me, pinning me against a wall. He grunts as he struggles to wrest the other knife from my hand, crushing my fingers and sending shooting pain up my arm.

Lightning explodes in the sky, blinding me. Beyond the spots in my vision, Smeeth leans his face close to mine, glowing with triumph. He pants, his breath brushing my face, smelling as foul as a cesspool.

"I've been stuck in this rotten city for a year. I am not about to let a little girl snatch away my ticket out of Everland just because she musters a moment of martyrdom."

"And I'm not about to let a traitorous Englishman have the cure!"

I shove him from me. Smeeth hardly budges but stumbles back just enough for me to wrench my hand holding the knife free from him. He lunges for me again, trying to grab the knife back, but he falls against me. The dagger plunges into his belly. Pain erupts in his dark eyes when the knife buries itself in his stomach. Sticky blood seeps onto my shirt as he collapses into my arms. Horror-stricken, my pulse runs hot beneath my skin.

Smeeth's eyes glaze over, and he crashes to his knees. He shrieks in agony as he wrenches out the weapon protruding from his stomach before dropping it.

My breaths come quick and gasping. It was an accident, wasn't it? He charged me, didn't he? Or was it the other way around?

Smeeth groans once more, his breath heaving before he becomes still. Panicked, I search for Bella. She wrestles with her captor, landing a knee in the soldier's groin. He crumbles to the floor. Bella launches violent kicks into her captor's gut as he lies moaning.

I snatch up the dagger I had dropped earlier and dash toward Bella. "Get ready to jump," I shout in Bella's ear, jabbing my blade toward an advancing soldier.

Her body stiffens. "It must be at least a three-story drop; there's no way we'll make it."

Shoving back the mounting anxiety, I glance at the ledge and take a step toward it. "We can do it," I say over the roar of thunder.

Bella shakes her head, her wet fringe sticking to her face. "No, Gwen, it's too high."

Reaching into my pocket, I pull out a handful of glittering gold powder. "All we need is a little bit of pixie dust," I say. I feel a smile tug at the corners of my mouth. The fear in Bella's face washes away and she takes my hand. We sprint toward the east wall as two Marauders struggle to their feet. A meter before the ledge, I throw a handful of dust into the air, step off the building, and we fly.

For an exhilarating moment, I feel weightless. A burst of lightning shines on the infrastructure of the building below us. Instead of the trail of gold I had expected to mark our hand- and footholds on the wall, only the brief flash of a balcony roof appears far below me. I have only a moment to realize that the impact is going to hurt when I hit the tiles with a heavy thud. Pain shoots from my wrist and into my shoulder as one of my hands grasps at the slick shingles. The apex of the roof grows farther away as I slide. Gravity hurtles me like an anchor toward the ground. My voice gives a squeal as my body slips from the edge, my hands clutching the rooftop ledge.

Bella slides down the roof above me.

"Help!" she cries.

I grab her wrist just as she slips past me, nearly plunging two stories toward the brick courtyard. She dangles, her small boots kicking beneath her.

My feet find something solid beneath me, a balcony railing. Grunting, I muster all my strength and hurl Bella up to the railing. Her petite hands clutch the wood, and she maneuvers a foot onto the ledge of the balcony, throwing herself onto the floor. I leap down and lie next to her, trying to quiet my heartbeat.

"Nice catch," Bella says through quick breaths.

Shouts from above draw my attention to the top of the building. Soldiers peer down at us, pointing. One Marauder screams orders to the other soldiers, but they are drowned out by cracks of thunder.

Bolting up, I help Bella to her feet. "We'd better get going," I say. I clutch the broken stone wall, preparing to climb down to the empty courtyard. Bella follows.

It takes what seems like several long minutes to get down to the bottom. When our feet are safely on the ground, Bella races toward me and wraps her arms around my waist. The sky opens up, rain washing away every trace of gold dust. "I thought you were really going to kill yourself," Bella whispers.

Kneeling down, I lock eyes with her. "After all we've been through, do you really think I'd leave you alone with those pirates?"

Bella shakes her head, relief evident in her slight smile. She holds a fist up, and I bump it with my own. "Lost Girls stick together," she says.

My breath hitches as she steps toward the courtyard. I don't follow.

"What is it?" she asks, looking over her shoulder at me expectantly.

I bite the inside of my cheek, weighing my words. "Bella, the first chance you have, run to the *Jolly Roger*. Don't stop. Don't look back, not even for me."

She shakes her head. "I'm not leaving you."

I place my hands on her shoulders. "Promise me that if things get dicey, you'll run. Find Pete and the other Lost Boys and leave Everland for good," I say. *"Promise me."*

She nods, though her face scrunches with worry.

"Now let's find my mother."

"What a touching moment," Hook shouts, applauding from the archway leading to the front terrace. Guards patrol just beyond the opening. Soldiers burst through a set of double doors, pausing when they see the Captain. Hook strolls into the courtyard, followed by Mikey wriggling in a soldier's hold.

"Mikey!" I yell. "Let him go, Hook!"

The Captain nudges my brother to the edge of a pit as another soldier serves Hook with a silver platter of raw meat. Hook pulls a hunk from the tray and throws it into the black chasm, coating his fingers in a dark red sheen. Reptilian hisses rise into the chilly night air, competing with the roll of thunder. Recognizing the crocodiles' menacing call, terror courses through my veins. The savage animals snap violently, growling and thrashing. Gazing down at Mikey, Hook wipes a finger across his cheek, leaving a red streak on his tear-stained face.

"I intend to. But first, the negotiations," he says.

"Negotiations?" I say. "There's no need for negotiations. I know exactly what you want." Placing my dagger against my palm, I cut a shallow groove into my hand. The blade bites into my skin, sending hot pain up my arm. Blood seeps from the cut and pools in my hand as I march toward Hook, holding my palm up to his face. "This is what you're after. Take it!" I spit.

"No! Don't do it!" Bella yells. I ignore her pleas.

"Gwen, no." Mikey's voice quivers as he watches me with wide eyes.

Scarlet streaks run down my arm and drip onto the wet brick. Hook stares at my palm, shakes his head, and throws the last of the raw remains into the pit. "I'm afraid that won't be enough," Hook says, confirming my suspicions. Of course he'd never let me go. My fate was written in the stars, the two I'd wished on: safety for my family, and for Pete and the Lost Boys. But not for me.

I drop my hand and feel the drip, drip, drip of blood from my fingertips like the ticking of a clock.

Hook wipes the blood from the raw meat off his hands. "Bring the other one," he says.

A Marauder escorts a vociferously protesting Jack from the palace doors to the reptiles' pit. Jack stumbles to the edge. He pulls his arms free from the soldier's hold and glares at him with disdain. His goggles tumble from his head and into the hole. Regaining his balance, he casts his gaze down. At the bottom of the pit, the two large crocodiles snap their powerful jaws, hissing at each other as they fight over the leather-and-chrome goggles.

"Careful. You don't want to get too close. Tick is all bark and Tock is all bite," Hook says, rubbing a pink scar on his arm. As if recognizing its name, the larger of the crocodiles growls.

"You have Gwen. Now let the Lost Boys go," he shouts, refusing to meet my gaze.

I glare at Jack.

Jack frowns. "How about it, Hook? Your turn to hold up your end of the deal."

"Not quite, little brother," Hook says.

"Brother?" Bella and I say in unison.

Mikey's bottom lip juts out in a pout.

Hook circles Jack. "Stepbrother, to be exact. Jack is a Marauder. He was the one who helped me find the Lost City."

I scowl at Jack and shake my head. "Traitor," I say with venom in my voice.

Bella breaks free from her guard and storms Jack. She beats on him with her tiny fists.

"We trusted you! Gwen is a Lost Girl—how could you give her up?" Bella screams.

Jack kneels, blocking her punches until he is able to pull her into a hug. She shoves herself from him, stumbles, and teeters at the edge of the crocodile pit. Jack lunges for her, grasping her wrist just as she loses her balance.

"Bella!" I scream.

Mikey wails.

Bella's arms flail, her feet kicking wildly beneath her. The crocodiles snap and growl, their jaws lifted in anticipation. Jack hauls her away from the lip of the pit and pulls her close. Breathing heavily, he asks, "Are you okay?"

Bella stares at him, her face contorted into rage. Her jaw tightens. "You're nothing but a bloody pirate," she spits. A soldier yanks Bella from Jack, but she doesn't break her enraged glare. Mikey wipes a tear with the back of his sleeve and wraps his arm around Bella.

Jack, still sitting on the wet stone, hangs his head. His ebony hair curtains his pale face.

Hook chortles and slaps Jack on his back. "Looks like it's going to be a pirate's life for you after all, Jack." Taking a katana from another soldier, he drops the sword in front of Jack. Jack doesn't move to pick it up.

Hook kneels so he is face-to-face with my brother. A soldier hands Mikey's dirty teddy bear to Hook. "I believe this is yours, young man," Hook says, holding the bear with an outstretched hand.

Mikey withdraws, clutching Bella's hand and scooting behind me. I shield him from Hook. My pulse increases, thrumming in my ears like the whir of a zeppelin.

"Leave him alone," I growl, slapping Hook's face, leaving a bloodied handprint on his cheek.

Hook hardly flinches. With his hand, he wipes the scarlet liquid from his face, inspecting it between his fingers. Standing, he turns. "Bring the child," he says.

"No!" I scream. I try to stop him, but my guard holds me back. His arms wrap around me so tight that he squeezes the breath out of me, and I tumble to my knees. Picking up Mikey, a Marauder follows Hook closer to the crocodile pit. My little brother wriggles violently in the Marauder's grasp, screaming loudly.

"Let him go!" I shout.

Hook tosses the bear into the pit. I can hear the crocodiles gnash at it. Mikey breathes heavily, but does not cry.

"What? No more tears? What a brave little Lost Boy you are. If only your mother could see you now," Hook says, peering down at Mikey. The Marauder swings my brother over the trench and dangles him by one arm. Mikey screams in horror.

"Please, please don't hurt him," Bella cries.

"Stop!" I shout, struggling in the guard's grip.

"This has gone too far!" Jack says, standing and picking up his sword. "You promised you wouldn't hurt any of the Lost Boys in exchange for information."

"I'm afraid you are mistaken. I promised that *I* wouldn't lay a finger on any of the Lost Boys. I have held my word. My men, on the other hand, have made no such promise."

"Dirty fink," Jack spits. He aims his sword at Hook.

"What more do you want?" I ask, holding my bloodied hand to him. "I know you need my blood. Take as much as you want. Take it all! I am not afraid of death. But let my brother go," I say, quickly and breathlessly.

Hook's eyes narrow, cold and devoid of compassion. "I don't want just your blood. I want you, *alive.*"

"What?" I ask, confused. I had expected to die at the hands of Hook.

"Do you think I'd let someone as valuable as you die?" He holds his hand up, his fingers stained with my blood. "Do you know what a drop of this is worth if the rest of the world is anything like Everland?"

An icy chill grates down my back. I had accepted that today might be the end of my life, but I had never considered the possibility of a greater horror: becoming Hook's prisoner, *forever.*

Hook holds his index finger up and looks greedily at the red liquid coating it, rubbing his forefinger and thumb together. "This is more precious than any treasure in the world." He wipes the blood off on his black trousers. "And I'm not leaving without it. *All of it.*"

A palace door slams behind me. I spin, my hands gripping the hilt of my dagger.

"Mum!" Mikey yells as a shoe slips from his foot and plunges into the pit.

"Mikey!" exclaims a new voice. My mother and Joanna, escorted by a soldier, take in the scene. Terror replaces the stunned look on my mother's face.

"Surprise, Professor," Hook says, grinning.

· GWEN ·

That's my son. Let him go," my mother demands. She races toward Hook. Before she reaches him, Hook pulls the trigger on his Gatling gun, spraying bullets in her direction. Shards fly as the bullets pierce the stone in front of her. She leaps back, but is struck in the leg. My mother collapses to the ground, groaning in pain while ribbons of blood drip from her wound.

"Mum!" I cry out, lunging toward her. When Hook turns the aim of his Gatling gun on me, I hold my hands up, terrified to move.

Joanna rushes to my mother's side and cries quietly next to her.

My mother grimaces as she sits up. She rips the sleeve of her lab coat off and ties it around the wound. The bullet appears to have only grazed her, but my heart crushes seeing her in pain. She fixes her daggered stare onto the Captain and stands, unsteady on her feet.

"I said let him go," she says through gritted teeth.

"All in due time, Professor," Hook responds with an unsettling calm. He approaches my mother and stops close enough that he is eye to eye with her. "We have some things we must discuss first."

Hook nods to the Marauder holding my brother. He sets Mikey down on the ground, keeping his grip on my brother's arm. Bella bolts to Mikey, wrapping her small arms around him.

My mother sighs, visibly relieved. "What do you want, Hook?"

"I'm a reasonable man. I'm certainly not a child killer. At least not yet," he says, circling my mother.

"Not a child killer?" I say. My voice trembles with rage. "*You* are responsible for this, for *all* of this!" I hold my arms outstretched. "You bombed London, you let loose a deadly virus, you killed the entire adult population, and who knows how many children? And you say you're not a child killer?"

"Casualties of war," Hook says, bowing. "Not murder."

"Get to your point," I insist.

Hook juts a finger in my direction. "You are my point. You and her." He points at my mother. "All I need is you and your mother, and the world will be mine. The rest of the kids, they're just sniveling dead weight. Extra baggage. They'll be staying."

Mikey bawls loudly as Bella hugs him tight.

Jack shifts unsteadily.

Hook stops in front of my mother. He caresses my mum's forehead, brushing the back of his hand against the stray lock of hair hanging in front of her transparent mask.

My mother jerks away, her lips pressed tightly together before she speaks. "You don't need Gwen. All you need is a small blood sample."

"Once the other nations find out she's the cure, who's to stop them from coming for her?" Hook says, pacing. Each step like a clock, counting down time. To what, I don't know.

Tick! Tick! Tick!

"She'll keep quiet," my mother says. "She won't tell anyone that the cure came from her. Take a sample. I'll come with you back to Germany to work on the cure—like you wanted. But leave Gwen here."

"No!" I protest. "You're not going with him!"

"I can't take that chance," Hook says.

My mother's eyes narrow and she gives him a smug look. "Well, you better take that chance, because I'd rather die than let my daughter go anywhere with you."

His complexion reddens and he shoves me from her. Towering over my mother, he raises a hand as if to slap her. My mother frowns at him, unwavering, as I throw myself in front of her. Hook clenches his fist and shakes it. "One year, Professor! For a year, you've been working with me. Hunting for the cure, and this whole time the cure was out there and it lay within your daughter, a daughter you never told me about. If you had just told me, we could have left this blasted place months ago." Hook takes a step back, straightens his military vest. "What else have you not told me?"

Hook turns his eyes to the stormy sky and screams so loud that I cover my ears. Fury crackles across his face, making him appear older than he is. Then he reaches for my mother's hand. She tries to pull it from his grasp, but he holds her tight. "I'm taking both you and Gwen, regardless. It will do me no good if you refuse to produce the cure. My proposal is this: No more secrets. No more lies. It's just you and me. With you by my side, I will rule the world."

I suddenly want to vomit.

"And if I refuse?" my mother says with venom in her voice. "What can you do to me that you haven't already done? You've kidnapped my children, killed my husband, and imprisoned me. You've taken everything!" she screams.

I'm startled by her reaction, but her defiance fuels my own anger.

Hook turns to me and throws me to the rain-soaked ground. Frantic, I crawl backward as he approaches, but he is too quick. He grabs my hand, slaps it on the brick, and pulls a knife out. My mother cries and struggles in the grip of a guard.

"See? There is still something left you care about. So you *will* produce the cure, even if I have to deliver your daughter's blood body part by body part," Hook says, snarling.

"Or there's always plan B," says a familiar voice. I look toward the courtyard entrance. Pete stands beneath the limestone archway. My pulse quickens. What's he doing here? He folds his arms across his bare chest. Under the light of the gas lamps, the inked cogs and gears glisten, and my heart swells with hope.

"Pete!" Bella says, bolting from her seated position toward the leader of the Lost Boys.

Doc also appears, a smirk spread wide across his face.

"Another Lost Boy, I presume?" Hook asks, his brows knit together so tightly they converge into one dark line. He releases my wrist and stands. "How did you get in here?"

"I'd like to say your men put up a good fight," Pete says, striding in with a smirk, "but I'd be lying. Turns out they get awfully squirrelly when you tamper with their masks." Pete holds up a Marauder's mask before he throws it at Hook's feet.

Hook reaches down and lifts the mask. "Impossible!" he says with a puzzled stare.

An explosion erupts from the royal gardens beyond the palace walls. The ground shakes, sending a few lanterns falling from the building, spilling gas on their descent and smashing onto the stone. Flames lick the night sky.

"Oh, our engineer, Cogs, wanted me to remind you that you ought not to leave volatile materials around for children to play with. They could start a fire or even blow up a few zeppelins," Pete says smugly.

Hook's dark eyes reflect flames as he watches the yellow and orange blaze dance above the limestone walls. He clenches a fist and nods to the building. "Go look into it."

"Aye, Captain," a soldier says, running past Pete toward the front of the palace.

"As for you two, I don't recall inviting you to this party," Hook growls.

Pete takes a few determined steps toward the leader of the Marauders. "What do you mean, Hook? You've been chasing me for months. All this time I've evaded you, and now I'm practically within reach and suddenly you don't want me. I'm hurt," Pete says with a mocking pout.

"I don't *need* you," Hook says, retrieving his revolver from its holster.

Pete ignores the weapon aimed at him. "Nice brand there, Jack," Pete says, folding his arms. "The only thing that's missing is the word *traitor* across your forehead."

Hook throws his head back and laughs. "Ah, yes. I forgot that you didn't know that my prodigal stepbrother has returned. Once a Marauder, always a Marauder."

Pete snatches his dagger and charges Jack, knocking him to the ground. He holds the blade to Jack's throat.

"It's not what you think," Jack says tersely. "I swear!"

His blade pricks Jack's neck, releasing a bead of blood. "It ripped me into a thousand shreds to leave you behind. You betrayed us! How could you?"

"No, I told him we'd give him Gwen," Jack grunts. "He promised he wouldn't hurt the Lost Kids. Gwen was all he wanted."

"She's more of a Lost Kid than you are," Pete growls through clenched teeth. He digs the knife slightly deeper. Blood leaks down Jack's neck.

"Pete, stop it!" I shout.

"I thought I was doing the right thing by giving up Gwen. He promised he'd take her and leave Everland. I knew you'd all be mad at me, but I did what I thought was right for the Lost Boys. I didn't think I could show my face again, so . . . so I pledged my allegiance to Hook."

"An honorable Lost Boy wouldn't have given up his clan, but even if he had, he'd have rather died than pledge his allegiance to a pirate," Pete snaps.

With Doc's help, I yank Pete off Jack just as he lifts his dagger, ready to drive it into Jack's chest.

"Let him go," Doc says with disgust. "He's not worth it."

Pete stands and spits on Jack's face.

"When I get my hands on you, you're going to wish you were dead," Pete growls.

Hook chuckles. "Good form, Lost Boy. Taking vengeance on my double-crossing brother. You'd make an excellent Marauder.

It's a shame I have to kill you." He aims his gun back at the boys and nods to a soldier. "Take them out to the garden and put them out of their misery. Then feed them to the crocs."

As the soldiers advance on the boys, Doc pulls a syringe from his back pocket. "If you kill us, you'll never have this." Hook stares at the vial in Doc's hand. Its iridescent tint glitters in the light. "It's the cure, Hook. This vial is all you will need to reproduce the antidote. You don't need Gwen or the Professor, but you do need this."

Hook scowls. "The cure hasn't been developed yet. I'd know if it had."

Doc hands the vial to Pete, who grips each end of it, poised to snap it in two.

"Maybe. Maybe not." Pete shrugs. "But this is the only vial. Are you sure you want to risk finding out?"

Hesitating, Hook stares at the glass container. "What's your proof?"

Pete nods to Bella. "Show him."

Bella rips off her gloves. Her tiny fingers reveal the pink tint of new skin where her open sores once were. A hush falls as we stare, astonished at her nearly perfect hands. "Less than an hour ago I was dying. My fingers hurt so bad I thought they were going to fall off. Pete gave me that antidote and now look!" She wiggles her fingers.

"But . . . how?" my mother says. "Even when we developed the antidote years ago, it never had the ability to heal that quickly. Some trials took years to show improvement."

"Two things," Doc says, with raised brows. "Stem cells and lizards."

My mother stares at Doc, bewildered.

Doc grins. "I've always been interested in the study of stem cells, mainly in the area of epimorphic regeneration."

"What is that?" Mikey asks.

"Good question, Lost Boy. You know how lizards can lose a tail and grow it back?" Doc asks.

Mikey nods.

"Same thing. If lizards can regenerate their tails, why can't people regrow body parts? In Bella's case, I created a solution combining Bella's cells with the protein that allows lizards to regrow their tails. Antibodies from the Lost Boys in the mixture helped Bella maintain her health, but did not cure the virus. It was too virulent. Something about Gwen's antibodies not only appears to heal, but is reacting to the original solution to accelerate the healing process."

Hook grabs Bella's hand and examines her pale pink fingers. He whips his head toward my mother. "Is what he says possible? Could this be done?"

My mother shrugs. "I suppose, but stem cell study is not my area of expertise. And even though my partners and I came up with an antidote, it took us years to develop. It was never as effective as that," she says, pointing to Bella's hands.

Hook's eyes dart toward the glass vial. Pete grins, still gripping either end of the container. "You ready to cut a deal, Hook?" Pete says with a victorious smile.

Hook doesn't respond.

"I developed what's curing Bella," Doc says, pointing at the vial. "I'm the only one who knows what is in it. You could take

Gwen and the Professor, but the Professor does not know what I mixed in with Gwen's antibodies. It will take her months, maybe years, to discover the solution."

"What do you propose?" Hook growls.

Stepping in front of Hook, blocking his view of the Lost Boys, Bella, and my family, I take in a breath. "Let everyone go. In exchange, you can have the cure," I say.

"The cure will do me no good without someone to help reproduce it," he says.

"I'll go with you to develop it," Doc says, stepping next to me.

"What?" I say, my heart skipping a beat. "You can't mean that."

Doc smiles weakly and winks at Bella. "I'd do just about anything for a Lost Girl."

Pete joins us and laces his fingers through mine. "We all would."

"But you never said that your plan would include giving Doc up to Hook," I say, shaking my head.

"And you never said that your plan would include giving *yourself* up," Pete says. He stares at me with intense eyes. He says nothing, but his steadfast and determined expression speaks a thousand words. He knew I'd sacrifice myself to save my mother.

"Have you lost your marbles, Doc?" Jack says.

Pete shoots Jack a dirty look. "Interesting choice of words coming from the Lost Boy turned Marauder."

Jack scowls.

"So what do you say, Hook?" Pete asks. "Do we have ourselves a deal?"

Hook rubs his chin in contemplation. He holds a palm out. "Deal. Give me the vial."

"Let them go first," Pete says, gesturing toward my mother, Bella, Joanna, and Mikey.

Hook turns his gun on me, pulling back the hammer. I gasp, my breath catching. "Fine, but the Immune stays."

"You won't shoot her," Pete says with a wide smile. "And even if you did, I'd crush this vial so fast you wouldn't have a chance to retrieve it. Then you'd have nothing."

"Valid point, boy," Hook says, but he grabs my wrist and pulls me into him, the barrel digging into my temple. "However, even you said we needed just a small sample of the Immune's blood. I shoot her, take a sample, and Doc still comes with me. Meanwhile, your girlfriend lies dying on the cold, wet bricks."

"Pete!" I say, writhing in the crook of Hook's arm.

Pete's gaze hardens as he takes slow, steady steps toward me. No, this isn't right. Pete would never allow Doc to join Hook. In fact, Pete would never let Hook have the cure. Curious, I glance at Pete. He winks. As fast as his wink, his expression returns to that of reluctance, defeat. He's up to something. He has to be.

"Give me the vial. He can't hurt you anymore. You can leave. The Lost Kids, my family, Bella . . . you'll all be safe," I say, blinking the rain from my eyes and meeting his. "Please, Pete. Let's just get out of here."

The stubborn resistance I have come to appreciate and admire in him slips. He nods with reluctance and hands me the vial of iridescent, milky liquid. Carefully, I close my fingers over the tube. Doc gives me a weak grin. A strange expression crosses Pete's face. He nods to Doc, and I get the impression that gesture is more than what it appears.

Doc starts walking toward Hook when Pete grabs him by the arm.

"Wait," Pete says abruptly, his hand gripping Doc's wrist. "It's been a great adventure. Thanks for everything . . ."

A crease forms between Doc's brows and he drops his gaze to the ground. "It's the least I could do. I know it doesn't absolve me from what happened with Gabrielle, but at least . . . well, maybe it . . ."

Pete pulls Doc into a hug. "All is forgiven," Pete says. Their exchange lasts just a moment too long. That's when I notice the glint of a dagger tucked at the small of Pete's back. Pete steps back, his hand still gripping Doc's. His eyes bore into Doc's.

My heart skips several beats. Hook barely acknowledges the exchange as his gun's aim stays fixed on me. I struggle to think of an alternative plan. Stomp on the vial myself? Make a deal with Hook? Run? None of the options seems viable.

"Let my family go," I say, holding the glass container up and drawing Hook's attention away from Pete and Doc.

Hook's eyes tear from the Lost Boys to me. From the corner of my eye, I see Pete quickly slipping the knife into Doc's hand. Hook nods toward the two soldiers accompanying my mother. "Escort them from the palace." The soldiers salute and turn toward my mother.

"No!" my mother screams, wriggling in the soldiers' grasp. "No, I won't leave her."

Mikey wails as Joanna helps him to his feet. She gives me a worried glance, but I nod to her, encouraging her to continue. She and Mikey follow behind the soldier dragging my mother away.

Another soldier escorts Bella out of the courtyard. Her voice fades in a trail of profanities.

Hook erupts in manic laughter. "And what about you, step-brother? Would you like to join the women and children?"

Jack aims his sword at Hook. "I might be a pitiful pirate and an inadequate Lost Boy, but I think I'll stay around just to make sure everyone keeps their end of the bargain."

Hook rolls his unpatched eye. "Good form, Jack. That's exactly what I'd expect from *you*." He sneers on the last word.

"What's that supposed to mean?" Jack asks.

"My mother was right about you. You've always been about what you think is right for everyone else, what you think is fair, and never about what is right for *us*, for our family," Hook says. "You're a disgrace to the family name."

Jack's shoulders stiffen. "And you think only about yourself."

" 'The fairest,' my mother mocked. 'A weak leader, bending to the needs of others,' she said of you," Hook says. "She never loved you."

"I never wanted to be a leader," Jack replies. "I just wanted my father's legacy, his compassion for his people, to live on long after his death. He was a kind and fair king. And as far as her loving me, at least I had a parent. A father who loved me. You know what your mother did? Think about it. Do you really think she didn't know what she was targeting? She sent her son to destroy the only weapons lab that contained the virus. She knew it was there. And guess who she sent to make sure it was a done deal? You, stepbrother. She sent you knowing that once you bombed it, you and the rest of the Marauders would die like everyone else."

Hook releases me as he spins and charges his brother, his boots smacking the wet brick. He slaps Jack's face, but Jack hardly flinches. "Lies!" Hook screams.

"You think?" Jack says, unmoved. "She gave you the targets. She chose you and her best fleet of zeppelins to make sure it happened."

Hook stops a few steps away, fury forming deep lines in his face. Turning toward the stormy night sky, he screams. Breathing heavily, he gathers himself together. "Well, life isn't fair, is it? Your father died a tragic death, and I was the scorn of my mother's eye," he yells, pointing the barrel of his gun at his patched eye.

"Your mother killed my father," Jack says, advancing on him. "She poisoned him for betraying her. For providing England with *her* weapon."

Hook aims his gun at Jack, but his brother is unshaken by the weapon aimed at his heart. He advances toward Hook. "The Horologia virus; how do you think England got it? Who do you think sent it to them?" Jack says, still moving forward with Hook's gun pressed firmly against his waistcoat. Rain-soaked hair hangs heavy in Jack's face, shielding his eyes as he shouts. "My father sent it to England, warning them of your mother's intentions, and he died for it!"

My breath catches; my heart stills. As the pieces connect, my heart is conflicted with anger, sorrow, and empathy for this Lost Boy. My saturated clothes anchor me as everything moves in slow motion.

Shock crosses Hook's face for a fraction of a moment before he regains his composure. "That is none of my concern. I came here to win England, not weep for your dead father."

"It appears no one got what they wanted. Not England, not her people, not even your mother. No one! No one except you, brother," Jack says. He steps back and gives an exaggerated bow. "The cure is all yours. Long live the Captain."

"I intend to," Hook says. He turns back to me, aiming the gun. "I've held up to my end of the bargain. Hand it over."

Wavering, I watch Pete, hoping he will tell me to stop, to run for our lives. Instead, he frowns. "There's no way out of this," he says. "He's won."

"No," I protest, counting four other soldiers including Hook nearby. Five against four—that is, if Jack is on our side. Blades against guns. Fear wells in me. Someone is going to die tonight, all because of me, because of what flows within my veins.

Doc's eyes flick between Hook and me. "Gwen, do as he says." His voice is stern, commanding.

Emotions collide inside me like a raging storm at sea. Tears burn my eyes, but I swallow back the lump in my throat, forbidding them to fall. I shake my head in protest. Doc gives me a slight nod and I see the glint of silver in his hand: Pete's second dagger. I place one hand on his cheek and kiss the other. My heart shatters as I pull away.

Please, please don't let anyone die. Not on my account.

Turning, I melt into Pete's arms. He buries his face in my hair, and I can barely hear his whisper in the rain. "The first opportunity you have, I want you to run as fast as you can. Don't look back no matter what. Don't come back for me or Doc. Just run."

His fingers comb through my hair, his heartbeat thrumming against my own. I place my hands on his face, my palms running along his stubbled cheeks. Finally, he leans his forehead against mine. He whispers again, "Run, Gwen. Run away, and don't you ever forget that you are always a Lost Girl."

Burning tears streak my cheeks. "*Your* Lost Girl," I say, my grief drowning in his stare.

"Well, isn't that sweet?" Hook says. He lifts the barrel of his gun toward Pete. "Young love. Now bring me the vial, Immune, or it'll come to an unfortunate end."

Reluctantly, I pull away from Pete's arms. Wet, angry, and battling the ache of defeat, I step toward Hook, his palm held out, waiting for me to give him his prize.

He grins wickedly. "Hand it over," he says.

He's won, and that simple fact chokes me like his fat fingers wrapped around my neck, stealing my breath. I fix my gaze on Hook's single dark eye and shove the vial into his outstretched hand.

"That's a good little girl."

"I am not a *little girl*," I say, tightening my jaw.

"Oh, aren't you cute? It's absolutely . . . ," Hook says, scratching his head, "darling."

As soon as Hook wraps his fingers around the glass tube, he turns to his soldiers. "Cuff the girl and the young doctor. We're taking the cure, the boy, and the Immune. As for Pete," Hook says, looking Pete up and down, "kill him!"

"No!" I shout as the soldiers move on Doc and Pete. A third guard moves toward me, but Jack steps in between us. He turns his sword on the soldiers. "No, that's not what you agreed on."

"Plans have changed," Hook says. "It's time you two get an up-close tour of the *Jolly*—"

Another explosion erupts outside the palace, followed by a dozen more. The ground shakes, sending lanterns smashing to the ground.

"Captain!" a Marauder says, running into the courtyard, breathless. "The soldiers! They've abandoned their posts. The ships . . . they're spooked! Phantoms, I tell you. Firing on our own men!"

"What?" Hook says.

I turn toward Jack, and he meets my stare. I nod toward the katana in his hand.

Hook regards the vial in his grip, like the wheels of a clock turning in his mind, trying to find a solution to his predicament. "No worries. We still have the cure and the little girl," he says. "As long as we have them both, I'll be the most powerful man in the world."

Rage erupts within me. I must end this. I *will* end this . . . for good!

I signal to Jack. He tosses the katana, and I catch it as Hook turns his attention to me.

Thoughts of my family flood my mind. Mikey's panicked face as he dangled over the crocodile pit. My mother's surprised expression after being held hostage, waiting for her children to be brought to the palace to save them. The night Joanna was taken from me, and the hurt in her eyes about broken pinkie promises to never grow up. And a final thought for my father, the clinking of his tags reminding me I will never see him again.

"I am not a little girl!" I scream. Lifting the sword over my head, I slam the blade down.

· GWEN ·

Hook's guttural scream is drowned out by the crack of thunder and the pouring of rain. I watch as his right arm, the antidote still clenched in his severed hand, one finger adorned with the skull-and-crossbones ring, falls into the crocodile pit. The coppery smell of fresh blood hangs in the air as Captain Hook falls to his knees. He tries to stop the blood with his gloved hand, but to no avail. With his teeth he rips his glove off his remaining hand and holds his bleeding stump to his chest. He stares into the dark chasm as the crunch of bones and broken glass echoes from the pit. In the distance, Big Ben chimes for the first time in a year, its clang announcing midnight in Everland.

The world around me slows. Out of the corner of my eye, I watch as the Lost Boys fight off the Marauders beneath a lightning-streaked sky. As the storm rages around me, I drop the sword, sending it clattering to the wet stone. When I lift my eyes, the leader of the Marauders is staring straight at me.

Hook turns his gaze to the sky, his square jaw clenching with a grimace. Pain etches the lines on his face, but I am certain it is from more than just his arm. Trembling in the heavy rain, he turns his dark, glassy gaze toward my sword and then locks eyes with me.

"I came to England to win her for my mother," he shouts above the roar of the rain. "For once in my life, to prove to her I'm more than just a worthless child. And now . . ." He scans the smoky clouds and the flames licking toward the night sky.

Hook covers his grief-stricken face with his hand. It is then I see them, the oozing blisters covering his fingers and the blackened fingernails, and I feel as if I've been punched in the gut. Why didn't I see it? Consider that he, too, could be vulnerable?

"You've contracted the virus," I say, hearing the shock in my voice. "All this time . . . this whole time your soldiers wore the masks, but you . . . you didn't."

Hook grimaces, averting his gaze. "When I discovered what I had done, when I killed nearly everyone in London, it was too late. Even for me."

Hesitantly, I kneel and place a hand on his shoulder. As if surprised by my touch, he flinches. He stares at me with the single frightened and wide eye of a boy, a Lost Boy. Acquiring the cure to rule the world may have been his goal, but it was never his primary agenda. He was after the cure because *he* needed it.

He hangs his head, anger twisting his features. "I couldn't go back to Germany like this," he says, holding up his infected hand. "I've destroyed England and possibly all of humankind. If I returned to my mother infected . . . she already sees me as a monster, but this . . ." He stares at his stump. "Now I can never go back."

The rain washes away my disdain for this boy, sympathy replacing it in the hollows of my heart. My soul shattered when I lost my mother, but I found her, was reunited into her loving arms. Hook, on the other hand, has never known nor will ever know a mother's love.

"I'm so sorry," I say, the words catching in my throat as I hold back my tears.

He smiles weakly and crumbles to the ground. "What have I done?" he whispers.

Despite my reluctance and weak stomach, I force myself to look at his stump. I have never purposely hurt another, not until tonight. "What have *we* done?" I whisper.

An explosion in the distance rocks the ground beneath us, drawing my attention to the wall of fire surrounding us. My pulse races and I search for an escape. Pete's face appears in my vision and he is shouting, but his voice is lost. He places a hand on each of my arms and shakes me. "Let's go!" he yells.

"We can't leave him here," I shout, gesturing toward Hook, who has curled into a ball around his ruined arm.

Pete glances at the wounded soldier. Hook stares back, unblinking, unmoving. Defeated.

"Come on, Gwen," Pete says, tugging my arm.

I shake my head, my wet hair clinging to my face. "He'll die if we leave him."

"We have to go. Your family is waiting," he says, wrapping an arm around me. He leads me away, but I don't take my eyes off the wounded boy.

Everything around me distorts in a fuzzy haze. I blink and I am running, Pete leading me by the hand. Ahead, Doc sprints, waving to us to follow him. I stop at a set of double doors and look back at Hook. He's curled in a crimson puddle, and he holds his bloody arm to his chest. He gives me one last sad glance, and my heart sinks as he is swallowed by the rainstorm. The palace doorway blurs as I run through it. The ground is littered with the bodies of soldiers. I blink the rain from my lashes again and I am racing through the garden toward the zeppelin fleet. Many of the ships are ablaze and the Marauders are nowhere in sight.

The whir of a zeppelin in the distance calls to me. A girl stands on the deck of the zeppelin, a girl waving to us. As we draw closer, I can see her wet, dark hair sticking to her face. Her black-and-gold sari hangs limply with rainwater. It's Lily. Behind her, Lost Boys run about, preparing the ship for its departure.

We sprint up the ramp. Lily extends a hand out to help me board. "You didn't really think I was going to leave Everland without you, did you?" she says with a smug smile.

"How did you know?" I ask her, helping Pete onto the ship.

She shrugs. "Because you're one of the most courageous girls I've ever met. A bit mad, but courageous nonetheless. To face Hook all on your own? Now that is brave."

Pete slips his hand into mine. "Agreed," he says.

"And there was no way Pete was going to leave Everland without you," Doc says as Lily helps him aboard.

Lily spins and shouts orders. I am greeted by my mother, Joanna, and Mikey. They wrap their arms around me tightly. From their embrace, I scan the royal gardens. The palace is ablaze. In the dancing light of the flames, a figure sprints toward the palace. The lanky boy turns to us. It's Jack. He takes one step toward the zeppelin and looks back over his shoulder at the palace.

"Take your places!" Lily shouts, her gloved hands gripping the steering wheel.

The whir of the zeppelin's engine vibrates beneath my feet. Across the garden, Jack spins, sprinting to the unguarded double doors. With a last glance at the ship, he places a hand behind his ear, touching the mark of the Marauders branded on his skin. Finally, he dashes inside the burning palace.

Lily calls to me, "Everyone is in place. Are you ready to leave, Gwen?"

Taking one last look as Everland burns to the ground, I turn and say, "Let's get out of Everland . . . for good."

· GWEN ·

All hands on deck!" Lily shouts.

Dozens of Lost Boys take their positions, cranking handles, feeding boilers, and pulling ropes, leaving the inferno of Everland in our wake. The zeppelin whirs with a subdued energy as we travel north toward what I've ached for over the last year, a place of promise for safety and peace.

Everland becomes just an orange flicker of light in the distance. Pete joins me by the rail.

"Will you miss it?" I ask as we fly away, leaving what's left of Everland and the storm behind us.

"I don't know. Absence makes the heart grow fonder . . . or forgetful," Pete says, frowning.

I peer up at the star-adorned sky as we travel north. Pete slips his hand into mine. The warmth of his touch soothes the anxiety that lies beneath the surface of my optimism for safer lands.

"What are you thinking?" Pete asks, whispering in my ear.

I drop my gaze from the stars and smirk. "I was just thinking about when you pointed out the second one to the right. It was a point of hope, a means to bring my family back together." I glance over my shoulder. Behind me Joanna and Mikey giggle as Gabs flaps his arms, teaching them a dance. My mother sits behind them, watching Gabs's dance moves. She catches my gaze and smiles, but it's mixed with relief and sorrow.

"And now?" Pete asks, watching the retreating clouds.

Returning my eyes to the clear night sky, I sigh. "Now I couldn't find it even if I needed to. It's lost among the thousands of other stars."

Pete pulls me into him and buries his head in my neck. "It's not lost, Gwen. It's still there, guiding you to the things you desire most. Leading you to your next adventure. You just have to look for it."

I roll my eyes. "Yeah, right. How can I follow a single point in a sea of stars?"

Pete's lips quirk into a crooked smile. He puts his hands on my shoulders and turns me to the north. He wraps his arms around my waist and whispers, his breath tickling my ear. His warmth chases the chill from my body. "Search for the brightest star in the sky."

Thousands of stars glitter in the inky black sky, each blinking to a rhythm of its own. One star shimmers brighter than the others, an iridescent display of colors in a single embedded diamond. I point to it. "There it is!"

Pete laughs. "That's Sirius. Next to the sun, it's the brightest star in the sky."

"It's beautiful," I say, watching its silver pulse.

Turning me back around, Pete brushes my cheek with the palm of his hand. "Not as beautiful as you," he says.

Blushing, I look away. With a crooked finger, he tilts my chin up so that our eyes meet.

"I'm serious, Gwen," he says. "You're beautiful. And what you did back there in Everland? That was brave, one of the bravest things I've ever seen."

Images of Everland cloud my thoughts. Visions of Hook brought to his knees by my hand. Smeeth's death. The sting of guilt pricks my heart.

I turn my stare to Sirius, and the star twinkles back. "What do you think is next for us?"

As the zeppelin flies us away from the ruins of Everland, Pete places his hand on my cheek, his fingers tangling into my curls. "I don't know, but no matter where our adventures take you, I hope you stay with us"—Pete dips his chin as his cheeks grow pink—"with me, forever."

"Forever is a very long time, Pete," I say, lifting his chin to meet my gaze.

With his brilliant green eyes fixed on me, he leans in. When his lips touch mine, it's as light as fairy wings, but an exhilarating rush I feel everywhere. I wind my arms around his neck, kissing him back, pulling him closer. I feel the pulse of my heart beating a tattoo through all of me, declaring me a Lost Girl . . . Pete's Lost Girl. Too soon, Pete pulls away, breathless, and the stars seem to shine brighter in the cloudless sky. Our fingers intertwine and he touches his forehead to mine, his gaze never leaving my eyes.

"A very long time indeed," he says with a crooked grin.

ACKNOWLEDGMENTS

Everland became reality thanks to the patience, determination, and advice of many. I am grateful to my husband, Stu—my best friend, biggest champion, and rock. Thank you for supporting me as I chase my dreams. And I owe the warmest of thanks and huge momma-bear hugs to my three sons. You're my favorite Lost Boys, and I'm so proud to be your mom. I wish you didn't have to grow up. K, thanks for the Steam Crawler idea.

My parents, Mary and Joseph, who against all odds still managed to help foster my belief in fairy tales and happily-ever-afters. Thank you for always loving and cheering for me, even when I deserved a swift kick in the butt instead. And also my siblings, Brandi and Jeffery, who make me the luckiest sister on earth. I will always love you both no matter what.

Bob, who loves me like a daughter, and Harriett, who was one of my best friends, thank you for always encouraging me to keep writing.

To the infamous BBBs, Erika Gardner, Jennifer Fosberry, Cameron Sullivan, Amy Moellering, Georgia Choate, Jerie Jacobs, and M. Pepper Langlinais, thank you, my sweet girlies. I'm so grateful to have you as my strongest cheerleaders—this story would never have come to life without you!

Ashley Hearn, Jennifer Dyer, Joseph Isaacs, Frank Anderson, and Anoosha Lalani, you are the best virtual critique partners I could have ever found. Promise me someday we'll meet and celebrate.

Daphne, thanks for being my very first fangirl.

A girl needs her BFFs, and I hit the jackpot with mine. Words can't express my appreciation and love for the three of you, Miriam, Audrey, and Erika.

I'm forever grateful to Ed Westmoreland and his staff, who let me take free residence at a prime table in Eddie Papa's restaurant. Special thank-you to Seth for bringing back Hahn.

Thank-you to Department 384, who are by far the best group of characters a writer could have and my most animated beta readers. Hug to you, Phil, for reading for me, loving me, and treating me like a princess, and to Guy for being my Pete inspiration.

Also, I can't leave out Marissa Meyer and Veronica Rossi for your continued support. While I fangirled over your successes, you took the time to cheer me on, too.

A Lost Girl couldn't have a more incredible agent than Thao Le. I am endlessly indebted that you took a chance on me and believed in my story—thank you for everything.

Special thanks go out to the rest of the team at the Sandra Dijkstra Literary Agency, including the lovely Sandra Dijkstra, Andrea Cavallaro, Jennifer Kim, and Elise Capron.

It's been a privilege and honor to work with the amazing Jody Corbett, my unbelievably awesome editor. You not only saw my vision but helped make it sparkle. I often wonder if you're secretly part pixie.

A gigantic thank-you to the entire crew at Scholastic. There are too many to name them all here, but I want to acknowledge a handful who have made *Everland* beautiful. Rebekah Wallin, thank you for your keen eye and attention to detail. Christopher Stengel, you made this book shine so much I nearly cried the first time I saw it. (Okay, I did cry.) Also many thanks to the wonderful sales team: Elizabeth Whiting, Alexis Lunsford, Annette Hughes, and the rest of you. Cheers to marketing trio Caitlin Friedman, Bess Braswell, and Lauren Festa.

And most of all, thank you to every reader who picks up this book. If I could count the ways I appreciate you, it would surpass the number of stars in the sky.

ABOUT THE AUTHOR

Wendy Spinale is a former character actor for the Disneyland theme park (so she's very familiar with the world of make-believe). *Everland* is her debut novel.

Wendy lives with her family in the San Francisco Bay Area.